# Black & White

# Black & White

## DANI SHAPIRO

ALFRED A. KNOPF · NEW YORK · 2007

THIS IS A BORZOI BOOK
PUBLISHED BY ALFRED A. KNOPF

Copyright © 2007 by Dani Shapiro
All rights reserved. Published in the United States by Alfred A. Knopf,
a division of Random House, Inc., New York, and in Canada by
Random House of Canada Limited, Toronto.

www.aaknopf.com

Knopf, Borzoi Books, and the colophon are
registered trademarks of Random House, Inc.

Library of Congress Cataloging-in-Publication Data
Shapiro, Dani.
Black & white / by Dani Shapiro. — 1st ed.
p.  cm.
ISBN-13: 978-0-375-41548-7
1. Women photographers—New York (State)—New York—Fiction.
2. Mothers and daughters—Fiction.   3. Psychological fiction.
I. Title.   II. Title: Black & white.   III. Title: Black and white.
PS3569.H3387B63 2007
813'.54—dc22    2006030424

This is a work of fiction. Names, characters, places, and incidents either are
the product of the author's imagination or are used fictitiously.
Any resemblance to actual persons, living or dead, events,
or locales is entirely coincidental.

Manufactured in the United States of America
First Edition

*For Jacob*

Stare. It is the way to educate your eye, and more. Stare, pry, listen, eavesdrop. Die knowing something. You are not here long.

—*Walker Evans*

# Black & White

# Chapter One

IT HAS BEEN YEARS since anyone has asked Clara if she's Ruth Dunne's daughter—*you know, the girl in those pictures.* But it has also been years—fourteen, precisely—since Clara has set foot in New York. The Upper West Side is a foreign country. The butcher, the shoe repair guy, even the Korean grocer have been replaced by multi-level gyms with juice bars, restaurants with one-syllable French names. Aix, Ouest. The deli where Clara and Robin used to stop on Saturday mornings—that deli is now some sort of boutique. The mannequin in the window is wearing blue jeans and a top no bigger than a cocktail napkin.

This is not the neighborhood of her childhood, though she can still see bits and pieces if she looks hard enough. There's the door to what was once Shakespeare & Co. She spent hours in that bookstore, hiding in the philosophy section, until one summer they gave her a job as a cashier. She lasted three days. Every other person, whether they were buying Wittgenstein or Updike, seemed to stare at her, as if trying to figure out why she looked familiar. So she quit.

Shakespeare & Co. is now an Essentials Plus. The window displays shampoos, conditioners, a dozen varieties of magnifying mirrors. A small child bundled up in winter gear is riding a mechanical dinosaur next to the entrance, slowly moving up and down to a tinny version of the *Flintstones* theme song.

Since the taxi dropped her off at the corner of Broadway and 79th Street, she has counted five wireless cellular stores, three manicure parlors, four real estate brokers. So this is now the Upper West Side: a place where people in cute outfits, their bellies full of steak-frites, talk on brand-new cell phones while getting their nails done on their way to look at new apartments.

It is as if a brightly colored transparency has been placed over the neighborhood of Clara's memory, which had been the color of a sparrow: tan, brown, gray as smudged newsprint. Now, everything seems large and neon. Even the little old Jewish men who used to sit on the benches in the center islands in the middle of Broadway, traffic whizzing around them in both directions—even they seem to be a thing of the past.

She crosses Broadway quickly, the DON'T WALK sign already flashing. Outside the old Shakespeare & Co., a man has set up a tray table piled with books. A large cardboard sign announces PHILIP ROTH— SIGNED COPIES!!! Above the sign, a poster-sized photograph of Roth himself peers disapprovingly over the shoppers, the mothers pushing strollers, the teenagers checking their reflections in the windows of Essentials Plus.

She has brought nothing with her. No change of clothes, no clean underwear, not even a toothbrush. She's not staying, no way in hell. That's what she told herself the whole flight down from Bangor. Ridiculous, of course. She's going to have to stay at least overnight. Broadway is already cast in a wintry shadow, the sun low in the sky, setting across the Hudson River. Her body—the same body that spent her whole childhood in this place—knows the time by the way the light falls over the avenue. She doesn't need to look at her watch. It's four o'clock. That much—the way the sun rises and sets—has not changed.

She's been circling for an hour. Killing time. Down Columbus, across brownstone-lined side streets, over to West End Avenue with its stately gray buildings, heavy brass doors, uniformed doormen just inside.

A man in an overcoat hurries by her. He glances at her as he passes, holding her gaze for a moment longer than necessary. Why does he bother? She looks like a hundred other women on the Upper West Side: pale, dark-haired, lanky. A thirtyish blur. She could be pretty if she tried, but she has long since stopped trying. Clara stares back at the man. *Stop looking at me.* This, too, she has forgotten about the city: the brazen way that people size each other up, constantly weighing, judging, comparing. So very different from the Yankee containment of Maine, where everybody just minds their own business.

The phone call came at about eleven o'clock, a few nights ago. No one ever called that late; it was as if the ring itself had a slightly shriller tone to it. (Of course, this could be what her memory is supplying to the moment now—now that she is here.) Everybody was asleep. Jonathan, Sam, Zorba, the puppy, in his crate downstairs in the kitchen.

Jonathan groped for the phone.

"Hello?"

A long pause—too long—and then he reached over and turned on the bedside lamp. It was freezing in their bedroom, the bed piled with four blankets. One of the windowsills was rotting, but to fix it meant ripping the whole thing out, which meant real construction, which cost money, which they didn't have.

Jonathan handed her the phone.

"Who is it?" she mouthed, hand over the receiver.

He shook his head.

"Hello?" She cleared her throat, hoarse from sleep. "Hello?"

"Clara?"

With a single word—her own name—her head tightened. Robin almost never called her, and certainly not at this hour. They talked exactly once a year, on the anniversary of their father's death. Clara sank deeper beneath the pile of blankets, the way an animal might try to camouflage itself, sensing danger. Her mind raced through the possibilities. Something had happened, something terrible. Robin would not be calling with good news. And there was only one person, really, whom they shared.

"What's wrong?" Clara's voice was a squeak. A pathetic little mouse.

"I'm going to tell you something—and I want you to promise me you won't hang up."

Clara was silent. The mirror over the dresser facing the bed was hanging askew, and she could see herself and Jonathan, their rumpled late-night selves. Through the receiver, on Robin's end, she heard office sounds. The muted ring of corporate telephones, even at this hour.

"Don't hang up. Promise?"

How like Robin to want to seal the deal, to control the situation, before Clara even knows what the situation is.

"Okay."

"Say 'promise.' "

Clara squeezed her hands into fists.

"Christ! I promise."

"Ruth is . . . she's sick. She's—oh, shit, Clara. It's bad. She's very sick."

"What do you mean?" Clara responded. The words didn't make sense. She was stupid with shock.

"Listen. I'm just calling to say that you need to come home," Robin said.

There it was. Fourteen years—and there it was. Home. She *was* home, goddammit.

"I've made myself insane, going around and around in circles."

Robin paused. "My therapist finally said it wasn't up to me—that you had a right to know."

"How long has this been going on?" Clara managed to ask.

"Awhile," Robin said. She sounded tired. Three kids, partner in a midtown law firm; of course she was tired. Clara couldn't imagine her sister's life.

Clara climbed out of bed and walked over to the window. She was suddenly suffocatingly hot in the freezing room. The lights from the harbor beckoned in the distance.

"Look, the truth is—I can't deal with this by myself," Robin said. Never, in Clara's memory, had Robin ever admitted such a thing. She was the queen of competence.

"I have to think about it," Clara said. Her sister was silent on the other end of the phone. Clara tried to picture her, but the image wasn't clear: round brown eyes, a tense mouth. "Okay, Robin? This is— I never thought I would ever even consider—"

"I know," said Robin. "But please."

After she hung up the phone, Clara climbed back into bed and twined her legs around Jonathan's, her hands on his belly. She closed her eyes tight and burrowed her face into the crease of his neck. He was asking her something—*What are you going to do?*—but his voice sounded muffled, as if suddenly there were something, something thick and cottony, separating her from her real life. She breathed Jonathan in, fighting the avalanche of thoughts.

She rounds the corner from 78th Street to Broadway. The wind is whipping, stirring up the litter. A flyer attaches itself to her thigh; she picks it off and glances at it: the opening of a new yoga studio. It has always been blustery right at this spot, only two blocks from the river, where the wide cross street meets the boulevard of Broadway. But now Clara feels the wind differently. After more than a decade of winters on an island off the coast of Maine, she has toughened up.

Her skin is thicker now; she is not as fragile, not as easily blown around—or so she hopes.

It took her four days to decide to come to New York. She went about her daily routine in Southwest Harbor—driving Sam to school in the morning, taking Zorba for long walks along the waterfront, doing Jonathan's invoices at his shop—but all the while, accompanying every step she took was a thrumming, ceaseless refrain: *she's sick, she's sick, she's sick.* Somehow, with a stubborn, self-protective naïveté, Clara never imagined that Ruth would ever fall ill. What *had* she thought? Certainly, that her mother would live well into her nineties, in perfect mental and physical health. By the time Ruth was failing, Clara would be an old woman herself, in her seventies. Maybe, by then, she'd be able to face Ruth without the fear of crumbling—the fear that the stuff she was made of was simply not strong enough. That her life, this life she's built for herself, would disappear—*poof*— and only she and Ruth would be left. Mother and daughter, just the way it had always been.

*She's sick, she's sick, she's sick.* Clara awoke on the fifth morning and began calling the mothers of Sam's classmates to arrange for Sam to be picked up at school and delivered to ballet, swim practice, jujitsu. She prepared a grocery list for Jonathan as if she were planning to be gone for weeks. All the way to the Bangor airport, she told herself that she could change her mind. Even on the flight to New York, she was unsure. Her feet have carried her here. Her heart is numb— except for the occasional skipped beat, hard against her chest wall, letting her know how terrified she is.

She stops in front of the Apthorp. The building takes up the entire block between Broadway and West End. She hesitates for a single second. If someone is watching her from a window up on the twelfth floor, they will not notice the faltering. She walks through the high arched gates leading to the center courtyard. A nanny sits by the empty fountain, taking advantage of the last moments of daylight with her charges: a boy and a girl. The boy looks to be five or so, and the girl, Clara thinks, is nine—the same age as Sam. This one is much more of a city kid, though, with long straight hair and a lime-green down vest that Sam would probably kill for.

Clara has not so much as brought a single photograph of her daughter. She thought of it as she was leaving home this morning. As the taxi honked outside, she removed the picture of Sam she carried in her wallet: Samantha's third-grade class photo, grinning against a sky-blue backdrop, her long hair shiny and braided. Clara slipped the photo into the kitchen drawer, under the phone book, where it would stay safe until her return. She might otherwise have been tempted. In normal circumstances—in some other family—it would have been the most natural thing in the world.

The doorman in the booth, a young guy, doesn't recognize Clara. Why would he? He's new. He was probably still in grade school the last time she set foot in this courtyard.

"Can I help you?" All business, with a slight professional hint of suspicion. Clara doesn't look like she grew up in this building. Maybe she doesn't even look like someone who might be visiting. She stuffs her hands into the pockets of her old down jacket, wishing, for a moment, that she had worn a nicer coat.

"I'm here to see Ruth Dunne."

"Who may I say is calling?"

*Her daughter.*

"Clara," she says softly.

He picks up the intercom phone—also new—and punches in a few numbers. She could still get out of here. She could take a taxi back to LaGuardia and wait for the next flight home.

"There's a Clara here to see Ms. Dunne," the doorman says into the receiver. She wonders who he's talking to. It occurs to her that Robin could be there. No. It isn't likely. Clara had left Robin a message at her office, letting her know she was coming. Robin would stay far, far away from this particular mother-daughter reunion. She would treat it like a toxic event. Besides, it's a workday.

"You can go up," the doorman tells her, gesturing to the set of elevators in the northeast corner of the building, as if Clara doesn't already know, as if her feet aren't already leading her there like a sleepwalker.

"Twelve A," he calls after her.

The elevator. When she and Robin were children, the elevator was still run by an ancient pneumatic system, water pushed through pipes, and to travel to the top, from the first floor to the twelfth, literally took minutes. Sometimes several minutes, with stops. A small bench had been built into the ornate wooden car. She used to sit there, listening to the sound of rushing water, her mind pleasantly blank, empty of all thought, as she often felt when arriving or leaving home.

Now, she barely has time to remember this. The elevator doors close efficiently, with a modern *ding,* and she is pulled quickly up, up, up. Hardly any time at all to remember her mother's voice, that surprisingly whispery little-girl's voice, saying, *I could read all of* Magic Mountain *in this elevator.* Once, when she was in high school, Clara actually tried. She carried a paperback in her book bag, whipped it out during every ride. She got to the part where Hans Castorp meets Herr Settembrini and gave up. It was easier just to float along, watching as one floor number slowly gave way to the next.

The door slides open on 12. She can still turn around. She can press the lobby button and head back down. Past the doorman, who would call *Miss? Miss, did you find everything okay?,* and out the gates. Gulp the air outside, filling her lungs. She should have brought Jonathan with her, for moral support. But she couldn't. Jonathan, here? It was an impossible thought.

Keep on marching. Out of the elevator and down the hall, the wide hall with just a few doors on each side. Many of these apartments have been combined over the years to accommodate growing families, or maybe just growing bank accounts. The walls are freshly painted, pale and glossy, the color of milk. The grungy carpet that Clara remembers is gone, long gone, replaced by something dark gray and forgiving.

She can hardly breathe. *You need to come home.* And here she is. Clara no longer uses her maiden name, hasn't since she married Jonathan. Clara Dunne no longer exists, at least not as a living, breathing person. Clara Dunne is only a flat black-and-white series of images, frozen in time: a toddler, a little nymph, a prepubescent creature, a teenager—hanging on the walls of museums and galleries, sold at auction to the highest bidder. She shakes her head hard. Not those thoughts. Not now.

She presses the buzzer on the side of the last door in the corridor. The sound is the same: a shrill high-pitched ring that could wake the dead. No chimes for Ruth. No melodious chords announcing visitors. Clara has been gone nearly half her life. She has truly believed that a moment like this would never come. Her past has fallen away. She has scrubbed and scoured, rubbed herself raw, until nothing of her history remains.

She flexes her fingers as she stands, waiting. Clenches her jaw, then releases it. If only she had a mantra, something she could repeat to herself right now, over and over and over, a calming phrase to hold on to if all else fails. She sees herself, convex in the mirrored peephole of the apartment door. She looks gnomic. A circus version of herself.

A rustling on the other side, and then the door is opened by a girl of eighteen or so. She's tall and reed-thin, wearing faded ripped-up blue jeans, a black tank top, black boots that look like they must weigh five pounds each. Two long dark-brown braids snake down her shoulders. Possibly an intern from ICP. Or maybe a very lucky Pratt student.

The girl cocks her head to one side.

"Clara," she says. "Robin said you might be coming."

Clara steps into the foyer, which is exactly as she remembers it: the pile of mail, the stacks of magazines. *The New Yorker, Harper's, Peo-*

ple, *The New York Review of Books, Vogue, National Geographic, Time, Newsweek,* the odd *National Enquirer*—her mother subscribed to every newspaper and magazine, from the highbrow to the low. It looks possible that not a single magazine has been thrown out since Clara left. They are piled waist-high on the console table and on the floor, teetering, threatening to fall over.

Above the console, the same Irving Penn nude, a woman curled around herself, her pale expanse of belly exposed, a single mole dotting her fleshy hip. It had been a gift from Penn, given to Ruth on the occasion of her first gallery show. There was hardly a great photographer who had not made a gift of his or her work to Ruth Dunne at some point over the years. Without even looking, Clara knows the rest of the photographs hung in the public areas of the apartment: the Cindy Sherman self-portrait, the Berenice Abbott nightscape of Manhattan, the series of Sebastião Salgado images of war.

Where the hell is Ruth?

The girl with the braids is still standing there like some sort of sentry. A last shaft of dusty light from a west-facing window slices across her body. There is something in the steadiness of her gaze, her self-possession, that is making Clara even more uncomfortable than she already is.

"My mother—" she says quietly, more a statement than a question. She is angry, she realizes.

"She's resting," the girl says, looking at Clara curiously.

Clara has no idea what this means. *Resting.* Ruth never rested. She slept four, maybe five hours a night, tops. Clara remembers wandering into the kitchen once—it must have been three in the morning—looking for her mother. And there was Ruth, slumped over the kitchen table, her head resting on her folded arms. The only light in the room was the glow cast from the city outside the window. *What are you doing? Why are you sleeping here?* she asked her mother. The look in Ruth's eye when she raised her head—it was as if she were staring straight through Clara, as if she were seeing someone else entirely.

"Is she in the studio?" she asks the girl.

"No. Her room."

Why is the girl here? She's acting like she knows things—important things. Ruth has always done this with all her little acolytes, these willing servants who think that somehow to be in the same room as greatness means they'll absorb it.

"Listen, I—" the girl starts.

"What's your name?" Clara interrupts.

"Peony."

Peony. Of course. It couldn't be a normal name.

"I guess you haven't seen your mother in a while," says Peony.

"You could say that."

The girl keeps staring at Clara while pretending not to stare— another trait endemic to New Yorkers that Clara has forgotten over the years.

"I wouldn't recognize you," the girl finally says. "I mean, from the photographs."

Clara feels this like a physical shock. Like someone has come up behind her, grabbed her around the waist, clamped a hand over her mouth. She waves a hand in the air, quickly trying to make the whole thing go away. *Not that. Anything but that.* The flood of images—she closes her eyes for a moment, a trick she learned a long time ago, and shuts them out.

"I'm going to see my mother now," she says. Her voice is thick. She doesn't sound like herself. She *isn't* herself, here in this apartment.

Peony nods. As Clara starts down the hall to Ruth's bedroom, she can feel Peony's eyes on her back, watching her.

Clara knocks softly. Is Ruth sleeping? For so many years, she tried to turn the doorknob without a sound, little feet padding across the hardwood floor. *Quiet as a mouse,* Ruth would laugh in the morning, opening her dark eyes to find Clara curled into a ball, tucked against her.

"Wait a minute," Ruth calls from the other side of the heavy door. Fourteen years, and these are her mother's first words. Clara stands still. She is surrounded by all the ghosts of her former selves that have ever occupied this space. The toddler dragging a red crayon down the length of the freshly painted hallway molding; the first-grader racing around the apartment, desperate to find her mother; the teenager sneaking in, avoiding the floorboards that creaked on her way to her own room. She tests her memory now, pressing one foot down on a slightly warped piece of the parquet. It groans, a low, almost animal sound, just like it always did.

"Come in," she hears Ruth say.

Clara's stomach lurches. The last thing she ate was a protein bar at the airport. Her intestines squeeze and rumble in protest against the combination of too much anxiety and too little sustenance. She imagines herself perched on the edge of a high craggy cliff, like a diver she once saw in Portugal when she was a kid. Arms raised high, back arched, and then that moment—it looked to her like faith—of slicing purposefully, cleanly through the air. She pushes the door open.

Ruth is sitting in a wheelchair by the window. No lights have been turned on, not even a bedside lamp. In the fading purple-gray dusk she is in shadows.

"Hi, Mom," Clara says. The word slips from her mouth, a lozenge, leaving behind the distinct taste of a young and bitter fruit.

"You're here," Ruth says. Even bundled into black sweatpants and a thick fleece sweatshirt, she is all bones. Her face, angular to begin with, looks sharply etched, like a pencil drawing. A brightly colored scarf is tied around her small head like a turban.

Clara's eyes sting. She looks around the room at the medical paraphernalia: the dull aluminum gleam of a walker, an ivory-tipped cane propped against the wall, a portable commode on the floor near the bathroom. Orange plastic prescription bottles litter the bedside table. Robin was right. Clara couldn't believe it until she saw it with her own eyes. Ruth is very sick. Ruth is—

She leans against the side of the bed. She isn't sure what to do. She's afraid to go near her mother, and she's afraid to stand too far away. There isn't anything in the self-help section for this, no *Idiot's Guide to Seeing Your Mother After Fourteen Years.*

Ruth flips the brakes on her wheelchair and struggles to stand. She makes it to her feet, then sways to the left, catching herself against the window. Her face is the color of a blank sheet of paper.

"Sit down!" Clara says. "Please don't get up for me—"

Ruth flashes Clara a look—there's the old Ruth, those dark eyes capable of seeing through anything—as if to say, *You silly child.*

"Could you fetch me my walker? I can't reach it."

The walker. Of course. Clara goes to the far wall and grabs it, grateful for something to do. Then she takes it to Ruth, who doesn't stop watching her—hungrily, possessively—a look that makes Clara feel smaller and smaller.

"Let's sit in the living room," says Ruth. "I can't stand being in this depressing place." She shuffles forward, using the walker, her feet barely leaving the floor. Her jaw clenches with the effort. One leg keeps turning inward, nearly tripping her with each step.

"Maybe if you just got back into the wheelchair, I could push you," Clara starts. "It might be easier—"

"God, don't tell me what to do," Ruth says. Her voice is reedy with sudden rage. "I'm going to walk into the—"

She trips on the fringe of the carpet and goes down. Her body hardly makes a noise as it hits the floor. "I'm okay," she says, even as she's falling. "I'm okay. Help me up."

Clara reaches down and grabs Ruth under both her arms. She hoists her back up—she is light as a child—and half drags, half carries her back to the wheelchair. She's trying not to think, just to act.

She can keep doing the next thing, whatever the next thing might be. Put one foot in front of the other. That, she can handle. Anything but talking. She just doesn't want to talk.

"Thank you," Ruth says. "That damn rug keeps getting in my way."

Her head scarf has been dislodged. Her hair—that black, wavy, waist-length hair—is gone. She's bald, the bony conical shape of her skull like something obscene, something not meant to be witnessed. Tufts of downy fuzz cover the top of her head. She looks new, like she has just been born. But no. The blue-black circles under her eyes, the skin so papery it might crumble to the touch. She is not new. She is—Clara does a quick calculation—fifty-seven years old. The last time they saw each other, Clara was eighteen and Ruth forty-three. She rests for a moment on the tide of numbers—infallible, controllable numbers—until the numbers start turning on her. Fourteen years: a lifetime. Samantha's lifetime, and then some. So much has been lost. So much has *always* been lost.

"Well, don't just stand there and stare." Ruth waves her hand in the air—the same gesture Clara used just a few minutes ago with the girl, Peony.

"I'm sorry," Clara says. "I just . . ."

"I know. I'm quite a sight." Ruth tries to replace the head scarf.

"What's happened to you?" Clara forces herself to ask. She leans against the bed again. She can just about make out the labels on some of the prescription bottles from here: morphine, lorazepam. She wants to reach over, grab a bottle, shake its contents into her open palm. *Stop it.* Oblivion is not an option. She can't soften the edges of this thing—a pain beyond dulling.

"Didn't Robin brief you? It appears that I have adenocarcinoma of the lung. Stage IIIB," Ruth says. "Which is a bad thing. Very bad." An attempt to keep her voice light. As if it hasn't been more than a decade. As if the thirty-two-year-old woman standing before her is no different from the eighteen-year-old girl who left.

Peony has slipped into the room, carrying a tray with a cup of something steaming—soup, tea—and some toast.

"You two have met?" Ruth asks, as if they're at a cocktail party. "Peony has been an absolute godsend."

Of course, they're all godsends, the girls and boys who worship at Ruth's feet. And Clara—ungrateful, terrible disappointment that she is—had fled. She had broken every pact and even one of the Ten Commandments.

"It's time for you to eat," says Peony. She sets the tray down on a rolling table, a piece of hospital furniture. "Can I get you anything else?"

Clara bets this isn't what she had in mind when she got the internship with Ruth Dunne.

"No, thanks," says Ruth. "I just want to be left alone with my daughter."

"Call if you need me," says Peony. And just as quickly, she slips back out.

*My daughter.* The phrase is not lost on Clara. Ruth has always used Clara's given name—the name Ruth gave her—sparingly. She'd much prefer to claim her as her own. *My daughter.* So many years since Clara has heard it, but still—it doesn't matter. Her mother's eyes are upon her. Boring into her. Darting back and forth, up and down. As a very little girl, Clara used to examine herself—each limb, every finger and toe—before going to sleep at night and again upon waking in the morning. She was deathly afraid that Ruth might have stolen away a piece of her. Once she knew about internal organs—heart, lungs, pancreas, liver—she searched herself all over for scars.

"Let me help you with your soup," Clara says, swinging the arm of the hospital table across the wheelchair.

"I don't want any soup," says Ruth. "I don't have time for soup."

Clara has kept tabs on Ruth over the years, typing her mother's name into search engines late at night, after Sam and Jonathan were asleep. She knew when Ruth switched from Castelli to Metro Pictures, and then from Metro Pictures to Matthew Marks. She knew about the retrospective at the Whitney last year, and in the weeks after the opening she bought the magazines in which postage-stamp-sized photos might appear. There was one, finally, in *New York* magazine, of Ruth, elegant in a black sweater and turquoise dangling earrings, her masses of hair pulled back into a ponytail.

Was she already sick then?

"Tell me something," says Ruth.

"What do you want to know?"

Ruth sighs, slumping down in her seat. She looks like she might slide right off the wheelchair and back onto the floor. "What don't I want to know," she says. She looks at Clara's left hand, her gold wedding ring no thicker than a wire. She scans Clara's whole body, looking for clues and signs.

"You live up north," Ruth says. More a statement than a question.

Clara nods. If she had to bet, she'd say that Ruth already knows quite a lot. Robin would have told her. Even though Clara and Robin have agreed, all these years, to stay off the subject of Ruth, nothing was stopping Robin from telling Ruth the little that she knew about her sister's life.

"Children?"

"A daughter," Clara answers. "She's nine."

Surely, Ruth already knows this. Even if Robin had tried to stay out of it, Ruth would have grilled her: *Who is your sister married to? How many children does she have?*

"Just one?" says Ruth dreamily. "You should have another. You should have two, like me."

Clara clenches a fist, then releases it. She keeps doing this, opening and closing her hand, feeling her nails dig into her palm.

"And there's a husband, I presume?"

Clara's about to say something—she has to say something—but she doesn't want even to utter Jonathan's name—or Sam's—in front of her mother.

Something crosses Ruth's face.

"Can you send Peony in, darling?" she asks.

"Why do you need Peony?" Clara asks. Insane as it is, she feels hurt.

"Please." Ruth's eyes dart over to the commode in the corner.

Ah. This is something she can't do. Thank goodness Ruth understands this. She doesn't expect Clara to hoist up her nightgown and wedge the commode under her buttocks. Perhaps this is a daughterly duty, repayment for the early years of diapering, but not this daughter. Not this mother. Suddenly Clara feels as if she might throw up. In which case the commode would be useful.

"Clara!" Ruth's voice snaps her out of it.

"Sorry," Clara murmurs. She goes looking for Peony, quickly, quickly, remembering some old childhood helplessness—*Mom! Mom, I've gotta go!*—and finds her sitting at the kitchen table, resting her legs on a chair, leafing through the arts section of the *Times*.

"My mother needs you," Clara says. It's all wrong. An eighteen-year-old student should not be changing Ruth's bedpan. Ruth shouldn't need a goddamned bedpan. Fifty-seven is so young. Peony is already halfway down the hall, past the two closed doors to what were once Clara's and Robin's bedrooms. Clara pours herself a glass of water, then picks up the phone. Tacked to the wall is a list of emergency numbers: the super, the alarm company, the insurance broker, and Robin's home, cell, office.

"Ms. Dunne's office," a male assistant answers.

"Is she in?"

"Who's calling?"

"Her sister."

An imperceptible pause. "Hold a moment."

As she holds, Clara tries to breathe all the way in. Her lungs feel tight, as if they are closing up in sympathy for Ruth. She struggles for more air. Sitting in the kitchen of her childhood—the refrigerator, oven, even the microwave are the same as when she left, no *Elle Decor* remodeling for Ruth—Clara is drowning. She needs to talk to Jonathan. She needs to hear Samantha's sweet, thin voice.

"You're here."

Robin's voice. So familiar, yet so strange. No comfort to be found in it.

"I'm freaking out," Clara says.

"Welcome home."

"Please don't keep saying that!"

"What? What am I saying?"

"Home. This isn't my home!"

"Sorry—just a figure of speech."

Clara hears papers rustling, the *ding* of e-mail being received. "She looks awful," she says quietly.

"Cancer isn't pretty."

"Robin, will you stop talking like that?"

"Like what? I have no idea what you mean."

"You're talking to me in news flashes instead of like a human being."

Robin sighs heavily into the phone. "It's been stressful," she says. "And now—I mean, I'm glad you're here, and it takes some of the pressure off me, but you've got to admit it also creates a whole new set of problems."

"Look—you called me."

"I had to call," Robin says. "I didn't want it weighing on me for the rest of my life that you didn't get a chance to—"

"To what?" Clara interrupts. "To make amends? To fix things? To say goodbye?"

The two sisters fall silent.

"Take your pick," Robin says softly, after a while. And she hangs up the phone, so gently that it takes Clara a moment to realize she's been disconnected.

# Chapter Two

RUTH'S STUDIO is pitch-black and empty. Clara slowly walks inside, feeling like a trespasser. The office is to the right of the front door. She could do this with her eyes closed, even now. She feels for the edge of the massive oak desk, then gropes around for the switch on the cord of the desk lamp. A bright halogen light floods the office. It seems as if no one has set foot here in months. Surely the girl, Peony, has been taking care of Ruth's business. Or Robin, stickler for all details. But the desk is piled with mail, most of it unopened.

Beyond the office is the darkroom, still with its faint chemical smell. And past the darkroom, the cavernous studio itself, with arched windows, all fitted with blackout curtains, facing Broadway. It feels like a cave. Deep inside a life, or a mind—her mother's mind—and far, far from the outside world. The walls are so thick in this old building that even the sounds of ambulances, fire trucks, and the occasional car alarm are muted. But Ruth, so easily distracted, had the studio professionally soundproofed. It's absence of noise is complete. It has its own disconcerting sound: total blankness.

The studio had once been a two-bedroom apartment, which Ruth rented in the mid-1970s. She gutted it and turned it into a pristine, white space. An enormous luxury, really, since most of her work had been set outdoors, in nature. It was only in later years—after Clara

left—that Ruth began to really use the studio. Clara had read somewhere, a few years back, that Ruth's wall-sized commissioned portraits were selling for $100,000 apiece.

She sits on Ruth's swivel chair, facing the desk, halfheartedly sifting through bills, magazine subscriptions, handwritten letters, probably from students and fans. Medical bills are stacked in their own
wire basket. Memorial Sloan-Kettering, Mount Sinai, Columbia Pres-
byterian, Beth Israel. Clearly, Ruth has gone from doctor to doctor,
hospital to hospital, in search of a cure.

Above the desk hangs a bulletin board covered with glossy invitations to gallery openings; the most recent is six months old. Some
postcards of Ruth's favorite photographs are tacked to the board: a
Walker Evans, an Arnold Newman, a Man Ray of two women—his
wife and her lover, if Clara remembers correctly. Now she sees the
yellowed edge of a small piece of notepaper poking out from beneath
the Man Ray. It occupies the same pushpin. Clara moves the post-
card to the side and traces the fragile edge of the note with one finger.

*Dear Ruth.*

Her own handwriting, loopy and round, embarrassingly girlish.

*Please don't look for me. You won't find me.*

Clara leans back in the swivel chair. So Ruth kept the note. It has
been so long since Clara has allowed herself to think of that time. It's
never far from her, of course, tucked high up in her mind like a box
on a shelf. She's hoped, stupidly, naively, self-protectively, that somehow the box would stay there forever, wedged into its own dark corner. That it would not come crashing down, full of its impossible
memories. It has been her life's work, really, to distance herself from
the past. She's built layer upon layer of a new self on top of the
old one.

But now the room goes blurry, her vision fading in and out of focus. Her hands are cold, clammy. The past is gaining on her, a predator, and the life she's built for herself seems like a flimsy thing, a thin shell about to be cracked wide open.

The note has a small rip, which has been carefully Scotch-taped. Ruth wanted to preserve this. She has kept it where she could see it every day for fourteen years.

*I can't be here anymore, I just can't. I love you, but I feel like I'm going crazy. I'll be in touch when I can. Love always, Clara.*

*Love always.* Something an eighteen-year-old girl would say and mean, even as she packed her belongings (jeans, sweatshirt, clean socks, change of underwear) in a knapsack and walked out the door of her childhood home. Clara can still feel the soft spring air on her face that morning as she stuck out her hand and hailed a taxi to Grand Central instead of boarding the crosstown bus to school. What was she thinking? Did she think at all? She had a destination but no real plan, her mind as blank as she could make it.

"How long are you going to be gone?" Robin had asked, when Clara called her at college the night before she left.

"I don't know," Clara answered. "Awhile, I guess."

She could hear Robin's breath over the phone. Steady, unruffled. Her mind going over the possibilities.

"I'm telling Mom," Robin said.

"No, you're not."

"How can you do this? You're throwing everything away. How can you leave school with only—"

"It doesn't matter, Robin," Clara said quietly. "I can't care about that."

They were silent for a while, the two sisters.

"You're not coming back," Robin said.

"That's not true."

"Oh, Clar."

Two small syllables—but her sister's voice carried inside it the knowledge of their shared family history.

Clara couldn't have done it—she couldn't possibly have left if she had known she was never coming back. She had five thousand dollars in traveler's checks folded into her sneaker. This money—an inheritance from her father when she turned eighteen—seemed like enough to last her until she figured out her next move. And so she hailed a cab to Grand Central and bought a ticket to New Haven. She had a friend from Brearley who was a freshman at Yale. Clara had made arrangements to stay with the girl in her dorm room. She had thought no further than that.

Lost. All she knew was that when she reached inside herself, searching for something to hold on to, there was nothing to grasp. She was a walking, talking echo chamber. This wasn't typical teenage stuff, adolescent angst. She had read the psychology books, crouched in the stacks of Shakespeare & Co. She knew all about adolescence and its discontents. This—this was something else. If she stayed, she might never find her way out.

*I'll be in touch.* Such a lighthearted phrase. *See you later, alligator. In a while, crocodile.* Clara tries to bring that girl to the surface. She had tossed off the word *love* as if it had no real meaning. Love requires dailiness. Love requires care and feeding. Being a wife and mother has taught her nothing if not that. But what did she know? She was just a kid—the same age as that little Peony—a kid who thinks she's a grown-up. That's the danger of the age. Clara's already aware of it, thinking of Samantha, at nine, just on the cusp.

She picks up the phone and dials home. Jonathan and Sam are probably eating dinner by now. Jonathan would have stopped at Little Notch on his way home and picked up a large pepperoni pizza and a six-pack of Coke. A far cry from the vegetable stir-fries and quinoa casseroles she usually puts on the table. Healthy food, enough sleep, cardiovascular exercise, yoga, meditation—she has spent the last nine years, ever since Sam was born, making sure that she does every possible thing right. As if maybe, just maybe, if she does everything right, she can keep the world from touching them.

She can picture them sitting at the kitchen table. Sam's long skinny legs are stretched out on Jonathan's lap. The pizza box lies soggy and open. The television is on, in the background. The dead of winter is Jonathan's slow time of year. His days are filled with overseas phone calls and faxes, doing the least favorite part of his job, ordering the materials he needs from Indonesia in time to make jewelry to sell in his shop to the summer crowd.

Clara walks over to one of the arched windows and pulls up the blackout shade. She wishes she had one of those video phones, so Jonathan could see what she sees. The cars zooming in both directions on Broadway below. The street never—not at any hour—empty. All of it unfurling like a silent film.

"Hello?"

It's Sammy. Clara still can't get used to the idea that her daughter is old enough to answer the phone. Since Sam's birth, the years have tumbled, one into the next.

"Sweetheart!"

"Mommy—when are you coming home?"

Sam cuts right to the chase. Clara told her so little before she left. Rushing to get her to school. Lugging her knapsack, art projects, a plastic container filled with cookies for the bake sale. No time to talk, really. Something about a quick last-minute trip to New York, as if such a thing were normal. No big deal.

"Well, I don't know, exactly."

The words come out before Clara even realizes what she's saying. What's this? The plan—at least the plan in her head—was to be here for as little time as possible. Assess the situation and get the hell out. But now she's here, in Ruth's apartment.

"What do you mean, you don't know?" Sam's voice quavers.

"I—"

"Why are you in New York?" Sammy asks.

Clara needs to change the subject. She can't tell Sammy what she's doing in New York—it's impossible. She has never figured out how to explain her history to her daughter, so she simply hasn't. Which isn't a *lie,* exactly. More like a sin of omission.

When Sam was a much littler girl, three or four, she used to ask Clara pointed questions from the backseat of the car as they drove the winding roads of Mount Desert.

*Mommy, do you have brothers or sisters?*

*One sister.*

*Just one?*

*Yup.*

*Does your sister have kids?*

*She does, sweetheart. You have three first cousins in New York City.*

*I want to meet them!*

*Someday,* Clara had said, wondering when that day would ever be. Hating herself for robbing Sam of the pleasure of first cousins. But how could she involve her family with Robin's and leave Ruth out of it?

*Where's your mommy?* Sam inevitably asked. Clara's hands tightened against the steering wheel. How could she do the right thing when she wasn't sure what the right thing was? She always figured there would be a moment—appearing clearly defined, outlined like an apparition—in which she would know, absolutely, that it was time to tell Sam about her grandmother.

*She's gone, sweetie,* Clara would answer.

Gone—that has certainly been true. Down on Broadway, a man stands in the center island, one hand on his chest, belting out an aria from *Don Giovanni.* Wow. *That* guy. He had been a fixture down around Carnegie Hall when Clara was a kid. He had a beautiful, professionally trained voice, and he sang on street corners, an open empty violin case at his feet.

"How was your swim meet?"

"I placed second."

"That's great, honey!"

"No. First would be great."

Clara can hear Sam squirming, the kitchen chair creaking. She's probably wearing the holey old gray sweats she puts on after swimming, her dark wet hair woven into a sloppy braid. She's skinnier than Clara ever was, but, other than that, Sam looks exactly like Clara did at nine. Last summer, Clara and Sam were at Jumpin' Java on Main Street, where the summer people go for their cold drinks, and an older gentleman in a windbreaker had stopped and stared at Sammy. Clara knew—even before he spoke, she knew. *My dear, you're the spitting image of that girl in Ruth Dunne's early photographs. The daughter. What was her name?* The man's crinkly blue eyes swept over the two of them, not really registering Clara. She had always been on guard for the day when someone would make the connection: a wealthy collector, a summer resident of the island. Clara had known it could happen. She pushed herself off her stool and grabbed Sammy's hand. *Come on, honey. We've got to go.*

"Mom, why are you in New York?" Sammy's not letting go of this one.

"I have some work to do."

"What do you mean?"

A reasonable question, since Clara doesn't really have work of her own. She helps Jonathan with a small amount of local advertising and marketing and makes sure the shop runs smoothly. Even a nine-year-old is going to detect the bullshit.

"Hey, can I talk to Daddy?"

There's silence for a moment. Sammy's chewing.

"He's not here."

"What do you mean, he's not there? Who's with you?"

"Elizabeth. We made nachos."

Elizabeth is the daughter of the next-door neighbors. Sixteen years old. An honors student. You couldn't ask for a more competent babysitter. But where is Jonathan?

"Daddy said he'd be home late."

*Goddammit, Jonathan.* Clara's skin feels too tightly stretched over her bones. Why tonight, of all nights? She's never been away from Sam before. Did she really have to spell things out?

Below, she can see two men arguing over a parking space on the east side of Broadway. One guy has climbed out of his car and is standing in the empty space, his arms crossed. Staking his territory. The other guy, in a sleek little sport car, has parked his car at an angle into the street, hazards flashing. He has one foot out the door. Middle-aged men acting like high school boys. Clara moves away from the window, once again lowering the blackout shade. She has been gripping the phone so tightly her hand aches.

"I'll be home as soon as I can. I promise. Tell Dad to call me when he gets home, okay?"

She blows a kiss, then hangs up the phone. She turns off the desk lamp, plunging the studio into darkness. She closes her eyes and imagines she is somewhere else, anywhere but here. She summons Flying Mountain at the mouth of Somes Sound—one of her favorite spots on the island—and tries, mentally, to put herself there. The view stretching wide over the great harbor. The Cranberry Islands in the distance. Next, she pictures her own house. Her small backyard. The dozens of bulbs she planted in the fall, waiting, sleeping beneath the snow-covered ground. Nothing is working. It's the silence, she realizes. It pierces every thought, every willful daydream. It is the dead silence of her mother's studio, a place where the rest of the world simply does not exist.

———◆•••◆———

A CRITIC once wrote that Ruth Dunne's work was a "hedge against memory." The phrase had wounded Ruth. *They don't understand,* she said at the time. *Why do they write about things they don't understand?* As a little girl, Clara thought she knew what the critic meant: Ruth's photographs were like a privet hedge—rising tall and green and dense, standing between her and her own memory. She struggled to remember things. At night, lying in bed, she would try to pry the branches apart, to glimpse a single moment, a sight, a sound. But it was impossible. So, instead, she kept a portfolio of Ruth's work by her bedside. Sometimes, when she couldn't fall asleep, she would rest the heavy portfolio on her chest and study the images of herself, searching for clues as to who she really was.

The first image is almost a memory. Clara is three. She is naked, splashing in the warm water of her bath, deep inside the claw-footed tub on the top floor of their first house in the country. The house is an early Victorian with a big front porch, the rooms painted in pastel sherbet-colored shades by its previous owners. It's late afternoon, and the sun is hitting the old glass windowpanes, a liquid orange light setting the room aglow. Plastic toys float all around her: a sailboat, a rubber duck, a foot-long green lizard. Clara's hair is long and wavy. It has never been cut. When she holds her breath and goes underwater, she keeps her eyes open and watches her hair move across her face like seaweed on the surface of the ocean.

Robin is sitting on the bathroom floor, flipping slowly through the pages of *Green Eggs and Ham.* She's five years old and can already read. She's asking questions in her high little-girl's voice: *Why is the train underwater? Why is that guy purple? Wait a minute, he can't fly!* Clara can tell that the questions are driving her mother crazy. Ruth's forehead is knotted, her mouth turned tightly down as she kneels on the bath mat, soaping Clara's back.

"It's a *story,* Robin," Ruth says. "Can't you just accept that it's a story? You're such a literalist."

"What does 'literalist' mean, Mommy?"

Ruth sighs. Robin is not a believer in make-believe. She wants an answer for everything. Robin knows that Santa can't possibly squeeze down the chimney, he's too old and fat. And she knows that the tooth fairy is just an invention. Fairies don't really exist. Her daughters are opposite in nearly every possible way. Robin is olive-skinned and tough, with short Buster Brown hair, and has frown lines at the age of five. And Clara—Clara is a frail little firefly, a head-in-the-clouds dreamer, with long Botticelli waves and amber eyes that seem to accept whatever they see.

"'Literalist' means," Ruth begins slowly, each word seeming like an effort, "someone who thinks that everything has to make sense." Her hands move smoothly over Clara's buttocks, efficiently soaping her private parts. But then something changes. The moment freezes, and Clara would swear, when she thought of it years later, that she could hear a shutter snap. Clara has put the foot-long green lizard in her mouth as she leans back in the tub, her hair floating all around her like a halo.

"Wait." Ruth's voice catches. "Hold on." She stands quickly, backing out of the room, still looking at Clara in the tub. "Robin, watch your sister."

"But what am I supposed to do?" Robin calls. "Mommy—I can't swim!" But Ruth has already run down the two creaky flights of stairs to the kitchen, where her camera bag is by the back door. Then her feet pound back up the stairs, two at a time, and into the bathroom. She snaps a lens into her Polaroid, crouches down.

Clara takes the lizard out of her mouth.

"Honey, could you put that back in there—the lizard? Keep doing what you were doing before."

"Why, Mommy?" The lizard has the chemical-sweet taste of plastic. Besides, the bathwater is getting cold.

"Just for a second, Clara." Ruth is poised, one knee on the bathroom tile, the other ready to pivot. She pushes her long hair behind her ears and squints through the lens.

"Mommy, why does he try the green eggs and ham?" asks Robin. "And anyway, why is the ham green?"

"Quiet, Robin. Mommy's concentrating."

"But I just need to know—"

"Hush!" Ruth's voice is sharp.

Clara leans back in the water, trying to remember what she had been doing at the moment Ruth ran down to get her camera. She allows her head to lean back, her hair to float again. The leaves from the huge white birch in the backyard are pressed against the bathroom window, and they look to Clara like hundreds of birds fluttering outside. Her whole pale body—long, for a three-year-old—is stretched out in the small claw-footed tub. She puts the lizard back in her mouth and tries to keep from shivering.

Her ears are underwater, so she doesn't hear the click and whir of her mother's camera. Ruth takes five or six shots in the fading afternoon light. Clara watches her mother's face as she snaps a frame, then lowers the camera.

"Honey, put one foot up on the side of the tub—exactly, like that." Ruth adjusts slightly, then snaps again. Ruth is not dreamy. The gauzy layer of absentmindedness that usually surrounds her has been replaced by a quiet and complete attention.

"Mommy, why won't you talk to me?" Robin asks. She has moved out of the way, out of the line of the camera's vision. Her back is up against the tile wall. "I'm just asking you a simple question."

"Okay," Ruth says as she clicks the lens cover back in place. She helps Clara out of the tub. Clara's lips are blue, her teeth chattering. She doesn't like the way her mouth feels. She needs to brush her teeth.

Ruth turns wearily to Robin. "What was the question again, sweetie?"

"You never listen!" Robin slaps the wall as hard as she can. The tips of her ears and her nose are bright pink. But she doesn't cry. In their entire shared childhood, Clara will never see her sister cry.

The photographs of Clara snapped that summer afternoon are merely studies for the work that will eventually become *Clara with the Lizard*. The following morning, their father takes Robin hunting for bugs in the swamp behind their house. They set off in their matching baseball caps and backpacks, magnifying glasses hanging around their necks, long socks and sneakers protecting their pale ankles from ticks. The bug hunting was Ruth's idea—though Nathan has no idea why she has suddenly taken an interest in entomology. They'll be gone for at least a couple of hours.

She doesn't ask Clara to come upstairs to the bathroom until she has set up the shot. Yesterday's Polaroids are taped to the bathroom mirror. The morning light through the flimsy lace curtains on the bathroom window has been blocked by several layers of black construction paper, masking-taped to the tile walls. Ruth's lights have been set up, along with a circular silver reflector. She has run the water in the tub hot enough so that Clara will not get cold too quickly.

It's the middle of the morning, a strange time for a bath. But it's so rare that Clara gets to spend alone-time with her mother, she doesn't complain. She sets aside her Barbies and allows Ruth to hoist her into the tub. The lizard is there, along with the toy sailboat, the rubber duck.

"Okay, Clara. We're going to do a little work now," says Ruth. "I want you to help me. You're my model."

Clara has vaguely heard of models. They're the beautiful older girls on the pages of the magazines that are always lying around the house. She feels proud that she's a model—her mother's model.

"Lie back. Let your hair get wet," says Ruth.

Clara dunks her head in the water. She lets her whole face get wet. When she emerges, she has tiny drops of water on her eyelashes.

Ruth bends over the tub, then holds a light meter near Clara's chin, just above the surface of the water.

"That's perfect. Now put the lizard in your mouth," says Ruth.

"But it tastes yucky."

"Just for a minute—I promise."

Clara does as Ruth asks. She strains to remember what she did yesterday. She puts one bare foot up along the porcelain side of the tub, just like Ruth wanted her to do before. She puts the lizard in her mouth and tries to ignore the taste. It isn't so bad, really. Kind of like the soft fat-free yogurt that her dad let her try one day when he was pushing her in her stroller down Broadway.

Ruth is completely still, except for the movement of her hands as she focuses and shoots. Time disappears. Five minutes go by, or fifty. Clara feels warm, even as the water starts to cool off. She has never had her mother look at her for so long.

"We're done," murmurs Ruth. She lowers the camera, places it on a dry spot on the bath mat. "Come on out, sweetheart." She wraps Clara in a big fluffy towel, then holds her close. Clara can feel both of their hearts beating.

"Thank you," Ruth whispers into the top of her soaking-wet head. "You're such a good girl."

Ruth made only sixteen prints of *Clara with the Lizard.* Not too long ago, Clara read on the Internet that the sixteenth had set a record at Sotheby's for Ruth Dunne's work, selling for $240,000. Even though it was work from very early in Ruth's career, the image was seen as iconic. It was the moment she had found her true subject matter.

Clara could picture the quiet frenzy of the auction, of course: the well-dressed crowd in their folding chairs, their suited legs crossed, hands fidgeting on their paddles. And in the front of the room, on an easel—as well as projected on a twelve-foot screen—there she was. Her mouth around the lizard, her eyes huge and glistening, her leg raised on the edge of the tub, her *private parts,* as Ruth liked to call them, splayed open. The soft smell of the summer day, the innocence of a three-year-old girl, who wanted to please her mother so much she would do whatever was asked of her.

———◆•••◆———

THE DIGITAL CLOCK reads 8:53 in the morning. For a long disorienting moment, Clara has no idea where she is. She hasn't slept this late since before Sam was born. The venetian blinds almost, but not quite, block the harsh light filtering in through the south-facing window. The ornate brass ceiling fan is motionless above her head. The walls are an improbable pink, so bright they look like a mistake. She sits up in bed, the fog lifting, then swings her legs around, her toes meeting the thick ply of the cream-colored wall-to-wall. Robin's apartment. The guest room. Never before in Clara's life has she felt like such a guest.

They're all gone for the day, just as Robin said. The three kids are off to their three different schools. Ed, Robin's husband, left at six for the gym, to get his workout in before arriving at his law firm. Robin's personal yoga trainer has come and gone by now—Robin mentioned that he comes daily at seven—and Robin herself is undoubtedly into her second cup of coffee (her yang to the yin of yoga) and cycling through her morning call sheet. The housekeeper is here. Somewhere, on the other side of the apartment, Clara hears the faint sound of a vacuum running.

How has Robin gotten so rich? Or is this simply how upper-middle-class dual-career Manhattan lawyers now live? She has no idea. She may as well have spent the past fourteen years in the Sahara. That's how little she knows about this universe—the world she left behind. Her eyes fall on the bureau, wood and orange Formica, a piece of fifties kitsch. On top of the bureau there is a framed color snapshot of the four of them—Robin and Clara, Ruth and Nathan Dunne. They're walking in Central Park: Clara and Robin in a double stroller, Ruth and Nathan looking young and disheveled. A young family out for a Saturday-morning walk.

Last night—Ruth sound asleep in a morphine haze—Clara called Robin and asked if she could sleep over. She didn't feel capable of checking into a hotel. It was too scary, too lonely. And besides, too expensive.

"The guest room is already made up for you," Robin said. She had just been waiting for Clara to ask.

Clara had hailed a taxi on Broadway, then given the driver Robin's address on 75th and Park. The meter started at a dollar fifty and clicked up in fifteen-cent increments every few blocks. The Plexiglas partition, so close to her face, made her nauseated. The park was barren, empty except for the taxis and cars speeding through the transverse. The taxi turned down Park, the oxidized green roof of the Helmsley building framed by the MetLife skyscraper in the downtown distance.

She wasn't nervous about seeing Robin—not really. Robin was incapable of surprising her. If Clara had been asked, as a teenager, what she'd imagine her sister's future to be, she would have pretty much predicted this. The three kids, *bing, bing, bing.* The stable attorney husband. The partnership in the law firm, no mommy track for her. The Park Avenue address. The country house in Hillsdale that had once belonged to Ruth.

As the taxi pulled up to the green awning just north of 75th Street, Clara thought about the last time she saw Robin, six years earlier. They had arranged to meet at the upstate New York cemetery, near Hillsdale, where their father had been buried ten years before. Clara was twenty-six, mother of a three-year-old. Robin was twenty-eight and already had her three kids, the youngest of whom was still an infant.

They didn't talk much that day, not really. They were both a little bit afraid of each other. Afraid of what would happen if all of it—the betrayal, the hurt, the abandonment—started tumbling out. Instead, they exchanged photos of their children as they sat on the low stone bench in the country cemetery, next to their father's grave. Robin's hair was streaked blond, and she was wearing a trench coat and high-heeled city boots. Even puffy from having recently given birth, she looked beautiful and sophisticated, like a creature from a glossy magazine. They each had brought flowers—Robin's city roses, Clara's a country mix of wildflowers—and they each had realized, at the same moment, that flowers were inappropriate. Their father had been Jewish, their mother Episcopalian. They had been raised as neither—as nothing.

*So what do we do now?* Robin asked, clutching her fancy city flowers in her lap like a bridal bouquet.

*I have no idea,* Clara said. *Jews don't believe in flowers, do they?*

And then suddenly—as had occasionally happened in their childhood—the two sisters started to laugh at the same time. The sound, ricocheting through the empty cemetery, might have sounded to a passerby suspiciously like weeping.

*Stones,* Clara finally remembered. *Jews leave stones on graves.*

*Stones,* Robin repeated, setting off new peals of laughter.

*Stop!* Clara gasped. *I can't—my stomach hurts—*

They pulled themselves together, gathered small rocks and pebbles from the damp, early spring earth, and placed them on their father's headstone. Then—their business finished—they stood there awkwardly, shivering in the cool breeze, wondering what to do next. Robin didn't invite Clara back to the house—now *her* house—for lunch. Clara didn't suggest grabbing a quick coffee before hitting the road. Instead, the two sisters touched cheeks goodbye, barely a kiss, the space between their bodies like its own separate person.

.   .   .

The housekeeper is now vacuuming the hall just outside the guest room, the edge of the vacuum cleaner banging against the bottom of the door. *You're going to stay awhile, aren't you?* Robin asked last night. Clara thought of what she'd said to Sam: *I don't know, exactly.* She could almost see the bewilderment cross Sam's small, delicate face. Too painful to even contemplate—that she would cause her daughter any harm. She'll stay for today. Only for today. She throws on the corduroys and black wool sweater she's been wearing since yesterday morning. She'll stop and buy a toothbrush at the Duane Reade on Broadway and grab a Starbucks coffee on her way back to Ruth's.

But first she calls Jonathan at the shop. They never ended up speaking last night. He must have been busy with his Indonesian suppliers. The time difference was a killer. But surely he got Sam off to school this morning, even if her socks weren't matching or she was wearing last night's underwear. And Sam could pack her own lunchbox—though God knows what she'd put in it, left to her own devices. Twelve packages of Fruit Roll-Ups and some piña-colada-flavored gourmet jelly beans for good measure.

"Jonathan Brodeur Jewelry," he answers, on the first ring.

"Hey," she says, relieved to hear his voice, her life—her real life—pulling her back. Jonathan, sitting at his wide old desk in his workroom behind the shop, small mountains of tiny plastic bags filled with semiprecious stones—watermelon tourmaline, fire opal, onyx, topaz—spread all around him.

"Sorry about last night," he says.

"Yeah, what happened?" She isn't angry, exactly, just off-balance. She can't afford to be angry. She needs everything to be normal. For her husband and daughter to be where they're supposed to be. She opens the guest-room door and walks into the hallway, cradling the portable phone. The walls of the long corridor are covered with family photos. Robin, Ed, and kids frolicking in the autumn leaves in Central Park. Robin, Ed, and kids posed in front of an elaborate

Christmas tree. Each child—two boys and a girl—smiling against a white studio backdrop. No Timothy Greenfield-Sanders for Robin. Not even a Jill Krementz. These are not commissions or favors from any of Ruth's friends.

"Oh, Charlie called from Bali. Minor crisis with one of the suppliers."

"And you couldn't deal with it from home?"

A pause. She usually didn't speak sharply to Jonathan. A gentleness existed between them—it had since the beginning. Key to their marriage was the sense that they always had each other's best interests at heart.

"No," Jonathan finally says. Keeping his voice light. "I couldn't."

"Okay." She lets it go. "Sorry."

"So where are you? What's going on?" Jonathan changes the subject.

"Robin's apartment."

"Wow—that's so bizarre."

"I can't even begin to tell you."

"How's your mother?"

A question he has never once—in all their years together—had reason to ask her.

"Really sick, Jonathan."

"Like—"

"She has lung cancer. I looked it up on the Internet last night. The stage she told me she has—people don't get better."

"She's so young," says Jonathan. "She smoked, right?"

"Still does, I'm assuming." The smell of tobacco clings to the drapes in her mother's apartment. Possibly a lingering scent, left over from the decades of cigarettes at bedtime, cigarettes with morning coffee, cigarettes left burning in ashtrays, their orange tips glowing.

"She's so frail," she says. "It's unbelievably weird to see her so frail."

He's quiet on the other end. Waiting. Giving her the space to say whatever it is she wants to say.

"Or to see her at all," she says.

"Of course it is."

"I don't know what to do."

"What do you mean?"

Clara walks across the foyer toward the kitchen. Her lips are parched and her stomach is rumbling. She never ate dinner last night.

"Staying, going. I'm just—" She passes a huge gilded mirror in the foyer and jumps at her own reflection. "I don't know what I'm doing here."

She needs a bowl of cereal, but first some juice. She looks around for the refrigerator. How hard can it be to find a refrigerator? The kitchen is the size of the whole ground floor of her house in Maine, an enormous marble island at its center. Finally, she spots the fridge. The front is covered with a painted wood panel, designed to seamlessly match the cabinetry.

"Do you want me to fly down there? I can be there in—"

"I wish you could."

"Nothing's stopping me. I can close the shop, pick Sam up early from school—"

"*God,* no."

"Listen, Clara, you can't—"

"Yes, I can." Her body suddenly shivers in the warm apartment. "I can and I *will.*"

"Let us be with you. Let us, for once and for all—"

Here they were again. If every marriage—even the most solid marriage—has fault lines running through it, this was theirs: Jonathan believed that secrets were a bad idea. There were no exceptions, no rationalizations. *Sam's old enough to make sense of this,* he's said to Clara more than once. *And she's also old enough to find out by accident. Is that what you want?*

"Can we not do this now?" Clara asks. "I'm barely holding myself together here."

"But—"

"I'm going to grab something to eat and head over to Ruth's," Clara says.

"She's asking when you're coming home," Jonathan says.

"I know. She asked me last night."

"What am I supposed to tell her?"

She listens to the sound of Jonathan breathing on the other end of the phone.

"Tell her, *Soon.*"

"That's not good enough. She wants to know why you're gone."

"Say I'm working."

"That doesn't make any sense, Clara. Listen—I know this is hard—"

"We're just going to have to wing it."

He sighs into the phone.

"Okay."

"I have to see how it goes."

What does she even mean by that? It's going to go all in one direction: Ruth will get sicker and sicker. What is Clara supposed to do? What's the right thing—and for whom? For the first time in many years, her mother's needs and her own feel all knotted up. On Robin's kitchen counter, a beautiful white spray of orchids curves from a delicate blue vase. Clara runs a finger softly over an orchid petal. Fake. She never would have known.


When Clara arrives back at the Apthorp, last night's doorman is back on duty. He gives her a brief nod of recognition as she walks past him, through the courtyard to the elevator. She has now registered for him. She is Ruth Dunne's daughter—Clara Dunne once more.

As she makes her way slowly to her mother's apartment, Clara wonders what's become of their neighbors. Mr. Lipsky, the old German piano teacher who lived next door, must be long gone by now. He had been in his late seventies when Clara left. She often passed him in the hallway on her way to school, when he was just back from his morning constitutional. He always inclined his head slightly, as he walked by her, and never said a word. And then there was Steven Hanson, the playwright. He had written one of the first plays about AIDS, which had run off-off-Broadway for a couple of years in the eighties. Clara notices his door, now festooned with bright Thomas the Tank Engine stickers, two small pairs of snow boots lined up on the mat. Clara would have heard if Steven had died, wouldn't she? It would have been news. Surely she wasn't that completely out of touch?

The door to Ruth's apartment is ajar, and as Clara pushes it open she hears voices.

"Ruth, I understand your point, of course—"

"Don't patronize me, Kubovy. You know how I can't stand—"

"My dear, I was hardly—"

"Peony, would you be a dear and bring us some tea?"

Clara closes the door quietly behind her. She moves through the foyer, her sneakers padding silently against the threadbare oriental. She resists the urge to flee, recognizing it as a constant fact of her time in this place. She can't bear it; she can't bear *not* bearing it.

Ruth's empty wheelchair is parked in the center of the living room, facing the fireplace. Ruth herself is precariously vertical, leaning on a handsome ivory-tipped cane. She's dressed in old jeans that look three sizes too large for her shrunken frame, and a striped shirt that Clara recognizes, with a start, as having belonged to her father. A Yankees cap covers her head.

Kubovy Weiss, Ruth's first art dealer, is standing in profile by the window, ostensibly taking in the view over Broadway. Kubovy is the only one among them who hasn't aged, though he must be sixty by now. His skin is golden in the dead of winter, his long mane of gray hair pulled back into an elegant ponytail. He's wearing a beautifully cut wool suit and orange-and-white striped sneakers. The only discernible concession to age are his green-tinted wireless spectacles. They remind Clara of the green spectacles that came with a pop-up book of *The Wizard of Oz* that she used to read to Sammy. The better with which to see the Emerald City.

"There she is!" Ruth turns and beams at her, as if Clara were her loving and devoted daughter who had, perhaps, just been away for a long weekend. "Look, Kubovy—it's Clara."

Kubovy crosses the living room in four long strides. He takes Clara's hands in both of his, his eyes moist behind the green lenses.

"My darling Clara," he says. "How amazing to see you."

He crushes her to his chest. She can feel his heart beating. He releases her, then gazes at her carefully, as if appraising a work of art.

"You've hardly changed a bit," he says. "Still so beautiful."

Clara feels herself disappearing. Who is Kubovy seeing? The little girl who grew up on the walls of the Kubovy Weiss Gallery, the images of whom earned him fifty percent of a small fortune? Which photograph is he seeing? *Clara with the Lizard? Clara in the Tree House? Clara, Napping?* She is disintegrating, becoming nothing more than thousands upon thousands of pixilated dots: gray and black and white. Each one, floating in space, separate from the rest—meaningless. She feels herself coming apart.

Clara tries mightily to hold Kubovy's gaze, but he is better at this awkward moment than she, and her eyes slide away. She's sure Ruth is watching, with a kind of carnivorous pleasure. Kubovy and Clara, together in a room. Just like old times. The movie reel of her life playing backward, stopping only at key moments characterized by the warm, milky comfort of self-delusion.

"Oh, please, Kubovy," Clara finally says, recovering. "That's hardly the case." Her voice is muted, as if coming from deep within the cave of herself. Even in the flattering light of Robin's perfect bathroom this morning, she appeared exhausted. Dark rings under her eyes. Hollows in her cheekbones that she hadn't remembered seeing before. Her hair cut into an efficient shoulder-length nonstyle. She has wanted for so many years not to resemble the girl in her mother's photographs. Now, by sheer dint of age, she may have finally gotten there.

Peony swings into the room, carrying a wooden tray with a teapot and two cups.

"Clara, I'm sorry, I didn't know you were here," Peony says. Her smile is a bit wobbly. She's scared, skittish.

"That's okay, Peony. I'm fine, thanks."

"Kubovy, tell Clara our plan," says Ruth. She's swaying slightly on the small tip of her cane.

"It's not exactly a plan, Ruth," says Kubovy. "As I've been trying to tell you, to move galleries, to come back to me at this point—believe me, as a businessman, I would like nothing better. But I'm saying this to you as your ally and your friend"—Kubovy's tan deepens—"it would be suicide."

"Suicide!" Ruth's whispery voice raises into a muted shriek. "Suicide!" She begins to laugh. She laughs harder and harder, until the laughter turns into a fit of coughing. She doubles over, nearly losing her balance. She hobbles over to the sofa, her left foot dragging, and maneuvers herself into a sitting position.

The three of them—Kubovy, Peony, and Clara—stand helplessly and watch. It's the Ruth Dunne show, and this morning's episode is featuring hysterical Ruth. There are so many Ruths, Clara can hardly remember them all. Jealous Ruth, competitive Ruth, manic Ruth, exhausted Ruth, lost-in-the-wilderness Ruth. But the scariest Ruth of all, at least to Clara, is this one. Hysteria spreads its map across her mother's face, a series of red blotches blooming on her cheeks, the tip of her small nose.

"I think I can afford to *commit suicide* if I want to, Kubovy," Ruth says, catching her breath. "I think I've earned that right."

"I apologize. It was a poor choice of words," says Kubovy. "But Ruth, we have a legacy to think about. It would be most prudent to leave the current works with Matthew, whose name, let's face it, is more bold-faced than mine at this point."

"I can't bear that place," Ruth spits out. The red blotches have faded, along with the hysteria, and now she looks completely spent. Her skin is translucent, a tangle of blue veins throbbing visibly in her forehead.

"He's done well by you," says Kubovy.

"He's a preening sycophant."

"Be that as it may."

Peony is watching the back-and-forth of this exchange as if it's the finals at Wimbledon. She is leaning forward, eager not to miss a single point. She is receiving a valuable education in the business of photography, as she is receiving an education in the business of dying. When she got the internship with Ruth Dunne, most likely she had been hoping to work in the archives, answer correspondence, or, if she were really lucky, apprentice in the darkroom.

"As your friend and adviser, Ruth—and I'm sorry to be speaking in such a direct manner—"

"Oh, bugger off, Kubovy."

Kubovy's tan deepens once again. This exchange is costing him. He loves Ruth—he has always loved Ruth. Clara realizes that she hasn't once—not once since she left New York—thought about what might have become of Kubovy Weiss. She has put him high up on the shelf in her mind where she keeps everything else related to her childhood. Now that he's here, right in front of her, close enough to throttle, she feels herself shaking.

Of course, she supposes, any good gallery owner could have put Ruth Dunne on the map with the Clara series. But it hadn't been just anyone. It had been Kubovy, and he had been brilliant at it: a master. All the more amazing that Kubovy had remained Ruth's friend, even after she left him in the late eighties for Leo Castelli.

"What, Ruth?" He sounds weary. "I'm trying to help you. I assume you asked me for my advice because you trust me. And what I'm trying to say here is that I'm in a better position to deal with your estate if Kubovy Weiss is not your gallery. Believe me, when it comes to the IRS I've been through this before—"

"Estate! The fucking IRS!" Ruth explodes. "I can't stand it. I won't listen to another word of this." She tries to lift herself off the sofa, struggling to her feet—an impossibility. She collapses back into her seat, her bony bottom barely making an impression in the cushions.

She turns to Peony. "Help me up."

Peony moves to one side of Ruth and swings her easily upward with her strong young arms. She pivots Ruth, whose feet dangle uselessly, and deposits her into the wheelchair.

"You could have a career doing this, you know," Ruth says to Peony. And then, as if she knows she may have just said something insulting, "Peony is a very talented young photographer, Kubovy. Interesting work in photo-collage. You should take a look at her slides."

"I'd be delighted," says Kubovy.

Peony doesn't know where to look. She keeps her eyes on her toes, but seems like she might levitate at any second.

"Ruth, we have unfinished business," says Kubovy.

"To be continued." Ruth waves airily from her wheelchair as Peony begins to push her back to her bedroom. Clara stands next to Kubovy and watches her mother's head, erect and bobbing on her narrow shoulders.

Kubovy puts an arm around Clara and steers her toward the windows. "She's going to try to make a bloody mess of things," he says. "That's what she does. It makes her feel alive."

"But she's *dying*, Kubovy," Clara blurts out. She is surprised by her own vehemence. Is she trying to convince Kubovy? Or herself? Despite all evidence to the contrary, despite the statistics on the Internet, part of her still believes that her mother is going to walk out of her bedroom, her long hair flowing down her back, her lungs pink as a baby's. And then Clara can leave for another fourteen years. Her past can stay right here in this apartment, locked up inside the gates, guarded by the doorman. Safe behind these thick soundproofed walls.

Kubovy gives Clara a long hard look, and again she tries and fails to hold his gaze.

"Don't judge me," she says quietly, her eyes on a bare patch in the murky blue of the oriental. Forcing herself to stand her ground. She is strong—she knows she is strong. She's done what she had to do to survive, hasn't she? What does Kubovy know about that?

"My dear Clara," Kubovy says, caressing her name. "Far be it from me. I was simply wondering . . ." He trails off, shaking his head as if to stop himself. "I know Robin is around, but you—Ruth is so delicate now, and after all these years—"

"What are you trying to say, Kubovy?" Goddammit, she's getting pulled in.

"Are you planning to see this through?" he asks.

She stares at him.

"Of course," she says. She is surprised by the force of her own vehemence. And then, as if to convince herself, "She's my mother."

# Chapter Three

IMPOSSIBLE to isolate a memory: to carve it out and separate it from what has come before or after, from what has been told and retold. Stories turn what we remember into a series of polished little gems. In Clara's case, impossible to isolate her own memory from what has been written about, taught in art classes, discussed as case law, hung in museums. Her past doesn't belong to her. She has long since stopped trying. Why make the effort when there is nothing new to be found?

But now, off the shelf it tumbles. Suddenly, glaringly accessible. All of it, her history, gleams—perfectly lit, silvery—in the darkened and cobwebbed corners of her mind. Each image is a looking glass into which she can disappear—like her favorite childhood heroine, Alice—until she finds herself on the other side.

She is four years old—the year before kindergarten—and she is sitting cross-legged on the floor of the Kubovy Weiss Gallery. She has never been down to this neighborhood before, a long taxi ride from their apartment on the Upper West Side. It might as well be a different city. It's quieter than uptown, and the light is much brighter over the low rooftops. Even the smells are different: turpentine, Windex, the sour scent of spilled white wine.

Her Barbies are strewn around her, their platinum hair all tangled up; she had tried to shampoo them the night before. She has been allowed to bring three Barbies, along with their assorted paraphernalia (tiny combs and brushes, a few changes of clothing) because her mother has told her it's going to be a long afternoon, and Clara needs to be patient.

The main rooms in the gallery are huge, cavernous—it is a converted warehouse in SoHo—with gigantic dark wood beams running across the high ceiling, from which small pinpoint track lighting hangs, creating oval-shaped pools of illumination on the spotless white walls. The front of the gallery is made entirely of glass, and from where Clara sits she can see people walking past on West Broadway. She's just learned to count, so she counts the number of ladies. The number of men. There don't seem to be any children. It's a school day. But Clara isn't in school, not yet. Robin is in first grade, but since Clara's only four, her mother wanted to keep her home. They have so much work to do.

"I think we should pare it way down, Ruth. Keep it simple." Kubovy is leaning against the front desk, smoking a brown hand-rolled cigarette. The surface of the desk is clear, except for a round glass vase containing a dozen pale peach roses, sent earlier that day by Clara's father.

"How simple, Kubovy?" Ruth's soft voice seems louder in this space, with nothing to muffle it. The heels of her cowboy boots click against the hardwood floors as she paces back and forth, looking at the various ovals of light. Her hair is pulled back with a large tortoise-shell clip, her face bare.

"I know we said we were going to hang the landscapes—but I'm having my doubts."

"But we only have eight Clara pictures," says Ruth. She folds her arms and stands in the middle of the room.

Clara is playing with two of her Barbies, trying to get one to comb the other one's hair. She pulls the comb through gently, holding up one small hunk of knotted hair at a time, the way her mother does with her—but it isn't working. Barbie's hair is more and more of a rat's nest. Serves Clara right, she's only half paying attention to the job at hand. She's listening to her own name, repeated over and over again, bouncing off the walls of the Kubovy Weiss Gallery. *Clara* pictures. *Clara.* Each time she hears her name, she looks up. But they are not talking to her.

"Eight. Exactly," says Kubovy. "Large format. One hung on each wall. Think of it, Ruth. It will be stark. Fabulous. A tremendous statement."

"But the landscapes," Ruth says. "I'm quite attached to the landscapes."

Kubovy takes a long drag on his cigarette and exhales through his nose and mouth. The white smoke swirls around his face. With his salt-and-pepper hair, long and curly around the collar of his shirt, he looks like a feline creature from one of Clara's picture books.

"If you put the landscapes on the same wall as the Clara pictures, they'll look like shit," says Kubovy. "Excuse my language."

Clara looks up. She's pretty sure he just said a bad word. And Ruth, who has been in a kind of dreamy contemplative mood, as blank as the blank walls, snaps to attention.

"What did you say?"

Kubovy shrugs. "It's my job to tell you the truth. The landscapes are derivative. Immature. I see nothing new or fresh in them."

"But you took me on after you saw those slides—"

"That's true," says Kubovy. "I suppose I saw some glimmer of talent. But nothing compared to the Clara photographs, Ruth. Surely you know that."

Kubovy walks over to a rolling cart, on which a series of large crates are stacked, each labeled with black Magic Marker on the light, splintery wood: *Clara with the Lizard. Clara, Napping. Clara in the Fountain.* He pries open the slats of wood on the *Clara in the Fountain* crate and carefully removes the photograph, bits of tissue paper floating to the floor. The photograph is five feet square—bigger than

Clara's whole body—and framed in simple black lacquer. Kubovy struggles to carry it over to the wall.

"Rico, Brian!" he calls into the back room, and two young men materialize. One of them is wearing a bandanna on his head, just like the bandanna Clara has brought for her Western Barbie outfit.

"Let's give this a try," says Kubovy.

Rico and Brian hold the photograph up to the wall. Clara gathers her three Barbies together on her lap and watches. She hasn't seen these pictures before—not in their final form. She's only seen the Polaroids Ruth has taken, sketches, ideas, the barest outline of the real thing.

Now, she sees herself. So gigantic! So much bigger than she actually is! She remembers the night—it was very late—Ruth woke her out of a deep sleep and bundled her into the elevator. *Where are we going, Mommy?* Clara had asked her. *Just to the courtyard, sweetheart. Everything's set up. It won't take long, I promise.* As the elevator made its slow descent, Clara looked at her mother in the dim old-fashioned yellowy light. Ruth always looked most beautiful when she was in this state. Clara didn't have the words for what the state was, exactly. But it seemed to her to be something akin to *bursting.* Bursting with what, she wasn't sure.

In the courtyard, the lighting was set up, two tall pole lamps and the silver reflector disk. Ruth had brought down a thick wool blanket, even though it wasn't cold out. She wrapped it around Clara.

"Let's get you undressed," she said. The blanket was itchy. Clara remembered they had used it for a picnic in Central Park earlier in the summer.

As Clara stepped out of her pajama bottoms, Ruth glanced up at the sky.

"Look, sweetheart," she whispered. "Look at the moon."

"It's a full moon!" Clara said, her clear voice piercing the silence of the night. "I see the man there—the man in the moon!"

"Ssshh," said Ruth. "We don't want to wake people up."

Where was the doorman? Ruth must have asked him to stay inside his booth. Maybe she gave him a tip, the same way she sometimes did when he hailed them a taxi on Broadway.

"Okay, Clara. Let's climb into the fountain," said Ruth.

"But we're not allowed," said Clara.

"Just for tonight."

Clara climbed up on the edge of the fountain and dipped her toe into the two inches of water inside the stone basin. It wasn't too cold. The water was still, because the fountain part had been turned off for the night. Beneath the green-black glassy surface of the water, hundreds of copper pennies, nickels, dimes, even quarters gleamed like stars.

Ruth quickly approached her with the light meter, holding it up to Clara's bare chest. She then adjusted the aperture on her camera. Clara knew better than to talk right now. She felt the heat of the lights on her body. Her mother was crouching, aiming the camera up at her, squinting through the lens.

"Hold your arms up in the air, Clara. Like you're a part of the fountain. Like you're reaching for the moon."

*Click.* Ruth checked the light meter again. *Click, click, click.*


Rico and Brian are holding *Clara in the Fountain* in the puddle of light cast on the gallery wall. The photograph slips a little, and they right it; their arms are getting tired.

"Perfection," says Kubovy. "I'm seeing it—the whole gallery, with just these eight extraordinary images."

"I don't know," says Ruth. She is standing in front of Clara, partly blocking Clara's view of her own naked body, pale and shiny as marble, arms flung wide in the moonlight.

"Ruth, please—listen. Listen to me. This is your introduction.

Your debut. No one knows you yet. Artists can spend their entire life-
times recovering from the wrong first impression."

"Mommy?"

Ruth doesn't turn around. She folds her arms, cocks her head. She
is lost in another world, the world she goes to when she's inside her
pictures. Sometimes Clara imagines that they are together in that
black-and-white world, that the place inside the pictures is the real
one and this—all this is just a rehearsal. A setup. Like the way she
and her mother stage the pictures before they actually get made.

"Mommy?"

Clara has to pee really badly. She doesn't know where the bathroom is. She looks around, but all the doors look the same. They
don't even have knobs.

"All right, Kubovy." Ruth sighs. "I hope you're right."

"I *know* I'm right."

Kubovy walks back over to the rolling cart of crates and begins to
open the next one, cursing as he nicks his finger on a staple.

"Let's start to sort out the placement," he says. "I think—"

"Mommy!"

Clara crosses her legs hard. She feels a tiny bit of urine wet her
panties. She never wets her panties. But now, out it comes. Down the
side of her leg. Pooling around her bottom.

Ruth wheels around. Clara is sitting in a puddle on the floor.

"Oh, no!"

"I'm sorry, Mommy." Clara begins to cry. She cries and cries, until
she feels wet everywhere: her bottom, her cheeks, the front of her
dress. "I tried to tell you—"

"God," mutters Ruth. She buries her head in her hands. "I can't
even . . . what the fuck is my—"

"I have an idea." Kubovy sweeps over, holding a paper towel with
which he quickly wipes up the offending pee. "Clara, I'm going to
take you for a very special treat. Let's leave your mother here for a few

minutes"—he motions to Rico and Brian to open the rest of the crates—"and you and I will go get some ice cream."

Clara stops crying.

"Have you ever had this very special Italian ice cream? It's called gelato," says Kubovy. He reaches a hand down and hoists her to her feet.

"But my dress," says Clara.

"It will dry in the sun as we walk," says Kubovy. He makes it all seem like a grand idea.

"Mommy?" Clara says. "Is that okay? Can I have gelato?"

Ruth turns to her. Her eyes are dim. She seems very far away.

"Please don't be mad at me," Clara says.

"Oh, honey." Ruth scoops her up and hugs her. She presses her lips hard against Clara's cheek. "You're the one who should be mad at *me*."

———◆•••◆———

THE STREETS of the Upper West Side are not made for wheelchairs. The sidewalks are uneven, an obstacle course. A cracked bit of pavement or a pothole can stop a wheelchair abruptly, tossing its inhabitant forward. The curbs, a series of little cliffs, sharp angles at every intersection. The only way to traverse them is to tilt the wheelchair back and carefully, with all one's strength, inch the back wheels forward, little by little, until they gently bump the street below.

Add to this, late-winter slush, icy patches, frozen gutters backed up with sooty snow. Clara isn't wearing gloves. She left hers at home in Maine, and she keeps forgetting to borrow a pair from Robin. In Clara's memory, New York is not a freezing-cold place. Not compared to what she's grown accustomed to, the endless string of twenty-below days, the thermometer outside the kitchen window permanently stopped, frozen somewhere well south of zero. Her hands—the knuckles red, the skin chapped—curl around the plastic handles of her mother's wheelchair as they wait for the light to change from red to green.

Thank goodness for Robin's clothes: a heavy oversized cashmere sweater, a pair of post-pregnancy jeans from before her sister snapped her body back to her usual size two. These, along with a few turtlenecks and some warm socks purchased at the Gap, have kept Clara going for exactly eight days. She cannot possibly lose count of how many days she's been here. Each morning, Sammy reminds her.

*You've been gone for five days, Mom. That's a long time.*

*Now it's six. Six whole days.*

*It's been a week now. Why are you away? Are you and Daddy getting a divorce?*

Clara has tried to reassure Sammy, but she knows that everything she says rings hollow. She can't give Sam an answer as to precisely when she's returning to Maine—though at least Clara has promised her that (my God!) she isn't getting a divorce. All these years—staying at home with Sam—they've been such a tight little threesome. It has to add up to something, doesn't it? To some sense of peace and security? Clara and Jonathan have never taken so much as a weekend away without Sammy. Surely, Sam will weather this absence. It will close up around her as soon as Clara gets home.

An older woman, bundled from head to toe in a black coat, moves expertly past Ruth's wheelchair, one hand holding a cane, the other a blue-and-orange Fairway shopping bag.

"Look at her," says Ruth, from the depths of the wheelchair. "She must be eighty."

Ruth's breath makes a vaporous cloud, disappearing as it wafts up toward Clara's face. Ruth is well insulated; she's wearing an ankle-length shearling coat, and Peony has tucked a soft blanket around her. A fur hat covers her head.

"I want to be just like that when I'm eighty," says Ruth.

The WALK sign lights up, and Clara eases the wheels down to the street.

"What do you think?" Ruth asks. She's a little breathless. Actually, they're both a little breathless. Clara's out of shape, hasn't been hiking in Acadia National Park lately. Who is she kidding? She hasn't been on a hike in more than a year. Her arms are shaking from the effort.

"Did you hear what I said?" Ruth asks.

"What?" Clara steers around a pothole the size and depth of a bowling ball.

"Eighty," says Ruth.

"Yeah, amazing. She looks great."

"You're not listening to me!"

They're on the corner of West End and 77th. Their destination, a holistic oncologist, just two blocks farther downtown. They should have taken a cab, but somehow that had seemed more daunting: folding the wheelchair into a cab's trunk, holding on to Ruth to make sure she didn't slip on the ice, sliding Ruth into the narrow confines of a backseat. That is, if a cab would even have stopped for them. Strollers, wheelchairs, walkers, canes, pets, suitcases—all these might make a driver speed on by, hoping to pick up a simpler, less demanding fare.

"I'm sorry," says Clara.

"I'm trying to give myself some hope here. Can't you understand that?"

"Hope," Clara repeats. This is today's news, a curveball. Ruth, it seems, is ricocheting around the five stages of grief: denial, anger, bargaining, depression, acceptance. At the moment, she has made a flying leap from acceptance to denial.

Or who knows. Maybe she knows something. Maybe, despite all the stark evidence on the Internet—eighty percent dead within eighteen months—Ruth has peered inside herself, inside the black caves of her own lungs, and seen herself rising above the statistics, climbing to the top of the highest curve of the most infinitesimal number and holding on, as if to a sturdy branch in a hurricane, waiting for the wind to die down all around her.

Who the hell knows. Clara rings a bell next to a brass plaque: ABRAHAM ZAMITSKY, M.D. A buzzer sounds, and she pushes Ruth's wheelchair through the door, only to be faced with two steep steps down to the office door below. How can an oncologist not have a ramp? How many patients are trotting in here on their own two feet? A holistic oncologist, in particular, might well be the last stop—after the chemo, the radiation, the trials and pills and potions of regular doctors have failed. Clara summons her strength, then tilts the wheelchair back and eases it down the first step. The wheels teeter precariously for a moment on the stair, threatening to slip too quickly down.

"Good job," says Ruth. As if this—the successful maneuvering of a metal contraption—is worthy of praise.

"Where did you find this guy, anyway?" Clara asks.

Their voices are deadened in the tiny vestibule. As soon as the words emerge, they are snuffed out. No echo, no reverberation. No sound at all.

"The *Today* show," says Ruth.

"The *Today* show! Since when do you—"

"I've had a lot of time to lie in bed."

A second buzzer sounds, and Clara pushes open the office door. The doctor's waiting room is furnished in a soothing blend of earth tones. An enormous fish tank is built into the far wall. The artificial aqua-blue water appears to be a distant ocean, and all these people— sick people, waiting—are stranded on the sandy shore of some interior decorator's idea of peace. Plants are everywhere, hanging from baskets by the windows, in terra-cotta pots in the corners. Low-maintenance plants. No African violets for this holistic oncologist. No ferns. Nothing that will die easily. A huge, hardy rubber plant spills out from behind a bald girl in her twenties.

"Can I help you?"

"Ruth Dunne, to see Dr. Zamitsky," Clara says quietly. They're on the Upper West Side, after all. Someone here will know the name, though it's possible, in this environment, that no one will care.

Pages and pages of forms to fill out. Paperwork. Clara wheels Ruth to an unoccupied corner of the office and brings her a months-old copy of *Vogue* on which to balance the forms as she checks off various boxes.

"Crazy," says Ruth, as she quickly runs down the list. "Diabetes, heart attack, stroke, high blood pressure . . . no, no, no." She jabs her pen against the box next to cancer. "Such a stupid thing," she says. "Nothing's ever been wrong with me. I've never even been in the hospital, except to have you two girls—and now this."

Ruth's eyes are watery from the cold. The tip of her nose is bright pink. She pulls off her fur hat, and beneath it is a silk scarf wrapped elegantly around her head. She wears no makeup, her bare face still surprisingly youthful. Ruth has always looked a decade younger than she is, and even now, even with no hair and pale, almost transparent skin, she is like a china doll. Soft and lovely and breakable.

"At least it got you here." She turns to Clara. She reaches over and takes Clara's hand. Her own hands are warm and dry. "Nothing short of this would have gotten you home, would it?"

Clara doesn't answer. Her mother's touch—the very fact of her hand encased in Ruth's—is almost more than she can bear. Ruth has been inching toward this—pushing Clara toward a greater intimacy—for the last few days. *So, darling, tell me about your life. Not just the broad outline; tell me what it's really like. Your days—what do you do? How do you feel?* Ruth wants to know everything about the last fourteen years, it seems. *And your daughter? I would give anything*—here she held Clara's gaze until Clara finally looked away—*I would give anything to meet her.*

Clara's mere presence, unlikely to begin with, is no longer enough.

Her mother wants more of her. And now the hand. Foreign. The skin thin and dusty. Clara closes her eyes for a moment, tries to pretend that the hand is Jonathan's. Or Sam's. But it isn't working. She pulls away.

"Oh, Clara. Please don't," Ruth says.

"I can't—I can't help it."

Clara starts to cry. Despite everything, despite every cell in her body struggling mightily to keep it together, she's losing it. Her eyes are flooded—the tears are almost horizontal. She swipes at her cheeks with the sleeve of her sweater. She had sworn to herself that she wasn't going to let her mother see a single feeling. Not rage, not grief, not loss, not a fleeting moment of tenderness. Fourteen years. It's just goddamned unacceptable.

In the upholstered chair across from them, a middle-aged woman in a velour sweat suit is thumbing through a copy of *People* magazine. She resolutely keeps her gaze on the magazine, but her brow creases in sympathy. She thinks Clara's crying because her mother is ill. Because they're at the last stop on the cancer train, the office of the *Today* show doctor.

"You hate me," says Ruth.

"It's not that," Clara says, her breath ragged. And it's true. She doesn't hate her mother. Not exactly. There may have been a time, a stretch of months or even years—but even then, inside the hate there was something else. Something she didn't want to look at or think about. A bright glowing thing—a core of softness. Clara never allowed herself near it. She had worked so hard to disconnect. To release herself from the bondage of Ruth. But now it isn't so easy. Ruth is in front of her: her mother—always her mother, forever her mother. Incandescent, beautiful, fragile, gravely ill. Ruth's smell hasn't changed in fourteen years, as if the mingled scents of the darkroom—the developer, stop bath, and fixer—have become a part of her.

Clara breathes her in. Tries to exhale her out. Tries to hold on to herself. Without even realizing it, she is gripping the sides of her chair.

"Mrs. Dunne?" A nurse looks around the waiting room. "Ruth Dunne?"

A few startled looks. An older man in a dark overcoat. The bald girl in her twenties. Ruth's name may be known, but physically she is anonymous. She is rare among photographers for never—not ever, not even once—having taken a self-portrait. It is Clara whose face is known. As she pushes Ruth's wheelchair through the waiting room, she keeps her head down. No one would think it, anyway. She has lost her girlhood face, along with its Ruth-like softness. No one will ever again look twice at her in confused recognition. Samantha is the one. The uncanny likeness passed down from one generation to the next. *My dear, you're the spitting image of that girl in Ruth Dunne's early photographs. The daughter. What was her name?* Not Sammy. She can't think about Sammy now.

The nurse leaves them in an examining room. What is there to examine? The X-rays Ruth has brought with her, large manila envelopes tucked into an aqua blue Metropolitan Museum shopping bag, should tell the whole story. Clara looks around the small, brightly lit space. She's never been good at small talk, but all she wants to do right now is keep the conversation with Ruth skimming along the surface of things. She searches for a subject. The weather— *Cold out there, isn't it?*—the news—*Did you read about those two guys who were arrested at JFK?* Anything to keep Ruth from pushing harder, probing deeper.

But there's nothing much to see, nothing to distract. No piles of well-worn magazines in here, no hardy plants, no striped neon fish swimming madly around faux-coral reefs. Only a life-sized diagram, tacked to the wall, of the human body. An acupuncture chart. In the sinew, the muscle, the nerve endings from the crown of the head to the tips of the toes, hundreds of small red dots are shown, each one illustrating a particular pressure point. Crisscrossed lines run throughout the diagram, linking one pressure point to the next and the next—patterns of energy. The arm bone is connected to the leg bone after all.

"So tell me about seeing this guy on TV," Clara finally says, filling the silence. The low buzzing of the fluorescent light overhead could drive a person crazy.

Ruth wraps the blanket around her shoulders, even though the room is already warm, the clanging radiator emitting a dry oppressive heat.

"It wasn't so much Dr. Zamitsky as some of his patients," she says. "He cured one woman of pancreatic cancer, using green tea colonics. And another woman, with the same kind of lung cancer as me—she's been in remission for six years now—he sent her to Mexico, where they use a special mud—"

"Special mud?" Clara repeats.

"They heat it up, like a compress," says Ruth.

Clara tries to keep her face expressionless. What does she know? Green tea. Special mud. Anything is possible. Particularly when it comes to Ruth, who has spent her whole life defying the odds.

A knock on the door, and then immediately the door opens, and Abraham Zamitsky, M.D., walks into the examining room. He's holding Ruth's paperwork in his left hand, his right hand outstretched.

"Mrs. Dunne," he says.

"Ms.," Ruth says faintly.

Clara can't tell: Is Ruth insulted that the doctor clearly has no idea who she is? To him, she's just another Upper West Side lady with cancer, or perhaps a housewife from Larchmont who has driven into the city after seeing him on TV. He's the famous one in this room. Illness, the great leveler.

"This is my daughter Clara," says Ruth. As if Clara is not thirty-two years old. As if she weren't about to introduce herself.

Zamitsky shakes Clara's hand. She's not sure what she had been expecting. She's surprised by how young he is. In her mind, a holistic oncologist would look something like Abbie Hoffman, with a curly mane of hair, a bushy beard, maybe an amulet strung on a leather cord around his neck. But Zamitsky is maybe thirtyish, wearing a good suit. He's bald—his head shaved in sympathy for his patients. His brown eyes are clear and limpid, radiating good healthy habits. He probably cleanses himself with green tea and takes Mexican mud compresses preventatively.

He gives Ruth's chart a quick read.

"I see you've been to Dr. Abelow," he says. "Ah, and Dr. Krellenstein." He reads farther. "And Dr. Chang."

Ruth watches him carefully. Clara remembers this look. Her mother's eyes—large, unblinking, as dark and impenetrable as a telephoto lens—taking everything in, processing it with her quick, visual intelligence.

"I brought my X-rays," Ruth says.

"Let's have a look," says Zamitsky.

He pulls the X-rays from their manila sleeves and attaches them with clips to an illuminated board. Six films in all—two of each lung, and two of another part of the body—liver? Spleen? Clara isn't sure.

Zamitksy stops in front of each image and examines it closely, as if it were hanging on the wall of a gallery. Clara can't possibly tell, looking at the X-rays, where the malignancies are located. That shadow on the far left? The white swirly material in the center? They look like the night sky, seen through a telescope. Bits of cosmic matter. The images are nothing more than abstract harmless shapes, if one hasn't been taught how to read them.

"Ah," Zamitsky says, tapping the last of the six films with the eraser end of his pencil. "And has Dr. Chang discussed these with you, Mrs. Dunne?"

"No," says Ruth. "Dr. Chang's office just received them from radiology yesterday, and I asked for them to be messengered directly to me."

"Why is that?" Zamitsky raises an eyebrow.

"I don't feel comfortable with Dr. Chang," says Ruth. "His receptionist was rude to me, and I . . ."

She falters. And in the space left where her words trail off, Clara knows that the reason Ruth has left Dr. Chang—as she has left the doctors before him—is that he's not telling her any news she wants to hear.

Zamitsky continues to tap the X-ray on the far right with his pencil.

"Here's our problem, Ms. Dunne." He waves the pencil around a wide area on the film, which looks grainy to Clara, full of hundreds of tiny specks. An aberration. An image left too long in the developer, breaking apart.

"What are we looking at?" Ruth asks.

"Your brain," says Zamitsky.

Ruth sits up straighter in her wheelchair.

"Can you see all these pinpoints in this area here?"

Ruth stares at the X-ray, uncomprehending.

"I don't see—"

Zamitsky points with his pencil. "They're hard to see, if you're not used to it; they're very small, like grains of sand."

She still looks a bit puzzled, her head cocked to one side. Clara sees her try to swallow.

"What are they?" Ruth asks.

Zamitsky turns off the light, plunging the films into darkness. They are now blank. The images disappear. As if Ruth can't be hurt by what she can no longer see. Zamitksy sits on the step leading to the examination table, so he is eye level with Ruth.

"They're tumors," he begins. "Very, very small tumors."

"Small is good," Ruth says. "Right? I mean, small is better than big?"

Zamitsky sighs. "I wish I could tell you that it matters, in this case. But what we're seeing here is that your primary cancer in the lung has metastasized to your brain. This is what usually happens, when—"

"Usually!" Ruth coughs from the effort. "I'm not interested in usually, Dr. Zamitsky. What can you do for me?"

"I'm sorry," he says. How many times a day does he have to do this? How often is he in the position of telling a patient there is no hope—that the illness has progressed beyond the miracle cures of green tea colonics and Mexican mud? And how does he relieve himself of that burden at the end of each day? He must be a marathon runner. Or maybe he smokes a lot of high-grade medical pot. He must have some way of escaping.

"But what about that woman you treated?" Ruth says. "The one who had lung cancer—"

"It was caught earlier." Zamitsky shakes his head. Clara's beginning to think he regrets having gone on national television. "She was extremely, unusually lucky."

Clara sees the fight go out of her mother's body, almost as if a shadow—the warrior part of Ruth that has served her so well—steps away from Ruth's physical self and leaves the room. Ruth's shoulders cave. She slumps down in her wheelchair. Her face falls, aging in an instant.

"That's it, then," she says softly.

"There's a lot we can do to make you comfortable," says Zamitsky.

"What's going to happen to me?"

Zamitsky isn't shying away from this. He hasn't backed off. He's looking at Ruth directly, his face no more than a foot from hers. Like a priest in a confessional, he is creating a sacred space, a space where hard things can be said.

"What exactly are you asking?" Zamitsky leans forward.

"How am I going to die?"

"Eventually your brain will stop telling your heart to beat—or it will stop telling your lungs to breathe. Your body will undergo a brief and painless systemic failure," says Zamitsky. He keeps his tone even. He's reporting the news.

Clara moves closer to Ruth. She stands behind her and puts her hands on Ruth's bony shoulders. Rests them there, just like that.

That evening, they gather around Robin's dining table. Clara would have preferred the impersonal din of a restaurant, the distraction of waiters offering wine lists, busboys depositing baskets of bread, pouring olive oil into small dipping dishes. Instead, there are the children. Two nephews and a niece—strangers to her—who keep staring solemnly at Clara from across the table. They have first names that sound like last names: Harrison and Tucker. The girl is called Elliot. At six, she's the youngest, but still she sits with perfect posture in her chair—Clara can almost hear Robin say *like a little lady*—as she lifts her cloth napkin off the table and smooths it across her lap.

Clara has been trying to get to know Robin's kids. Her third day in New York, she went to a toy store on Lexington Avenue and bought them each gifts she couldn't really afford—gifts she wouldn't just go out and buy Sam—video games for Harrison and Tucker, a karaoke machine for Elliot. She has asked them each questions about school, teachers, friends—all the usual stuff that eventually works to get kids talking. But still they continue to look at her with polite disregard. What have they heard about her, over the years?

"You shouldn't have gone to such trouble, sweetheart," Ruth says to Robin, as the first course is served by one of the staff. Clara is having a hard time keeping count of just how many people her sister has in her employ.

"Oh, I didn't," Robin says airily. "Edjinea is a fabulous cook. She can do anything Brazilian, of course, but she also follows recipes."

"Delicious," pronounces Robin's husband, Ed. The puree of pea soup is garnished with tiny bits of earthy-looking matter that turn out, upon tasting, to be black trumpet mushrooms. A delicacy, out of season.

Clara feels like she's walked into an alternate version of her life. *This is the path not taken.* If she hadn't left home at eighteen, would she have been sitting at this dining table all along? Would she have graduated from Brearley, gone to an Ivy League school, carved out a career for herself in—what? law—like her father and Robin? Not likely. Something in the art world? Impossible, it would have killed her. No. Her job in life has been to survive. And that, she has done. She has done that brilliantly. She's here, isn't she? She has a family of her own, doesn't she? She's even managing to survive being in the same room as her mother again—something she had never thought possible. Clara realizes that she's gripping her soupspoon too tightly. When she releases it, her fingers ache.

"Mama, may I please have more soup?"

This from Tucker. The children call their parents Mama and Papa—nothing so common as Mom and Dad for them. Clara can't imagine what Sam would make of this, these New York City first cousins she has longed to meet. Sam would be intimidated, that's for sure. Sam is right between the two boys age-wise, but they might as well be creatures from another planet. Handsome kids whose lives are already mapped out for them; the type people refer to as *well-rounded.* They take after Ed's side of the family—strapping sandy-haired jocks, destined for Ivy League eating clubs and varsity lacrosse.

Ruth sits at the head of the table, in her wheelchair. She has some color in her cheeks from the two glasses of wine she's downed since arriving at Robin's. She fills her glass once again, then raises it and clinks the edge with her salad fork.

"A toast," she says. She's looped, Clara realizes. Fine bordeaux and the benzodiazepines Ruth is taking three times a day cannot possibly mix well. "To my beautiful family," says Ruth, slightly slurring her words. "I can't possibly tell you how much this means to me—to see you all together."

Robin and Ed exchange a quick marital look. Ed passes the open bottle of wine down the table, toward Clara. The only thing worse than a terminally ill Ruth would be a drunk terminally ill Ruth.

"Mama, what's the matter with Grandma?" the little girl, Elliot, asks in a loud whisper. So she isn't such a grown-up after all.

"Ssshh, darling," Robin says. Robin looks—despite the yoga, despite the therapy—so tightly wound that she may just uncoil from the table and start spinning around the room like a top. She's put together perfectly—a personal shopper sends her bags full of each season's latest Jil Sander, Narcisco Rodriguez, Georgio Armani—but none of the pieces quite fit. She is all angles and absences, a puzzle with the corners done but the center missing.

"That's all right," says Ruth. "Elliot, you've asked a very good question. Grandma's going to tell you—"

"Stop!" Robin says. Her tone is so sharp that all three kids snap to attention. "Mother, think for a moment. Just think about what you're saying."

The soup dishes have been cleared away, and now a fish stew is being served. The scent of cardomom and a faint whiff of ginger waft up from Clara's plate.

Ruth continues determinedly. "Grandma's going to tell you, Elliot, and I want you to remember this forever and ever—"

The little girl's eyes are huge with wonder.

"Mother, I'm warning you." Robin's voice is shaking.

"—that I will always love you," Ruth says. "Whether I'm in this room with you or someplace else entirely."

With that, Ruth keeps her eyes downcast, as she uses all the strength in her thin arms to wheel herself backward from the table.

"Mother—Mom, where are you going?" Robin asks.

Ed shakes his head, then spears a shrimp from the fish stew.

"O ye of little faith," comes Ruth's voice, faintly. She turns her wheelchair—it must take every ounce of strength she has—and moves slowly through the French doors and into the living room.

"Oh, please." Robin drops her head into her hands. "What a drama queen."

"What's a drama queen?" asks the younger of the two boys.

"Grandma thinks . . . Oh, never mind."

"I'll go see her," says Ed.

"No." Clara rises quickly from her chair. "Let me."

"We need to talk about what happens next," Robin says. "Clara—"

"What do you mean?"

"She's deteriorating. She can't be alone in that apartment with just that girl, what's her name—"

"Peony," Clara says. "And we can talk about it later." She's feeling something almost impossible to contain, a welling up of sympathy for her mother so huge that it seems to fill her, spilling from her very pores.

Ruth has moved to the far side of the living room, her wheelchair parked beneath a large lime-green vintage poster of a devil wrapped around a Tanqueray bottle. In the polished surroundings of Robin's living room, with its white art-deco sofas and Regency chairs, yards and yards of shimming silk curtains spilling artfully to the floor, Ruth looks small and lost.

"Mom." Clara walks over to her. "Robin didn't mean to hurt your feelings."

Ruth shakes her head. Her chin is trembling.

"She was just trying to protect the kids," Clara goes on. The wrong thing to say, judging from the way Ruth sinks deeper into her wheelchair.

"Please. All Robin's done for the past ten years is try to protect those children from me." Ruth pauses, takes a ragged breath. "As if I'm some kind of monster."

"Well, you can see that they don't feel that way about you—you're their grandmother," Clara says, blindly trying to soothe. What is she saying? So hypocritical. Sam's face floats before her. Eyes accusing, mouth trembling with confusion.

"Thanksgiving, Christmas, New Year's Day," Ruth says bitterly. "That's exactly how many times a year I see them. At parties— surrounded by hundreds of people."

Clara is just hoping the tide doesn't turn toward her now. *And what about you? You left me—for all these years.*

"This is too hard," says Ruth. "I want to go home."

"Nonsense," says Robin, startling them both. Clara hadn't heard her approaching, in her soft velvet slippers. "We're about to have dessert."

Ruth just keeps staring at some invisible point in space, as if she sees something in the air in front of her. A vision, a ghost. The color has drained from her cheeks, the wine-induced euphoria gone in an instant.

"Look, Robin. I can take Mom back to her apartment," Clara says. "If that's what she wants."

A long-forgotten familiar look crosses Robin's face. Ah, she sees. Clara is here now. Clara, who will fulfill her role as the favorite daughter and do her mother's bidding.

"I guess I thought—" Ruth begins. Then she stops, squeezes her eyes shut, summoning the words. She tries again. "I don't have much time left to see you all—to make sense of you."

"What exactly did the doctor say?" asks Robin, ever practical.

"I wanted to be able to fix you in my mind," continues Ruth. Her voice gets softer and softer until it's almost an echo of itself. "So I can take you with me when I go. Like those carvings they find on the insides of caves, those carved figures that have been there for thousands of years—"

"What are you saying?" asks Robin. She sounds just like she did when she was five years old. *Mommy, you're not making any sense.*

Clara's breath catches. It all makes sense to her, of course. She has always understood. Ruth lives for the images in her mind—she has never been able to live for anything else. For a long time, Clara was that image. And during those darkest, most golden years, her mother lived for her.

"Mama?" Elliot's voice, calling from the dining room. "The ice cream's melting!"

"Coming, sweetheart," Robin calls over her shoulder. She turns to her mother. "Please. This isn't easy for any of us. Let's try again."

Ruth nods, almost imperceptibly. And the three of them—the Dunne women—go slowly back to the table.

# Chapter Four

Ruth's apartment is abuzz with activity, just as it has always been—but now, instead of assistants and interns, ringing phones, and FedEx deliveries, there is a revolving door of home aides. Clara has hired them through an agency—despite Ruth's feeble protests that she can *manage just fine.* In the past two and a half weeks, there have already been a series of them: women exhausted by jobs that usually come to an end when the person they are caring for dies.

*She's too difficult,* one of them said, before she quit on her second day.

*Nobody talks to me like that,* said another.

A package of adult diapers leans against the wall beneath the Edward Weston. The line of amber plastic bottles along the kitchen counter—morphine, Lorazepam, Prozac (Prozac? What possible point can there be in Ruth taking Prozac?)—offers Clara the comforting thought that if it all becomes too much, she can numb herself with one of Ruth's sedatives. At least for a few hours, she can medicate herself into a semblance of peace.

This morning's call home ended badly. Each day, Sammy has grown ever so slightly less communicative. *How's school? Fine. What's new? Nothing.* Jonathan took the phone from Sam, then sent her upstairs to get her socks and shoes on. He whispered fiercely into the phone, his voice a hiss.

"You're putting me in an impossible position."

"I know." Clara had closed her eyes. "Believe me, I—"

"And I've got to tell you, I really resent it."

"Please, Jonathan. Don't say that. It makes me feel—"

"This is *bullshit*, Clara. You're in total control of this situation—in fact, that's part of the problem. You're acting like a control freak. You're telling me what I can and can't tell Sammy. You're forcing me to lie to her."

"No, I'm not, I—"

He barreled right over her, interrupting—something he almost never did.

"I can't keep doing this."

"What are you saying?"

"I'm saying that something's got to give. Either come home now or let me tell Sam why you're away."

"No!"

"Will you stop it already?"

She could picture Jonathan—the look on his face—one she had seen only a few times in their years together. He rarely got angry, but when he did it transformed him. His handsome, craggy face became at once hard and vulnerable. She couldn't bear the thought of it.

"Please, Jon—"

"No. It's enough." His voice was devoid of all sympathy for her. "I'm hanging up now."

Peony has just come into the kitchen. She's carrying a batch of photographs encased in large manila folders—back to being the photography intern she was meant to be.

"Oh, sorry. I didn't know you were in here!" she says. "I was just going to make myself a fruit smoothie. Do you want one?"

"No, thanks," Clara says. The girl is always apologizing.

Peony's wearing three tank tops, one layered over the next over the next. White, gray, black. A red grease pencil is stuck behind her ear and she smells familiar, slightly musty—she's been in the archives, Clara realizes. A photograph is peeking from the top of the folders, revealing the top of a shiny dark head, a slice of white forehead. Without even knowing what she's seeing—a fraction of an image, taken out of context, it could be anything, couldn't it?—Clara draws in her breath.

"What are those . . . Why are you . . . ?" she stammers.

"Oh, these?" Peony hugs the folders to her chest, gently caressing them. "Ruth wanted to edit them this afternoon. She's not getting out of bed much now, and—you know. For the book?"

"The book?" Clara repeats.

A dark-skinned woman in a purple satin blouse, several lengths of gold chain wrapped around her neck, bustles down the hallway.

"Good morning, Rochelle," Clara says. The hospice nurse, arranged for by Dr. Zamitsky's office. A real pro—and, unlike the home aides, no behavior of Ruth's is going to faze her.

"Your mother's resting comfortably," says Rochelle. "No changes. I'll stop back in a few days."

A few days? What does she mean, a few days? And what's this about a book? Clara's head hurts. She can't make sense of anything and finds herself suddenly, improbably, wishing that Robin were here. Robin would know what to do. She would break each thing down into small manageable bits.

"She's great, the hospice nurse," Peony says, after Rochelle leaves. "I don't know how these people do it, going from apartment to apartment where everybody they take care of is—"

She stops abruptly.

"It's okay, Peony. You can use the D word," says Clara. She's still staring at the corner of the photograph, the slice of white skin, the shiny dark hair.

Peony looks at her blankly.

"Dying," says Clara. "I know my mother is dying."

Peony ducks her head to the side, the color rising in her cheeks. Clara has a flash of sympathy for the girl. Of all the well-known photographers in New York, of all the studios where she might have picked up a few tips, maybe found herself a mentor, she had to wind up here—in the house of craziness and death.

Down the long hall leading to the bedroom wing, Clara hears a door creak open, then shut with a solid click. Ruth's door. A childhood sound, the sound of her mother, restless, tiptoeing past Clara and Robin's bedroom in the middle of the night. Back then, Ruth would wander into the kitchen, fix herself a cup of tea, then pad quietly into the studio. There were so many closed doors between Ruth and her daughters—her bedroom door and theirs, the studio door, the darkroom—each one another kind of barrier. *Where's Mommy? Let's go and find Mommy.* Ruth was always, finally, in the darkroom, blue light seeping from beneath the crack. *Don't open it!* Ruth's sharp voice. They knew she didn't mean to sound angry. *Ssshhh, Mommy's working,* they whispered, holding hands as they made their way back to their rooms.

But wait—Clara pulls herself out of the quicksand of the past. What is Ruth doing out of bed?

A small red-haired woman wearing the gray uniform of a hospital orderly approaches them. Not Ruth, of course not. Had Clara been hoping that her mother might have improved these last few days? That perhaps those pesky tumors had taken a look around, realized that they were in Ruth Dunne's brain, and dissolved out of respect for her artistic genius?

"Marcy, this is—" Peony begins.

"I'm Ruth's daughter," Clara interrupts. "Clara."

"Yes, we spoke on the phone last night," Marcy says.

"Oh, of course."

The new home aide—sent to replace yesterday's.

"Well," Clara says faintly. "How's everything going so far?'

"The nurse gave her some morphine—put her out cold," says Marcy. "But she's been agitated on and off—thrashing about. I told your sister I think we need to order a hospital bed."

"Why's that?"

"The railings, hon. So she doesn't fall out and break a hip."

"I'll get on it," Clara says. That is, if Robin hasn't already checked it off her list.

"Where's the incinerator?" Marcy asks.

"Out in the hallway, to the right."

*Please, God*—Clara doesn't ever pray, but lately she's found herself offering up these silent beseechments—*let this one work out.*

Marcy heads into the outside corridor, carrying a white plastic trash bag stuffed with God-knows-what. Meanwhile, Peony straightens the edges of her folders, the stray photograph—the sliver of pale skin—disappearing from view.

"I'd better get these back into the archives," says Peony. "Until Ruth feels up to working on the book."

*What book?* The question screams through Clara's head. But she doesn't want to play her hand. Peony has no idea how little she actually knows.

"I'd like to take a look at them," she says coolly. Surprising herself.

"Oh, yeah—of course." Peony hands her the pile of folders. So easy—just like that. Who, after all, would argue with Clara's right to see them? She tries not to tremble. There must be a dozen in all.

Slowly, Clara walks down the hall to Ruth's room. She turns the knob and opens the door soundlessly; she knows exactly how to keep it from creaking. Ruth is lying on her side, curled up in the fetal position. She appears not so much to be sleeping as to be in another, more altered state: *out cold.* Sedated, resting comfortably, agitated, thrashing: What does any of it mean? It seems the language of dying has its own code that Clara has yet to begin to crack.

She stands by the bed, looking down at her mother. She can't remember a time in their shared lives when she has ever been able to simply watch Ruth—with no static interference, nothing in the air between them. Now, she takes it all in: the bony still-beautiful face, the elegant profile, the shadow cast by her long lashes, a delicate blue-green vein throbbing along her temple. She is so human. Stripped, for the moment, of her gaze. Her eyes shut, lids fluttering as if, even now, with all the morphine in the world pumped into her system, she still can't turn off the pictures in her mind.

No chance she's going to wake up—not from this stupor. Clara sinks into an armchair by the corner window, the pile of folders in her lap. Now that she has extracted them from Peony, she isn't sure she has the nerve to look at them. For so many years, she's avoided the possibility of stumbling across her mother's work. No visits to museums. No gallery-hopping in any city she has ever visited. Once, on a trip to Portland with Jonathan and Sam, they were browsing through a Barnes & Noble when she caught a glimpse of a familiar image—it appeared to her like a fragment of a remembered dream— on the cover of a photography magazine misplaced among stacks of *People* and *Newsweek*. She quickly rounded the corner, her throat thick with panic. *Let's get out of here,* she had said to Jonathan, pulling at him.

Ruth's breathing is labored—from illness, drugs, deep sleep, or a combination thereof, Clara isn't sure. She listens to the uneven rhythm of her mother's breath, willing herself to have whatever it takes—courage, hubris, a wild overestimation of what she can bear— to open the folder.

The phone next to Ruth's bed rings. Ruth stirs, flinging one arm up over her eyes as if shielding them from the sun. The sound is more of a purr, actually, fancy phones with intercom systems and caller ID being Ruth's only concession to modern life. Clara understands her mother's need to screen calls—she has the same need herself—and leans over to see KUBOVY WEISS spelled out on the small lit-up screen.

Kubovy. Well, she won't be answering that call. In an almost reflexive gesture, more of a tic than something carefully considered,

Clara opens the first folder. There, as she suspected, is the first image ever taken of her, the one that started the whole ball rolling: *Clara with the Lizard.* The wet shiny hair, the sliver of forehead—how had she known? The bit she had seen peeking from the top of Peony's folder could have been from any one of dozens of photos of her. Her hair was often slicked back off her face, her forehead smooth and pale as milk glass. But she did know—she did—because those images have always been more vivid and immediate to Clara than anything she might actually be seeing. Each one a vast bottomless whirlpool into which everything surrounding it is sucked in and drowned.

But wait. There are more photographs in these folders than Clara had originally thought. Each folder contains several photographs, separated by thin, archival tissue. *Clara in the Fountain. The Accident. Clara and the Popsicle.* As she studies the images, she crosses her legs tightly, pressing them together, cutting off her circulation. Pins and needles. Half of her is numb.

Interspersed among the familiar photographs are a few she's never seen before. Each is encased in vellum; a yellow Post-it is attached to the vellum on which is written, in Ruth's shaky hand, *never shown or published.* Clara, curled up on the sofa in the living room in Hillsdale, a patchwork quilt crumpled on the floor next to her. Clara, standing framed by a doorway—she must be eight or nine—her hip bones as fragile as bird's wings. She doesn't remember these pictures being taken. Not a glimmer, not a flash. It is as if these moments never happened—but here they are. She was there.

She skips the middle batch for the moment and flips all the way to the last folder, the final series of images. She has a hunch, a quick flood of feeling—terrible, foreboding, but also impossible to stop now that she has begun. She is shaking—the paper itself is shaking—as she opens to the final picture, *Naked at Fourteen.*

*Naked.* Ruth had used the word purposefully when she titled the photograph. Not *nude*—an artist's word—but *naked.* Stark and absolute. No bullshit about it. As if to say, Let's call this what it is.

Her own eyes stare back at her, angry, vulnerable, accusatory. *How could you?* Her pubescent body, breasts already forming above the rib cage, a shadow darkening between her legs. Arms crossed defiantly, hips cocked to one side. Clara reaches back—she grasps at the past—but it is like she is in a free fall, clutching at the air. There is nothing to hold. No memory. Only this.

"What time is it?" A hoarse voice—Ruth's voice—nearly makes Clara jump out of her chair. Her mother has rolled over and is now lying on her side, facing Clara. How long has she been watching her?

"Tell me about these," Clara says quietly.

"Sorry, dear?"

Clara holds up a few of the photographs.

"Careful with those—my God, Clara, your fingerprints!"

Ruth's all there, all right. Plenty of *compos* in her *mentis.* Over the past few days, Clara has wondered if her mother has started to mentally lose it—but no. Clara is overtaken by a violent, intense desire to rip the pictures in two, all of them, one by one—as Ruth lies there, a prisoner on her bed. She wants to do it—but she is paralyzed. She feels as if she's floating, hovering above herself and Ruth. Are the photographs hers to destroy? Her mother's days in the darkroom are over. Each of these prints are the last ones in Ruth Dunne's possession. The last that will ever be made.

"Why are you looking at these, Mother? Why has Peony taken them out of the archives?" Clara asks. She sits on her hands—literally sits on them—to stop them from shaking, to stop herself from doing something she can never take back.

Ruth flinches slightly. *Mother.* Clara has spoken with such disdain, such sarcasm, after these weeks of increasing kindness and sympathy. The old feelings rush back—nothing has changed between them.

"Would you mind calling Peony, darling? I need some help—"

"That's no longer Peony's job, remember?"

Ruth's nose wrinkles.

"But these women from the agency are so . . . I don't know . . . I can hardly carry on a conversation with them," she says.

"They're here to help you, not to provide intellectual stimulation." Clara finally snaps. "Stop avoiding my question."

"What question is that?"

Is Ruth messing with Clara's head? She is capable of many things, but has never been capable of guile. With Ruth, what you see is what you get—so what's this? She seems to be wavering in and out of focus. Sharp, then blurry, then sharp again.

"The photographs. They're all here—every single one of them, as far as I can tell. All your photographs of me, even ones I never knew about."

"Of course." Ruth struggles up on one elbow. "For the book."

"What book?" Clara's voice is raised. She hears a shuffling outside the doorway. Is Peony standing there? Or Marcy? Or some other person from the phalanx of Ruth's helpers?

"Kubovy is helping me put it together," Ruth says. "I've wanted to do it for years, and now—"

"Jesus Christ," says Clara. It dawns on her in an overwhelming rush, a shock so profound that it actually feels electrical. Her spine is on fire. She understands now. It has taken longer than it should have—but now she understands.

She thumbs through the folders resting on her lap. She feels reckless. Nothing she discovers could possibly make things worse. She opens one that appears to be slightly smaller than the rest and finds a mock-up of a book jacket inside. There she is, close-up, closer up than she has ever been before. It's one of the images she's never seen. How old is she, perhaps seven? It is summer—she can tell by the waviness of her hair—and she is lying on a braided rug, her hair spread all around her. Clara remembers the rug; it smelled of lemons and dog hair and was soft from a thousand washings. How can she remember the rug but not the photograph?

A black paper sash runs across the middle of the mock-up.

CLARA. Just her name, nothing more—each letter cut out from the black paper. The design is brilliant; she sees this even now. The sash can be removed so that only the image of the little girl remains. And the name CLARA itself—her own name!—is an absence rather than a presence. Cut out. Each letter an empty hole in the blackness.

"What do you think of it?" asks Ruth.

"You can't do this," says Clara.

"What do you mean? It's already—"

"I won't let you do this," Clara says, more forcefully.

Ruth has managed to sit up now and has shoved two pillows behind her. She looks at Clara indulgently, as if she were an adorable but misguided child.

"Oh, Clara," she begins, "it's my work. It's not about you—it was never about you."

"That's bullshit! Of course it's about me—it *is* me!"

"You've refused to understand this," says Ruth. "Light, shadow, texture—the pictures are scenes, compositions—"

"You stole me away from myself!" Clara digs her nails into the soft flesh of her palm, willing herself to stop—but there is no stopping. Not at this point.

Ruth doesn't react. She just takes it all in, wishing—Clara is certain—that she had a camera in her hand. Even now, she is framing her subject: her grown daughter, face contorted by outrage, sitting in the old wing chair with a pile of photographs on her lap.

"I'm sorry," Ruth says, sounding anything but. "I wish you weren't still so worked up about all this. It's ancient history. How can it possibly matter?"

Clara is crying now. For such a long time—all her adult life, really—it has been difficult for her to muster tears. She has moved past her feelings as if they were scenery seen from a moving car. Anger, sadness, regret, loneliness—she kept going, and her painful thoughts remained stationary, like dusty signs on a road. But all Ruth has to do is . . . to be Ruth. Ever since first arriving in New York,

Clara has felt tears gathering in the corners of her eyes. She has sprung a slow leak.

"It matters," she says. "How can you not understand that it matters? I've been trying—" She breaks off, gulping for air.

"Oh, Clara, please, you must—"

"You stop." Clara finds her breath. "You stop this right now."

Ruth shakes her head.

The phone rings again. KUBOVY WEISS. Ruth reaches for the receiver but doesn't have the strength. She collapses back against her pillows, breathless even from that small effort.

"Could you answer that for me, Clara?"

"Why the fuck would I do that?"

"Clara!"

There's that feeling again—unfamiliar, both terrifying and liberating. If Clara had to describe it, she would say it is a complete lack of caution. The sudden improbable removal—as if surgically excised—of a key aspect of her careful, guarded nature.

"Fine," she says. Her body is coiled, tense, like an animal ready to spring. She grabs the ringing phone.

"Hello, Kubovy."

A split second of silence on the other end.

"Is that Clara?"

"Yes, Kubovy. It's Clara."

"How are you, my beauty?"

"I've been better." And then, in a rush of words—"Kubovy, this book you're doing with my mother. Please think—think about what you're doing."

Another pause, slightly longer than the last. Even as a little girl, Clara imagined Kubovy's mind as a calculator. Always computing, adding or subtracting, finding a way to make the equation work to his advantage.

"I can't accept it." Clara fills the silence. "It's too much."

"What are you saying?" Kubovy asks.

She waits him out.

"Clara, Clara," he finally says. He has chosen his tack, adopting the weary, admonishing tone that Ruth already tried on her. "There's another way to look at this, you know."

"Oh, really? And what is that?"

"You've had a remarkable life. An *interesting* life. And part of the reason for that remarkable, interesting life is—"

"My life hasn't been so goddamned interesting," Clara interrupts.

Ruth shifts her weight on the bed, sinks lower into her pillows.

"Well. I can't speak to your current life in . . . where is it again—"

"Maine," Clara bites off.

"Ah, yes. I would agree. Perhaps not so fascinating. But your childhood, my dear—you were a star!"

Clara closes her eyes. Squeezes them tight so there is nothing but darkness. No images of flashbulbs popping outside the Kubovy Weiss Gallery. No frank stares, no sideways inquisitive glances from strangers on the street. None of that—but still, it all seeps in around the edges. Poison finding its mark.

"I just wanted to be a kid." Clara's voice drops to a whisper. She can't seem to stop crying. The images blur beneath her lids.

"And you would have wanted your mother to be . . . what . . . baking cookies?"

"You don't get it."

"No, my dear, it's you who don't get it. You've been in such a privileged position. It's sad that you can't see it for yourself."

"Stop it, Kubovy. You don't know me anymore. You don't know anything about me." She is breathless, unaccustomed to saying what she thinks. "Don't you dare treat me like a child."

"But you are acting like one."

Clara slams down the phone. She has momentarily forgotten about Ruth. Ruth stares up at her from the bed, seemingly unfazed by her behavior—or maybe she really is stoned on morphine.

"I really do need that woman—what's-her-name—to come in here," says Ruth. "I'm sure she's trying to give us some privacy, but—"

"I'll go get her." Clara jumps to her feet. Glad to get away for a moment. Afraid of what she might say next.

The phone rings again. Ruth doesn't even try to reach for it. It rings and rings. Clara pictures Kubovy on the other end, pacing the floor of his gallery, cursing her under his breath in his native Turkish.

"Clara." There is an unfamiliar tone in Ruth's voice. "I really don't want to hurt you." She seems almost to be pleading.

Clara stops, one hand on the doorknob. She waits for more. She waits for her mother to say she's made a mistake. That she understands. That she'll leave ancient history where it belongs, locked up in the dusty archives of the past.

"Did you hear what I said, Clara?" Ruth's voice is weakening. "The last thing I want to do is hurt you—"

"Then don't," Clara says. And walks out of the room.

<hr />

"RAIN!" Ruth looks out the fogged-up window of the Checker cab. "Why does it have to be pouring on this night—of all nights?"

"It doesn't matter." Clara's father soothes her. He's sitting on a folding metal jump seat, facing Ruth, Clara, and Robin. He reaches over and pats Ruth on her knee. Clara recognizes the expression on his face, though she's used to seeing it directed at her or Robin. Pride. Nathan Dunne is proud of his young, beautiful wife who is about to have her first gallery show. He hasn't seen any of the photographs; Ruth has kept them under wraps. She wants him to be surprised—to see her work hung on a gallery wall for the first time, the way the rest of the world will see it.

That is, if anyone shows up. A rumble of thunder. Lightning flashes across the sky like a strobe. Clara loves these Checker cabs, with their rounded hoods and roomy insides where you can sit across from someone while you bounce along. And she loves to be able to look at her father, who has put on his downtown best for the occasion—black jeans and a black sweater—the freshly ironed crease along the center of his jeans legs the only giveaway that he's really an uptown lawyer.

"Of course it's going to matter, Nate!" Ruth looks like she's going to cry. She never wears makeup, but tonight her face is painted. A slash of red across her mouth. Eyes lined with charcoal, lashes thick and dark. Clara wants to wipe her mother's face with a damp tissue, the way Ruth does when she has a runny nose. She doesn't like all that color on her mother's lips. It makes her look hard. Like a stranger.

Clara had watched Ruth as she got ready for the evening. Her mother looked almost like a little girl in her fuzzy slippers and panties, squinting at herself in the harsh light of the bathroom mirror. Ruth smiled unnaturally at her own reflection, then let out a deep sigh.

"This is supposed to be fun." Ruth turned to Clara.

"What is, Mommy?"

"The opening," Ruth said, dusting powder over her cheeks. "The party."

"Parties are fun," Clara said. She wasn't sure what her mother meant. All she knew is that Ruth looked tense. All bottled up.

"The work is the best part," Ruth said, crouching down so she could look at Clara directly. "The stuff we do together. The rest—I'd just as soon skip it."

The taxi stops at a traffic light in Times Square. Dozens of small storefronts covered with iron gates, a blur of seedy, flickering neon. A car alarm is going at full tilt, a series of syncopated staccato blasts. A tall woman in a short skirt steps gingerly over a puddle in her high-heeled boots.

"Daddy, look—is that a man?" asks Robin, pointing to the tall woman.

Nathan peers out the window, through the pelting rain. "Seems to be, sweetheart."

"Why is she dressed like that?"

"Some adults like to play dress-up."

"But why?"

"Oh, please don't start with the whys," Ruth says under her breath, so softly that only Clara can hear it.

"Why, Daddy?"

Clara knows this bothers her mother—the way Robin never stops asking questions, the way these questions are always directed at their father. Clara wishes she could tell her mother that Robin never asks her anything because Ruth never answers. But even at four, she knows the way things have lined up in the Dunne family: Ruth has Clara. Nate has Robin. A perfect mathematical balance.

"Look, Daddy—that sign says s-h-o-p, that spells shop!" Robin pipes up again. She looks at the pink flashing lights that precede it. "s-e-x. What does that spell, Daddy?"

Nathan and Ruth exchange a parental look: amused, shoulders shrugging. As if to say, *What do we do now?* But Robin's already on to the next thing, her mind fixed on what's right in front of her, like a small animal foraging for scraps.

"Will there be food at this party?" Clara wants to know.

"Wine and cheese," says Ruth.

"What about juice?"

"I'm sure Kubovy has thought of that," says Ruth.

"He does seem to think of everything," says Nate.

The rain has slowed to a drizzle by the time the taxi stops on the corner of Broome and West Broadway. It's a few minutes before six—Ruth doesn't yet know about being fashionably late to her own openings. A few people are already gathered outside Kubovy Weiss. Thursday nights are reserved for these downtown openings; the galleries on the strip of West Broadway between Broome and Houston are lit up, doors propped open. Small groups move in the darkness from one well-lit space to the next. A man in jeans and a motorcycle jacket is walking alone, drinking from a plastic cup.

"Look, Mommy, there's your name!" Robin says. She elbows Clara. "And yours too!"

Sure enough, painted in large bold type, across the glass front of the gallery, are the words RUTH DUNNE: THE CLARA SERIES. Clara spots Kubovy. He's standing just inside the entrance. He sees their taxi and dashes outside, holding a huge black umbrella.

"Here you are," he says excitedly. Ruth climbs out, and Kubovy looks at her from head to toe, taking in the floaty black ensemble, the crimson lips. "Magnificent," he says, kissing her on both cheeks. "Nathan—welcome," he adds, shaking Clara's father's hand. "Glad you could make it."

Nate's eyes flicker away. Clara can see that Kubovy makes him uncomfortable. *Glad you could make it?* Welcoming him to his own wife's art opening? But Nate rises to the occasion, summons his lawyerly self, forces a smile.

"Wouldn't miss it for the world," he says.

Kubovy has already moved ahead of them, shepherding Ruth inside under his big umbrella, even though the rain has all but stopped.

"Gary Indiana's on the confirmed guest list," Clara hears him say. "And Ingrid Sischy's supposed to come—I think she'll show up, but you never know."

Ruth's hand covers her mouth as she walks in the door. Many years from now, Clara will wonder how her mother did it: how she stepped over the threshold of the Kubovy Weiss Gallery that rainy Thursday evening, bringing with her all her terrors, her insecurities and fears. What was going through her mind? Did she understand what was at stake? It was not the possibility of failure. Failure wouldn't have changed her life. Nor, even, would a modest success. If her first solo show had come and gone the way so many first shows do, with perhaps nothing more than a two-line notice in the *New York* magazine listings, a brief mention in *The Village Voice,* Ruth would have just kept going, kept making her pictures—she might even have moved on to another subject. No, it was the slim but very real chance that RUTH DUNNE: THE CLARA SERIES would become an overnight sensation, as envisioned and orchestrated by Kubovy Weiss. That Ruth would go from art student anonymity to the beginnings of fame.

"Young ladies." Kubovy takes Clara and Robin over to a table covered by a white cloth. "Have either of you ever had a Shirley Temple?"

Robin and Clara both shake their heads no.

"A perfect drink," says Kubovy, handing them each a red concoction in a plastic cup. Then, over their heads, he notices someone walk in the door. "Please excuse me."

Robin nudges her. "Look," she whispers. She's pointing to one of the photographs, but Clara is afraid to follow her sister's finger. She takes a sip of her drink—sickly sweet—and fishes out a maraschino cherry. In her peripheral vision, she sees herself looming, huge images hanging on each of the white walls, illuminated by tiny powerful spotlights.

"You're naked," Robin whispers.

"I know," Clara whispers back.

Where is her father? Where is her mother? She looks around the enormous space and sees Ruth, who is now surrounded by a small crowd: a man holding a spiral-bound notebook, a woman with frizzy red hair and platform shoes, an older gentleman in a suit, and a few people dressed identically in faded jeans and leather jackets.

One of them turns and notices Clara and Robin, standing near the bar. Ruth believes in letting the girls pick out their own clothing. For tonight, Robin has chosen sensible wide-wale corduroy pants and a forest-green sweatshirt she got last summer in Colorado. Clara is wearing a pink skirt and purple top; she picked it out because she thought it looked like something in Barbie's wardrobe.

"That's her," the frizzy red-haired woman says, sotto voce. "That's Clara."

Ruth is deep in conversation with the older man in the suit. Her head is tilted forward, and she's nodding intently. Kubovy brings over a small elegant woman with severe dark bangs.

"Ruth, this is Roselee Goldberg, from The Kitchen," he says.

Clara's ears, stereophonic, take in sound from all four corners of the gallery. She isn't looking, she's only listening. And the bits she hears, over and over again, contain her own name. *Clara. That's the girl. Dunne's daughter. No, darling—the younger daughter. Clara. What about the other one? No, just Clara. Her muse . . .*

Blood pounds in Clara's ears. She's so small—only up to the waists of these people. The crowd is growing, visitors spilling in from the street. The floor is dotted with water splattered from shoes and dripping umbrellas. She reaches for Robin's hand. Small, damp, quivering slightly, Robin's fingers wrap around her own.

*I'm scared, Robin,* Clara wants to say. But the words are trapped somewhere between her heart and her mouth, stuck; nothing escapes. *I don't like this.* Can she articulate the thought, even to herself? The room is blurry, the images thankfully receding into dim memories of themselves. Robin tries to pull her hand away—she needs both hands to drink her Shirley Temple—but Clara holds on tight.

*Original, never seen anything quite— Sold-out show, have you heard? Subversive in their own way—quite brilliant really.* Conversation swirls around her, words she doesn't understand. High pointy heels, platform boots, fat veiny ankles. The hems of black skirts. Bellies straining over belt buckles. Someone bumps into her, nearly spilling her pink-red drink all over her special outfit.

*Excuse me, young lady—oh, it's you! It's the girl in the pictures!*

Finally—through the sea of legs—Clara sees her father. He's the only man standing alone in this room full of cliques and packs. At the sight of him, her gaze clears. He is in front of a single photograph, his back to the crowd. She looks—for the first time this evening, she looks directly at what's hanging on the wall.

Blown up so that it actually appears life-sized, most of the foreground of the picture is taken up with a bed. Soft ivory sheets, the kind that look as if they've been washed a thousand times and dried on a country laundry line. Sheets that smell like lavender and freshly cut grass. A striped Navajo blanket, pushed to the edge of the mattress by the little girl at the center of the bed, who is lying on her stomach, her legs splayed carelessly open. Her head is turned to the side, eyes closed, as if in sleep. Next to the little girl—this is the first but hardly the last time in her life that Clara will think of herself as *that girl*, as someone entirely other than who she is—is a big stain, spread out from beneath her bare buttocks.

A shiny white plaque is affixed to the wall to the right of the photograph. Robin, still holding Clara's hand, walks over to the plaque and squints at the small lettering.

"The A-C-C-I-D-E-N-T," she spells out. "What does that mean, Daddy? What's that word?"

"Accident," Nate says hoarsely.

Clara remembers—it's a little hazy now, since Ruth took this picture more than a year ago, when she was only three—the way she had peed in her bed during the night, when they were staying at the house upstate. The way Ruth, when she saw the stain on the sheets, the room bathed in sunlight, Clara lying there—*I'm sorry, Mommy!*—didn't get mad like some other mothers might. She didn't even strip the bed. Instead, she waited until nighttime and set up the shot, pole lights and silver reflector in place. *Like that, sweetheart. Pretend you're really sleeping. Pretend you're dreaming about something wonderful. Move your chin down a bit, Clara. Open your legs.*

"Quite something, isn't it?" Kubovy appears at Nathan's side. "To my mind, it's the most—"

"We're leaving," Nathan says, very quietly.

"Excuse me?" Kubovy takes a half step back.

"You heard me," says Nathan. "I'm taking my girls—" He glances over at Clara and Robin, then leans closer to Kubovy. "How could you encourage this?" His voice is shaking with rage. "What were you thinking?"

Clara isn't sure why her father is so angry, but she knows it must have something to do with her. She looks over to her mother. Ruth hasn't moved from her spot in the center of the gallery. She's surrounded by a new group of people. Someone brings her a glass of white wine and then clinks the plastic rim. A murmured swell of congratulations.

"Nathan, calm down," says Kubovy. Beads of perspiration appear, like droplets of condensation, on his high shiny forehead. "I don't think you understand."

"I understand perfectly," says Nathan. He bundles Clara and Robin under his arm. His black cashmere sweater is soft against Clara's cheek. "And I'm taking them out of here—right now."

"Nathan, please don't make a scene. If you take Clara, people will—"

"Do you think," Nathan says slowly, "that I give a flying fuck what these people will say?"

It is perhaps the only time in Clara's life when she will ever see Kubovy unprepared. He had anticipated the excitement, the critics, the art world press. He had even allowed himself to imagine a sold-out show. But he had not taken into account the way a father might view the images of his little girl, blown-up, life-sized, naked—more than naked: exposed. No, he hadn't given a second thought to Nathan, the uptight, uptown lawyer husband. The one who, Kubovy was certain, would be no more than a footnote in the ultimate biography of Ruth Dunne.

"Ready, girls?" Nathan crouches down and hugs them both.

Clara finally lets go of Robin's hand.

"Daddy"—she starts to cry—"I want to go home."

———◆◆◆◆◆———

EVERY NIGHT SINCE she's been in New York, Clara has crept into Robin's apartment, careful not to disturb the equilibrium of family life. The boys doing their homework at the kitchen table. Elliot already asleep in her pink ruffled room. Ed closed off in their bedroom, watching basketball on a muted flat-screen television. And Robin—perched on the edge of a delicate antique chair behind her gleaming desk in the corner of the living room. The only sound in the whole apartment is the rapid clicking of her computer keys.

But tonight Clara makes no attempt to be quiet. Into the pristine, expensive silence of Robin's apartment she flies, hair a mess, face red and sweaty from a fast walk through the city. She smells the sharp scent of her own body as she shrugs out of her down jacket, not bothering—for once—to hang it up. She needs a shower, though as priorities go it isn't at the top of her list.

Robin looks up from her usual spot in the corner, her fingers frozen in midair above her computer like a pianist's. She's been to the hairdresser today; soft bangs sweep across her forehead, making her look years younger. A cup of tea—her favorite, Serenity Blend—rests on a coaster. Serenity tea, private yoga, alpaca throws neatly folded on ottomans and draped across the backs of armchairs—as if all this will keep Robin safe. As if the perfect paint chip, the best staff, the right schools, the lovely clothes will keep the past at bay. *You're wasting your fucking time!* Clara nearly screams. She imagines—the image just slams into her mind—a wrecking ball demolishing the whole thing.

"What's the matter?" Robin asks quickly.

Clara's heart is racing. It's been racing all day, galloping like a runaway horse. She's told herself to calm down—she's tried to calm down—but she can't seem to catch her breath.

"Did you know?" she manages to ask. She doesn't move from the spot in the foyer where she dropped her jacket. She's afraid to walk all the way in. She's been sucked in far enough—back into the vortex of their shared history.

"Did I know what?" Robin swivels around and watches Clara carefully as if . . . what? Is she afraid Clara is going to throw something perhaps? Break a precious piece of Murano glass?

"Mom's book," Clara says.

"What are you talking about?"

"All the photographs from the Clara Series—"

Her breath catches. Saying it out loud—saying it to Robin, of all people—makes the book even more real, somehow. All day long, she has walked miles around the city, trying to push it away. She left Ruth's apartment and walked through the park to the East River, where she stood across from the entrance of Brearley and watched the girls and their mothers come and go. Had she ever simply been one of them, in her navy blue jumper? Or had she always been different? She walked down the streets of the Upper East Side, past newsstands and shops, her childhood haunts. She ate lunch at the soda fountain in the pharmacy on Lexington, summoning the past. Trying to force herself back into it, if only to see if she could survive the journey.

"Calm down, Clara. Take a couple of deep—"

"I can't."

"Let's have a look." Robin faces her computer screen once again. "Come over here."

Clara approaches her sister. So Robin hadn't known. There was some small grace in that, at least. She stands behind Robin and peers into the small screen of her computer as Robin types RUTH DUNNE and CLARA into Google. A few seconds later, a list appears. There are more than seventy thousand entries. Robin begins to scroll down: first, the online biographies of Ruth, then a series of home pages from Ruth's galleries—Paris, Madrid, Berlin, London—and then academic papers. Hundreds of them. Art students from all over the place, writing their dissertations about the role of Clara in the work of Ruth Dunne.

"Unbelievable," says Robin. "I haven't done this in years."

Clara's never been able to bring herself to look at any of this stuff. These perfect strangers who have their opinions—people who have spent years of their lives thinking about Clara and Ruth—studying the photographs as if they might find answers there.

Robin clicks randomly on one, written by a graduate student in women's studies at Berkeley. *The child acts as both metaphor and provocateur in Dunne's early work.* Clara skims the page, restless, jumpy. *These images, at first, might be misunderstood as pornographic. But in fact, at its subversive best, Dunne's work speaks to the profound and collaborative nature of mothering itself.*

"I don't know how you stand this," Robin says.

"I don't," says Clara. "I don't stand it."

"There's nothing here about a book," Robin says, after a few more dizzying minutes of scrolling down. Robin's about to close the laptop when Clara remembers the name of Ruth's German publisher, Steiffel. It floats into her consciousness like a detail from a dream. It sounds huge and looming—a tower, a steeple.

"Let me." Clara comes around the side of the chair and sits next to Robin. She does a quick search for the publisher, and there it is, what she's been childishly hoping she wouldn't find. CLARA. It pops up instantly—the design she saw earlier in the day, the price in euros, the date of publication. December, nine months from now.

"Mom?" Tucker calls from the kitchen. "Mom, I need some help with—"

"Not now," Robin calls back. "Go ask your father."

"But he—"

"Just do it!"

Robin folds her hands in her lap, but not before Clara notices that she's shaking. Her whole body is taut. The tiny muscles in her arms twitch beneath the smooth surface of her skin.

"I'm so sorry," she says, not looking at Clara.

"You didn't do anything," Clara says.

"I know. I know, but—"

"Mom?" Another child's voice pierces the moment. "I forgot that I need my guitar tomorrow, at school."

"I'm busy, Harrison," Robin calls. "You're going to have to wait a few minutes."

She turns now and looks directly at Clara.

"What are you going to do now?"

"What do you mean?"

But Clara knows. She knows exactly what Robin means. She can hear Robin's younger voice—fourteen years younger, to be exact—as if it has been trapped inside of Clara all these years. *You're leaving, aren't you? You're not coming back. How can you do this?* It has never gone away. None of it has. The past is alive inside of them—it will die only when they do, and maybe not even then.

"I haven't thought about it—" she falters. And then she realizes that it is, in fact, all she's been thinking about as she's circled the city. A knowledge, just out of reach. She's already gone, in fact. Back to Maine, back to the life she never should have left, not for a minute. She's brought about Jonathan's fury at her, Sammy's sadness and confusion—for what? What had she been thinking, that it really could be different?

"Come on, Clara."

"I'm not like you, Robin, I don't just—"

"You're leaving."

A long pause, a free fall.

"Yes."

Clara hadn't noticed—hadn't allowed herself to notice—how much Robin has grown to look like their father. She has Nathan's gray-green eyes, Nathan's strong jaw. Clara wishes she could wrap her arms around her sister and hold her.

"Is that it, then?" Robin's face tightens further.

"Yes," Clara says softly.

Robin's cheeks redden. "Please. I know this is bad," she says. "And you have every right to be furious at Ruth—but I've been dealing with her for so goddamned long by myself—"

"I just can't," Clara says. "Especially now, after I started to—"

She breaks off, shaking her head.

"What? Started to what?" Robin stands up now and moves a few steps back. As if she can't bear to sit so close to Clara.

"To let myself feel something for her again. To believe that maybe—"

"She is who she is," Robin says. "I've known that forever."

"Well, maybe it's less complicated for you," says Clara.

Robin blinks hard.

"What did you just say?"

"I'm sorry, I—"

"You think my relationship with Ruth has been—uncomplicated?"

"No, that's not what I—"

"Fuck you," Robin says, her tone improbably soft.

"I meant—"

"I know what you meant," Robin says. "It's all about you, Clara. It's always been all about you."

"No, that's not it!"

Clara stands up. She can't afford to be sitting down with Robin towering over her like this. Robin's hands twitch at her sides, and for a split second Clara thinks her sister might slap her. But then all that rage seems to slide off—Clara can almost see it puddling on the floor around Robin—and what is left, instead, looks like grief.

"I spent my whole life"—Robin's mouth contorts—"by myself. Mom was always taking you away. You spent hours in the studio—"

"I didn't want to be doing that," Clara interrupts. "I didn't want—"

"And then in the country," Robin goes on. "You'd be gone all afternoon. What did you think I was doing, especially on the weekends when Dad was away? I was alone in that goddamned house—"

"She was torturing me," Clara says softly. "I hated it."

"She was paying attention to you."

"Mommy?"

Elliot appears in the archway of the living room, rubbing her eyes. She's holding a well-worn stuffed kitten, and her cheeks are creased from her pillow.

"Oh, Ellie, would you ask Daddy or Edjinea to put you back to bed, honey? Mommy's busy."

Elliot turns and pads back down the hall, looking for her father.

"God, you'd think that for once I could have a little space." Robin bites her cuticle, then stares at her fingernails. She's trying hard not to cry. "Please, Clara. Stay a little while longer."

It costs Robin something to ask, and Clara knows it.

"Listen," Clara says. "I was trying to let go of it—trying to tell myself that it all happened a long time ago—"

"And it did!" Robin interrupts.

"But now she's bringing it back," Clara says. "It's all coming back. Don't you see?"

"Please," Robin repeats. Her mouth quivering.

"I can't."

Something shuts down in Robin's eyes. Clara sees it happening— as if two tiny window shades have been pulled down. Her whole face becomes opaque. Robin gives a nod, then a small tight smile.

"Okay, then," she says. "When's your flight?"

# Chapter Five

THE TAXI from Bangor drops Clara off in front of the Bar Harbor YMCA. The trucks and SUVs in the parking lot are in their usual spots. Mary Ann Rowe's metallic blue Toyota with its SUPPORT OUR TROOPS bumper sticker is next to Ali Mulvey's white Land Cruiser, so caked with mud and snow that it appears gray. Susanna Haber's Lexus—the only luxury SUV in the lot—is parked halfway into the yellow line of a handicapped space even though there's plenty of room around it. If Clara bothered to look, she knows she would see keys dangling from the ignitions of most of the cars and open handbags resting on passenger seats. They all do this, the mothers. They even leave their engines running sometimes, as they dash into the Y to pick up their kids after swim practice.

Four-thirty on a Wednesday, and everything is exactly as it was before Clara left. She can hear the sound of splashing, the shriek of the coach's whistle as she walks past the front desk to the double doors leading to the Olympic-sized pool. She inhales sharply. The warm damp air stings the insides of her nostrils. The air around the pool smells slightly of chlorine.

The last two and a half weeks close around her—constricting her movements—and for a moment she stops. Tries to calm down. *You're home now. You're home now. You're home.* Fourteen years—what hubris, what staggering innocence—to think that those years would double and redouble, that she would live out her whole life as she intended. As if her past could be chopped away. She remembers once, at Sawyer's Market, ordering a butterflied leg of lamb. She watched as the butcher carefully sliced away the fat, his knife as precise as a scalpel. When it came time for him to flatten the meat, he turned to Clara with a wink. *Thinking of my mother,* he said, as he grabbed a meat cleaver. He raised the cleaver high and started pounding on the meat, whacking it until it quivered under the thick metal blade. A vein popped out in his forehead from the effort.

*Thinking of my mother.* As Clara pushes the doors open, the sound of splashing grows louder. The thin voices of girls (Sammy!) echo off the tile walls and ceiling. The humid air, usually oppressive, hits her not at all unpleasantly. Often she finds it hard to breathe in here, but today—after the taxi to LaGuardia, the hour-long flight to Bangor, the two-hour car service back to the island—her pores open up to the heat. She wants to sweat New York out of her system. Feel her mother and her sister—and the rest of them, Kubovy, even the hospice nurse—dripping out of her. Detoxified. Gone.

Where's Sammy? Clara's need to see Sammy is frantic, physical. She scans the pool for Sammy's small head in its bathing cap and goggles. There she is, poised to dive into the pool at the far end—the long muscles in her thighs tensed, arms angled perfectly over her head. It's all Clara can do not to lurch toward her daughter, dive into the pool, and grab Sammy's wiry little body, breathe into the back of her sweet wet neck.

Two and a half weeks. A fucking eternity. And for what?

The moms are sitting on the bleachers, surrounded by piles of towels, down jackets, snow boots, knapsacks, brown paper bags filled with snacks for the ride home: juice boxes, single-serving yogurts, and packages of peanut butter crackers. This group of women has been together for years, loosely formed by the fact that their daughters are swimmers. Clara has always thought of them as *the moms.* As if she herself were apart from them. As if she herself has not perched on these bleachers, year after year, making small talk about play dates, chorus, the need for a new tennis coach.

Laurel Connolly spots her at the door and waves. Her daughter Emily has been swimming with Sam since kindergarten.

"Hey there, stranger!" Laurel moves a pile of towels out of the way and makes room for Clara next to her on the bleacher. She leans over and gives Clara a hug. "How are you? I've been thinking about you so much."

"I'm fine," Clara says. "Thanks for all the carpooling. It was a huge help."

"No problem." Laurel is looking at Clara strangely. Too intensely. "Are you okay? I mean—really?"

Inwardly, Clara bristles. She isn't ready for this—the way people in Southwest know all about each other's comings and goings. They know who's sick, who's having problems meeting their mortgage payments, whose child needs remedial help at school. They pass each other's houses in their cars, and they notice who stays up late at night, the blue flickering lights of television visible from the street.

"I just had to be in New York for a while," she says. Hoping Laurel will leave it at that.

"Well, thank God you were able to get to the best doctors," says Laurel.

Clara is watching Sam slice through the water in a graceful backstroke. So determined, so purposeful. Sam has no idea Clara is here, and she won't notice until practice is over—she's in another world when she's swimming.

But then Laurel's words sink in.

"I'm sorry?" Clara turns to Laurel, whose dark curly hair has been made wild by the humidity, springing all around her soft, pretty face. In her sweat suit and sneakers, she could be mistaken for a high school kid.

"The specialist," Laurel repeats. "In New York."

Clara feels apprehensive—suddenly on guard—though she has no idea why.

"Sammy told Emily that you were sick," Laurel falters. "That you needed to be away because—"

Clara looks at her, unable to hide her bewilderment.

"You mean you're not—"

"No," Clara says slowly. "I'm not sick."

"She told the whole class," says Laurel. "I was going to call Jonathan, but he's so private, and I thought—"

Laurel breaks off. She looks down at her hands, embarrassed for Clara.

*Oh, Sammy.* Clara's stomach clenches. She can see it, of course, all too clearly. Sammy holding court with her friends as they stand by their open lockers. Flushed, eyes glittering. The tumble of words that seem to fall, on their own, from Sammy's lips. The sweet, slightly sickening relief at having something—anything—to say about her mother.

"Shit," Clara says, under her breath. She keeps her eyes on Sam. Doing the butterfly now. Ahead of the pack. Her small curved back rising and falling through the water like a dolphin's.

"It's okay." Laurel tries to fix things, good mommy that she is. "Really—all our girls exaggerate sometimes."

Clara tries to steady her heartbeat, quiet the thumping against her rib cage as she watches Sammy climb out on the far edge of the pool. Sam pulls off her bathing cap, her long dark hair spilling over her shoulders, her body glistening. She stands with a gaggle of her girl-friends, laughing at something, their heads bent together. *Sammy!* she wants to shout. *Over here!* She wants to wrap Sam in a towel. Wrap her around and around and around—

The shriek of the coach's whistle, the splash of arms and legs scissoring through water, the high-pitched voices of the girls—it all becomes muffled, cottony. *Be still, Clara. This is a very slow exposure. Don't move . . . That's it, darling. That's beautiful. Try not to breathe.*

Clara digs her ragged fingernails into the fleshy part of her palms. Has that whispery voice—Ruth's voice—been with her all along? Surrounding her throughout her whole adult life like a toxic gas, noxious and undetectable? Now she can't seem to make any of it go away. *Stay absolutely still, sweetheart. The moon is in the perfect spot.*

"Clara?"

Laurel's voice seems to be coming from a far-off place.

"Clara, did you hear me?"

"What?" Clara shakes her head. "I'm sorry, I was just—"

"I was supposed to drive Sammy home," Laurel says. "Did you come straight from the airport?"

"Yes, actually." Clara feels a rush of gratitude. "I had planned to call Jonathan, but it would be incredibly helpful if you could give us a lift home."

"No problem."

The girls are starting to move toward the bleachers. Shivering, smooth arms covered with goose bumps. Any minute now, Sammy will see her. Any minute now, Sam will look over to the bleachers and—

Emily notices Clara first and points. Even from twenty yards away, Clara can see Emily saying, *Look, there's your mother.* Sammy's head jerks up. Her eyes quickly race over the dozen women standing there, towels in hand, until she lights on Clara. She stops absolutely still for a second—frozen in surprise—then defies the number one rule at the pool and sprints the rest of the way on the wet tile floor.

"Mommy!"

Sammy runs straight into her, dripping wet bathing suit and all. She wraps her arms around Clara's waist and holds tight. Some of Sam's friends have already stopped hugging their mothers in public. They're too cool for school, these girls. Clara sees them sometimes at drop-off, shrugging off any gesture of affection, any acknowledgment of parenthood. They pretend they hardly know their mothers.

And the mothers, smiling their brave, wavering smiles—*not me,* Clara thinks. *Not yet. Not today.*

"I didn't know you were coming!"

"I wanted to surprise you."

Clara's voice catches in her throat. Sammy's face opens up to her like a flower. How could she have left this precious girl for more than two weeks? What could possibly have justified it? *Tell me everything, darling. Tell me about your life in—where is it again? Northern Maine? How do you stand living in such a place? Is there culture there?* Clara pushes Ruth away, mentally shoves her so hard that she goes careening off the planet. Limbs flailing. Mouth cartoonishly open into a scream. *Fuck you, fuck you, fuck you.*

"Hi, Clara," says Emily, sidling up next to Sam. Is it Clara's imagination, or is Emily looking at her funny? The girl is staring at her; she's sure of it.

"What's the matter, Emily?" asks Clara, a bit too sharply. She gives a quick, sidelong glance at Sam.

"Mom, let's go," says Sam, her voice thin and reedy. Anxious to get out of here. To avoid being caught in her big lie—and how big is it, anyway? How elaborate? Did she give Clara a particular disease? A number of months to live? Clara feels a wild surge of protectiveness toward Sam. If the other kids at school find out that Sammy has lied, she'll have a hard time getting past it.

Sam pulls a huge navy-and-white Yale sweatshirt—one of Jonathan's—over her head, then shimmies out of her Speedo, crouching down to remove the waterlogged bathing suit from around her ankles. She yanks up her jeans and stuffs her bare feet into her fleece-lined snow boots. Then she stands there expectantly, holding her knapsack.

"Laurel and Emily are giving us a ride home, sweetheart."

Sam's face falls. Clara sees the anxiety marching across it. Clara's not used to seeing Sammy this way, tense and self-protective.

Amid the goodbyes and see-you-tomorrows, the social dance of nine-year-old girls who spend almost every waking hour together, Sam and Clara follow Emily and Laurel out of the building and through the parking lot to Laurel's truck. The girls have recently graduated from their booster seats—Sammy weighing in at just over sixty pounds—and they climb into the backseat, strapping themselves in with their seat belts.

Laurel throws the truck into reverse and pulls out of the parking lot of the Bar Harbor Y with the ease of someone who does it nearly every day.

"Thanks for the ride," Clara says. She looks out the window. In the two and a half weeks since she's been gone, the thin crust of snow and ice that covered the island—coating the lawns, the docks, the edges of the streets—has all seeped away, leaving in its wake a dirty, grungy brown. The icicles that hung from every windowsill and gutter have melted, taking with them chips of paint, shingles from rooftops. The town looks like a sad old lady with sagging skin and missing teeth. It's mud season, the time of year when the year-rounders go a little crazy.

"It's not out of our way at all," says Laurel.

This isn't strictly true—Laurel and her family live ten minutes inland from Clara's house—but Clara lets it go. This neighborliness is a fact of life on the island, an unwritten code. It has taken Clara forever to get used to it, but in recent years—especially as Sam has gotten older—she's grown to appreciate it. Carpooling and sleepovers, the ease with which people help each other out, the casseroles delivered to doorsteps when there's an illness, a death, a new baby.

"So what have I missed?" Clara asks Laurel as they turn onto Eagle Lake Road, past the multicolored Christmas lights still strung along the roof and windows of the Perettis' house.

"Oh, not a whole hell of a lot," Laurel says.

"Mommy?" Emily pipes up from the backseat.

"Yes, sweetie?"

"Can Sam sleep over this weekend?"

"Oh, I don't know, Em. Sammy's mother has been away for a long time—she probably wants her all to herself."

Laurel keeps her eyes on the road. Slows to a rolling stop at the intersection of Sound Drive and Route 102, concentrating—Clara thinks this—probably more than she needs to. Carefully avoiding eye contact. Avoiding any possibility of intensity or discomfort.

"Hey, Sammy," Clara says. Knowing better. "Tell me what's been going on at school."

"Nothing."

This is always the hard part. Getting the dribs and drabs, the pieces of the puzzle of a nine-year-old girl's life. Sometimes Sam volunteers a lot. Other times, she talks in monosyllables. The thing is, Clara isn't sure how far to push.

"Oh, come on. Something must be going on!"

She sounds like an annoying mother, and she knows it.

"I *told* you." Sam's voice raises, and Laurel's expression shifts almost imperceptibly, a ripple across her brow. *"Nothing."*

"Fine," Clara says softly. Sammy never speaks to her like this. Especially not in front of other people. "Never mind."

They fall into silence, the mothers and daughters. After a few minutes, Laurel bends forward and fiddles with the radio dial. The local weather report crackles through the truck's old speakers. *Well, folks, looks like we have some snow headed our way. Boston already has . . .* The broadcast fades into static, so Laurel switches it off.

"Really?" Clara asks. "How much are they guessing?"

"Not much," says Laurel. "A couple of inches overnight."

Clara thinks about Jonathan; he's probably spent the day in his workroom. Whole days, as he solders twenty-four-carat gold around semiprecious stones, as he cuts slices of watermelon tourmalines and dangles them from the most delicate wires strung with seed pearls. His eyes covered with goggles. His head filled with his favorite lo-tech music from his iPod. At the end of such a day, he emerges as if from a long involved dream. Blinking his way back into reality—sweet, spent, emptied out.

As for reality, Clara is just trying to hold on. Reality feels a bit out of her grasp at the moment—her daughter is unfamiliar to her, whispering and giggling in the backseat. Suddenly the sharer and keeper of secrets. She lowers her sun visor and tries to get a glimpse of Sam in the mirror. Is it possible that Sam's face has changed in the past few weeks? She appears less girlish. The bones of her face are more prominent, angular.

And Jonathan—Clara knows she should have told Jonathan she was coming home. She should have said it on the phone last night—it was stupid, really—but he's been so angry at her. His voice had nothing left for her—no sympathy, none of his usual gentleness. She thought it would be better if she simply showed up. Back home for good.

"So, I noticed that Jonathan redid his windows," Laurel changes the subject.

"Yeah? Are they good?"

"His windows are always gorgeous. It's like an underwater reef—and all the jewelry is coral."

"There are pearls too," Sammy pipes up from the backseat.

Clara swivels around. "Did you help Daddy with the windows?"

"Yeah," Sam says. "It's pretty cool. We tried to make it look like a shipwreck."

Even though Jonathan's business caters almost entirely to the summer crowd, he takes great care with his windows this time of year. It's his little contribution, his attempt to inject some beauty into the dismal gray stretch of mud season. For the regular folk on the island, his stuff is too expensive even for special occasions. Jonathan has tried to produce some less pricey lines: silver and copper pieces imported from Bali. But those haven't sold well. Year-rounders don't tend to have extra money for luxuries, and if they do they buy a new tricycle for their kid or upgrade their snowblower. Fancy jewelry—

well, that's for the people who drive across the causeway on the Friday of Memorial Day weekend, their Range Rovers packed with tennis rackets and golf clubs, titanium bicycles hanging from a rack, wheels lazily spinning in the breeze.

"Here we are." Laurel slows to a stop in front of their house. Clara hears the click of Sammy unbuckling her seat belt, the rustling of papers as she gathers her books. And Clara—Clara sits still for a minute, gripping the handle. She takes a deep breath. She is surprised by the beauty, the solidity of her own house standing tall and proud in the blue-gray dusk. The wide front porch—painted with a fresh coat of white last summer—its wicker furniture pushed to the side and protected by heavy green tarps. The boxwoods on either side of the steps to the porch, wrapped in burlap for the winter months. The yellow light pouring from the tall windows of the living room. *Home.* The caw of seagulls as she opens the truck's door. *Home.* The brackish smell of the harbor. *Home.* Her heart seems to beat the word over and over again.

"See you tomorrow," calls Laurel, as she pulls away from the curb. "Thanks again!"

Clara stands with her arm around Sammy, waving goodbye.

"They're such good people," Clara says. She's buoyed for a moment, by a sense that all is well. She's back where she belongs.

But then Sammy shrugs. "I guess. Whatever."

"Samantha, what has gotten—" Clara starts, then stops. *What has gotten into you?* She can't ask the question. And the brief wave of optimism rolls away from her, back to sea.

Through the glass panels by the front door, Clara sees a shadow moving. Of course, Jonathan is home waiting for Sammy to be dropped off. It's after five. He's expecting Sammy, but not—

The door opens and Jonathan fills the frame. The bulb in the porch light has blown; he squints down the front walk, his eyes growing accustomed to the twilight. Tall and rangy—Clara has always loved his largeness—in his jeans and T-shirt. Longish gray waves tucked behind his ears. The glint of his wire-rimmed eyeglasses. Jonathan. *Home, home, home.*

"Hey, Dad!"

Sammy takes off, bounding up the steps to him.

"Hey, lovey. How was your day?"

Clara's still standing there. She feels the oddest sensation. As if she herself is invisible. As if Jonathan is looking straight through her body at the McCulloughs' house across the street. Maybe she's lost her mind. Maybe she's gone completely insane—she always wondered if she might—and really she's still back in New York. Sitting by Ruth's bedside. The soft white sheets, the amber plastic bottles, the vague and constant stench of urine—

"Well, well, well."

Jonathan's voice. Directed at her. His eyes—exhausted from painstaking attention to his work—finally focusing on her. Taking her in.

"I'm here," she says.

"I see that," he says.

Sammy is looking back and forth between them, her antennae set to the highest frequency. How much of the tension between her parents has she picked up on?

It takes Jonathan four long strides to reach Clara. He wraps his arms all the way around her, pulling her close to him. Enveloping her. She is small in his arms—fitting neatly into his chest, her head tucked beneath his chin—*like two pieces to a puzzle.* Hasn't she always marveled at that? The way she seems to just click into his body as if she had been made for him? But now—now the puzzle is more complicated, the pieces harder to sort out.

"This doesn't mean everything's okay," Jonathan whispers. "It just means I love you."

Tears spill down Clara's cheeks, and she wipes them on Jonathan's T-shirt. She doesn't want Sammy to see her cry.

"Where are your bags?" Jonathan asks.

"I don't have any."

"What do you mean?"

"I didn't bring anything with me," Clara says.

"Oh," says Jonathan. "So that when you go back—"

She pulls away from him. Looks into his green eyes—she has always felt able to see all the way into him—and speaks slowly. Wanting to say it only once. Wanting the words to sink in.

"I'm not going back," she says.

---

NEW HAVEN. Clara was eighteen years old and constantly afraid. Fear wasn't new to her, but this was different. She felt jostled and bumped, as if passersby couldn't *see* her. She felt as though she might have melted, or somehow crumbled into nothing. The Gothic steeples and spires of the Yale campus rose gray and menacing all around her, piercing the soft blue membrane of the sky. The students walked in packs, oblivious of the girl wandering around by herself. They hugged their books to their chests, deep in conversation. Clara watched them—with envy, with greed, with something like remorse. She could have been one of them, next year—if she had stayed home, if she had finished school. If she had put her college applications in the mail instead of ripping them into shreds and feeding them to the incinerator.

She was jumpy, anxious—her whole body tensed like a sprinter's at the starting gate—waiting for the sound of a gunshot, ready to take off. Every time someone caught her eye, she was sure Ruth had sent them to spy on her. Of course, no one was looking at her. No one at all. With her hair spiky and jet-black, fifteen extra pounds on her delicate frame, and a silver stud in her nostril, even the most dedicated art student would have had a hard time recognizing Clara as the little girl in the photographs of Ruth Dunne.

But it wasn't just that. Surely, Ruth would have called the police.
*My daughter Clara is in grave danger, I'm certain of it.*
*How old is she, ma'am?*
*Well—she's eighteen.*
*Sorry, ma'am, but there's nothing we can do about it.*

Every professor, every man in a suit, looked like a detective. Clara kept reminding herself that she wasn't a kid running away from home. She was an adult. She had a right to do whatever she wanted. And what she wanted was to disappear. Didn't she? After a lifetime of being stared at—the second glances, the frank appraisals—she was finally invisible. She hardly knew what to do with herself.

She is living on Tamara Stein's floor. Tamara had been a year ahead of Clara at Brearley, and honestly they hardly knew each other. Clara chose her precisely because Ruth wouldn't even know her name. Tamara—the math geek—would not be on the long list of people whom Ruth would certainly call, frantic, searching. Tamara's parents were professors of religious studies at the Jewish Theological Seminary.

On her third night, Clara is lying on her makeshift bed of blankets when Tamara rolls over and switches on the light.

"So why did you do it?" she asks abruptly. She isn't one for social graces. Too smart to waste time on small talk.

"Do what?" Clara has been hoping that Tamara would just leave her alone.

"Run away."

"I didn't run away. I'm eighteen."

"But you quit school."

"Yeah," Clara says.

Tamara waits. Expecting more.

"Yeah, well, I just couldn't handle being at home anymore."

Tamara sits up in bed. Her hair is a halo of curls. Everything about her is round: her face, her belly, even the calves poking out from beneath her nightgown.

"Because of your mother's pictures?" she asks, her voice gentle.

Clara's throat constricts. Tamara Stein's expression—the grave empathy—is almost more than Clara can bear. She pushes herself up on both elbows, grinding her bones into the hard floor, willing herself not to cry. So Tamara—even Tamara—knew about the pictures.

"I thought maybe you didn't—"

"Oh," said Tamara, "everyone talked about it."

Clara's friends at Brearley always used to tell her how lucky she was. *You're famous,* the other girls would say to her—that is, the ones who didn't jealously turn their backs. Certainly, Brearley had its share of big-deal girls—Caroline Kennedy had been a student years earlier, and each class had a smattering of the children of well-known artists and actors. It wasn't unusual for a Brearley girl to perform in the Christmas production of *The Nutcracker* at Lincoln Center or fly off for the weekend on her family's private jet. But somehow, Clara—or the image of Clara—captured the imagination of her classmates. *You're in your mother's photographs; that's so cool. Did you know my uncle bought one at Christie's last week?*

"It was horrible," Clara whispers—to Tamara Stein, of all people. "I wanted to die."

"I'm sure you did," Tamara says.

"What?"

"Want to die. I mean, it's sort of like your mother was"—Tamara struggles to get the words out—"abusing you."

Even though Clara is on the floor, she feels like she's tumbling through the air in free fall. Some part of her wants to defend Ruth. Some other part of her wants to hug Tamara Stein.

"I used to wonder if you had any choice," says Tamara. "I mean— did your mother pay you? Did she make you do it?"

"I don't want to talk about it," Clara says. "Please."

She lowers her head back down to the floor and hopes Tamara will stop. She focuses on a poster, thumbtacked to the wall above Tamara's desk: Albert Einstein, his white shock of hair, his gentle smile.

"Of course," Tamara says. "Sorry."

She leans over to her bedside table and switches off the light. The creak of bedsprings as she settles herself. *Her fat little body,* Clara thinks. And then—*she was only trying to understand.* Down at the other end of the dorm, somebody's having a party. The clink of beer bottles. The steady thump of music.

Tamara's voice floats in the darkness. "Don't take this the wrong way, Clara—but I always felt sorry for you."

And so Clara wandered the campus of Yale University, surrounded by *real people,* as she thought of them, living *real lives.* She herself had forfeited that right—or perhaps she'd never had it at all. Perhaps it simply wasn't possible for her to find some sort of normal terrain. Was there a place in the world for someone like her? A special place—a lost land of child muses? These were the kinds of thoughts that buzzed through Clara's head as she blended into the fabric of New Haven life.

Days turned into weeks turned into months. She looked very much like a college student. She borrowed Tamara's library card—the librarian didn't so much as glance at the photo—and spent hours in the stacks, comfortable there, picking through this and that. Kant, Nietzsche: shelves full of answerless questions. She abandoned philosophy in favor of psychology—in particular, child psychology. Here was D. W. Winnicott on the subject of the good-enough mother. Had Ruth been a good-enough mother? Clara saw Ruth's face, superimposed, a transparency, everywhere she looked. The pale skin, the angry curve of her lips, her accusing eyes. *How could you do this to me? How could you?*

Last week—worn down by loneliness—she found herself feeding coins into a pay phone. Calling home. She hardly knew what she was doing as her fingers dialed the numbers she had known all her life.

*Studio,* an intern's voice said, young and fairly bursting with self-importance. *Studio.* A bit more forceful this time. *Hello—who is this?*

And Clara—Clara gently replaced the pay-phone receiver back on its hook. She stood still for a moment, trying to regulate her breath. Ruth was okay. Ruth would survive. Ruth had found another eighteen-year-old to take Clara's place.

She is sitting at a long library table, looking through an atlas of North America, when she hears a voice behind her. So startling—to hear a voice at all.

"Plotting your escape?"

A man's voice, not a boy's.

She jumps in her seat, turning in the direction of the voice.

"I'm sorry. I didn't mean to disturb you."

Wavy gray hair—longer than he'd wear it in coming years. Clear green eyes, not yet behind glasses. And a young face—later she will realize it is kindness she sees—smiling down at her. A shark's tooth hangs on a leather strand around his neck. He doesn't look like a student, but he doesn't exactly look like a professor either.

"Jonathan Brodeur." He extends his hand.

"Clara Dunne," she says, without thinking—then instantly regrets it. What if he—but he doesn't. No blink of recognition. No sense of a reaction at all.

"Nice to meet you, Clara Dunne."

She waits—suddenly, strangely calm—to see what he'll say or do next. Why has he come up to her? He doesn't seem to want anything. He's just standing there, his arms loosely folded. Taking her in.

"May I sit down?" He gestures to the empty chair next to her.

*It's a free world. Whatever.*

Tough-girl phrases bubble up inside of her, but she stops them. Holds them in her mouth like something to be spit out.

"Sure," she says. She slides the atlas farther down the table. She had been looking at the western states—Montana, Idaho—but he doesn't need to know that.

"So, seriously," Jonathan says, "why are you looking at the map?"

Clara shakes her head. Slightly worried now. Is there any possibility that this guy has been sent by Ruth? He doesn't look like a private investigator—in Clara's mind, private investigators wear poorly cut suits and have potbellies—but you never know.

"I've been watching you," he goes on. "You've been sitting at this table every day staring at that thing."

"So?"

"So, nothing." He stops. "Sometimes my curiosity gets the better of me. Sorry."

"No problem," Clara says. But she doesn't entirely mean it. Maybe she should get out of here. She pushes her chair back, the wooden legs scraping loudly against the floor—ready to flee, to race down the aisles of this cavernous room and out the glass doors of the library into the bright sunlight.

"Wait," he says. "I didn't mean to ask so many questions."

"Okay."

Clara pulls at a hangnail on the side of her thumb.

"Do you want to get a cup of coffee?"

She looks at him. "That's another question," she says.

Jonathan laughs. And when she hears his laugh—the way it seems to bubble all the way up from somewhere deep in his belly—she feels herself relax.

"I'm here on a fellowship in the geology department," offers Jonathan.

Ah. That makes sense.

"And you?"

"And me, what?"

"You're a student?"

She doesn't answer. Stuck. She can't tell him the truth—but something stops her from being able to lie. The library is so quiet that she can hear the ticking of the clock above the reference desk. Again, the panic rises inside of her.

"Did my mother send you?" The words fly from her lips.

"What?" He looks genuinely taken aback. "Your *mother*?"

She feels herself turn bright red.

"Sorry. Never mind."

"Your *mother*?" Jonathan repeats. "Who the hell is your mother, and why would she— I mean, what are you saying?"

"Never mind!"

Clara wants to flee, but something keeps her rooted to the spot. Maybe it's her loneliness. Maybe she's been so isolated these past months she doesn't mind talking to a perfect stranger. Who is he, anyway? She doesn't know him. What does he mean, he's been watching her? She's never seen him before.

"Come for coffee. Or lunch, even. I don't bite."

His eyes are the green of a pond. They remind Clara of daybreak in Hillsdale, the way she and Robin would crouch at the water's edge, looking for tadpoles.

"No—I can't."

But still, neither of them moves.

"You're not a student here, are you," Jonathan says. More a statement than a question. How does he know? What has given her away?

"No," Clara says. Her voice is almost inaudible. "I'm not." A few small words, and relief washes over her. Finally, to say it—to someone other than Tamara Stein. She's tired. Exhausted from the sheer effort of day-to-day survival. She has been existing on falafel and burnt coffee—university food—and sleeping only a few hours a night on Tamara's floor.

Jonathan extends a hand to Clara. And—much to her surprise—

she takes it. She watches herself as if from a great distance, as if she were not even herself but, rather, a character in a play. *Here she walks out of the library with a strange man. Here she sits at a café table and allows him to buy her lunch. Here she knows—from this very first moment, she knows—that something has shifted. She is eighteen years old and her life is beginning again.*

———◆◆◆———

DINNERTIME at the Brodeurs. Spread before them are unfamiliar casseroles and Tupperware containers—food that has been left on their doorstep by friends and neighbors who assume that Jonathan couldn't possibly manage dinner. Here, Sylvia Grausman's famous beef stew in a cast-iron Crock-Pot. There, glazed carrots and parsnips from the Habers in disposable plastic. Single-sized servings of mac-and-cheese wrapped in foil.

"Well, you haven't been starving, I see," Clara says. Her vision of frozen pizzas and microwaved popcorn had clearly been off the mark.

"I've had to turn them away," says Jonathan, chewing. "The only thing I could figure is, they're angling for a discount at the shop."

"Daddy!" Sammy exclaims.

"Jonathan!" Such a cynical thing for him to say. And so unlike him. He never thinks anyone has an ulterior motive, unless proven otherwise.

"Well, Tess Martin did manage to work the topaz necklace with the tourmaline clasp into our conversation."

"She didn't!"

"She did."

"No way."

"Way."

It almost feels like a normal evening. The easy banter. Sammy's bare feet warming themselves under Clara's thighs, wedged in there like she's done since she was two years old. Zorba under the table—naughty dog—his tail wagging madly, foraging for scraps. Jonathan, his chair tipped back on its hind legs, arms folded behind his head. Clara can almost hear him thinking: *my girls.* He wants nothing more than what is right in front of him. No striving, no yearning for paths not taken. This is everything—his lovely complicated wife, his precocious sweet daughter, his shop—the Tess Martins of the world notwithstanding.

Maybe, just maybe, this world Clara has built will close up around the gaping hole of her absence, smoothing it over. A wound becomes a scab becomes a scar becomes—nearly invisible. Clara holds on to the wish tightly, like a child. Maybe these crazy weeks can fade away. No real damage done. And Ruth—Ruth is in New York, almost four hundred miles from here, probably deep into her late-afternoon nap. The brown eyes drifting beneath closed lids. The clawlike hands resting on top of the soft white sheets.

Sammy pushes her plate back.

"May I be excused?"

An unusual request from Sammy. She never leaves the table before they do; she wants to be with her parents all the time. Besides, she's barely touched her dinner. Macaroni and cheese—her favorite—and she hasn't taken a single bite.

"Aren't you hungry, Sam?"

"No."

"Come on, honey, stay with us. I haven't seen you in so long—"

But that thing comes over Sam's face again, the slight hardening that Clara saw at the pool. Self-protective. An angry edge.

Clara tries to catch Jonathan's eye, but he's focused on his beef stew. She feels like she's been gone months, not weeks.

"Is there anything you want to talk about, Sammy?" Clara asks.

A scary question, but she has to ask it.

Sam just glares at her. Under the bright yellow lights, her cheeks look sallow, hollowed out. She's lost weight, Clara realizes with a start. Sam was always thin but now, even in the bulky Yale sweatshirt, she's pale and bony. Dark circles under her eyes—no nine-year-old should have dark circles. Has she been sleeping? Eating? How did Clara not see this at the pool? Of course—she was looking for other things. She was looking for the happiness and surprise on her little girl's face, herself reflected there as a good mother.

"Do you want to talk?" Clara repeats. Soft, insistent. Trying to quiet the hammering anxiety that has started up inside of her.

"No," Sam says, her mouth tight.

"Okay," Clara says. She doesn't want to push things—not right now. "You may be excused."

Sammy takes off like a shot. Her footsteps pound up the creaky old stairs to the second floor. She races down the hall to her bedroom; her door slams. One of the things Clara has always loved about this ancient, drafty house is that she always knows where everyone is. But right now—right now there is no comfort to be found in the thought of Sammy throwing herself on her bed. Covering her head with a pillow, the way she does when she gets upset.

"What's going on?" Clara asks. "What the hell?"

Jonathan is sitting there, just watching her. He is infuriatingly calm.

"Say something!"

But he doesn't.

"Jesus," Clara says. She gets up from the table and looks for an open bottle of wine in the kitchen. There aren't any, so she pulls a bottle from the wine rack without even looking at it. The corkscrew is halfway in before she realizes it's a good bottle, an expensive Oregon Pinot Noir. A gift from one of Jonathan's summer people. *Oh, who the fuck cares.*

"I told you," Jonathan says, very quietly.

She whirls around, corkscrew in hand, and looks at him.

"You told me what?"

"That things were getting bad around here."

"But you didn't say—" She falters. He didn't say what? That Sam was becoming unreachable? That she had stopped eating? What good would the specifics have done, except to make Clara feel even more torn than she already was? Jonathan had been trying—impossible as it was—to protect her. And it had cost him dearly. She could see the price all over his exhausted face.

"Look." She sits back down at the table and hands him a glass of wine. "I'm done there, Jon. In New York."

She can't bring herself to say Ruth's name out loud.

"What happened?"

"I don't want to talk about it."

"Did your mother—"

She shakes her head. "Please. Not now."

His hand comes down hard on the table, rattling the dishes and glasses, scaring her.

"You can't do that!" he shouts.

"Ssshh. We don't want Sammy to—"

"No, Clara, you can't cut things off, just because—"

"You don't know anything about it!"

She's yelling now too. Forgetting, for a moment, about Sam upstairs.

"That's because you won't let me in!" Jonathan says. "It's like a fucking fortress in there." He waves at her whole body, his hands flailing, dismissive.

She goes cold, her blood pooling away from her extremities. She knows what he's saying. She knows, even if he doesn't.

"That's a low blow, Jonathan." Her voice steely. She can find the strength inside herself—she knows she can. She always has.

"That's not what I—" Jonathan reaches for her hand but she pulls away. This has gone on forever—since the beginning, or certainly since Sam's birth. Jonathan thinks she's closed off. Shut down. *You won't let me in.* His hand on her body, tracing her limbs, fingers gently prying, exploring, searching for the hidden places. And she—

there's only so far that she can let him go before she stops him. Grabs his hand and holds it tight. *No, honey. I just can't—not tonight.* He can't know how scary it is, how many locked doors there are inside of her. They don't really talk about it—although every few years he broaches the subject—because where is there to go with it, really? Jonathan—no one would believe this, but it's true—Jonathan is the only man she's ever been with.

"Let's talk about Sam," she says.

Jonathan nods slowly. Here they are again, pushing it all away.

"She's awfully thin," she says.

"Yes."

"And Laurel Connolly told me that she lied—at school. She told her girlfriends that I'm sick—"

"What?"

"—and that's the reason why—"

"Christ."

"She must be really angry at me," Clara says, "to come up with such a thing."

"I don't think that's it," Jonathan says. He empties his glass of wine, then pours another. "I think she had to make something up because she was terrified. She doesn't understand, Clara. Her mother just up and left home for more than two weeks with no explanation."

"Okay," Clara says. Above their heads, she can hear Sammy moving around her room. Sweet, beautiful, wonderful Sammy. "I'll talk to her."

"When?" Jonathan isn't going to let her off the hook.

"Soon," Clara says. A dive into thin air. "I promise."

# Chapter Six

IT WAS JONATHAN who had come up with the idea of Mount
Desert Island. Jonathan who studied the map with her, their fingers
tracing routes from New Haven to—well, they didn't know exactly
where to. They were giddy, in love, stunned to have found each other.
Reveling in their freedom to go absolutely anywhere. Arizona? New
Mexico? Too vast and dusty. California? Expensive—and besides,
they shared a disdain for chronically good weather. Europe? Clara
spoke good Brearley French, and Jonathan spoke passable Italian.
But how would he start his business in a foreign country? They considered the possibilities—over long afternoons at the Middle Eastern
café they tried on their future lives for size—but nothing felt quite
right.

"I've been thinking," Jonathan began. Clara was naked, lying on
top of Jonathan's old quilt, the midday sunlight pouring in through
the skylight of his room in graduate student housing. "My aunt has a
house in Southwest Harbor. She's old now and she never uses it.
Maybe she'd let us rent it for a while."

"Southwest Harbor? Where's that?"

She had never even heard of it.

"Maine," Jonathan said.

"You're distracting me." Clara felt his hands traveling over her. Exploring her body for its lakes and valleys, ridges and disparate climates, as if she herself were a map. She closed her eyes, tried to allow the good feelings in. Tried to allow her nakedness to be the most natural thing in the world. The warmth of the sun, lighting her—the gentle hands moving her this way and that—

"Relax," Jonathan whispered. Parting her legs. His tongue moving in a straight line down from her belly button. Clara willed her muscles to let go, her limbs to soften. This was Jonathan—Jonathan!—and she trusted him. He was not like those boys from Trinity or Collegiate, boys who wanted to fuck her because they'd seen her naked. They had seen her go from little girl to adolescent before their very eyes.

"I can't." She squirmed and rolled away from him. *I can't.* The first of so many times Jonathan would be the recipient of that tiny, nearly invisible wound.

He climbed back up to her, his lower face wet. She resisted the urge to wipe him with the sheet. To remove all traces of herself from him.

"So," he went on, as if nothing had just happened, "let's talk about Maine."

"Isn't it full of—I don't know—lumberjacks?" she asked. "Who would buy your jewelry?"

"Well, Southwest Harbor is sort of unique," Jonathan answered. "It's on an island. There's a wealthy summer community, and—"

He went on, but Clara had stopped listening. *Island.* He had said the magic word. *Island.* A place disconnected from the mainland. A place floating on its own, separate, apart.

"Yes," she said, interrupting him.

He raised his eyebrows.

"Yes?"

"Let's do it," she said. She, who had vetoed every idea from Rome to Albuquerque. "Let's move to Mount Desert Island." Even the name itself was perfect: round and American and comforting—but also somehow strange and new.

The house—the first time she saw it—was like a figment from a dream she had forgotten but now remembered with all the power of a déjà vu. White, crumbling, Victorian—like an abandoned, melting wedding cake perched a block from the harbor—it possessed a lop-sided charm, as if the house understood its own improbability. *Don't take me seriously!* it seemed to shout from its high perch. When had Clara dreamt of it? And in what kind of dream? She had no reference point for a place like this. It was nothing like the old farmhouses in Hillsdale, which were simple clapboard affairs.

"Well, here we are." Jonathan's voice is tense, excited. He's nervous, Clara realizes. He wants her to like this place.

She slowly makes her way up the steep, painted front stairs, holding on to the rickety banister. Is she seven months pregnant? Eight? The preparations to come here have taken longer than either of them had thought. Jonathan had to finish his fellowship, and Clara got a job making cappuccinos and lattes for the New Haven crowd: Yale students, professors, actors and stagehands who worked at Yale Rep, the crew from the public radio station. At first, Clara could hardly tell them apart, but by the time she left her job she was able to match the drink to the face: The girl with the Mohawk always got the hot chai. The older man in the blue sweater—a famous historian, she had been told—got the double espresso. And the skinny lady who carried a brown paper shopping bag at all times, she got the half-caff cappuccino.

Jonathan pulls the house keys from an envelope addressed in a spidery old-woman's hand. He fumbles for a moment, dropping the keys—they fall to the weathered porch in a clatter—and then finally fits one into the lock and pushes the door open.

"Hold on. I should carry you over the threshold."

"Don't even think about it," Clara says. Thirty pounds heavier than she usually is.

She makes her way slowly through the front foyer. No one's been in the house in many months. The shades are drawn; she can just begin to make out the shapes of furniture in the dim light. A sofa. Two club chairs. The dull gleam of silver frames lining the fireplace mantel.

"I haven't been here since I was a kid," Jonathan says. "I spent every summer—"

"What's that smell?" Clara asks.

Jonathan sniffs the air.

"Something dead," he says. "Mouse, probably."

She nods. Keeps walking into the kitchen, which is cheery in that old-fashioned way of kitchens that have never been updated. Yellow-and-green tile floor. Old enamel double oven. A pot rack hanging in a corner, copper pots dangling over abandoned plants. She imagines the kitchen with a paint job. New leafy plants to replace the old ones. A bright tablecloth covering the speckled linoleum table.

Behind her, she hears Jonathan opening the curtains. Cracking windows. Letting the ocean air inside.

"I guess the caretaker hasn't been doing his job," Jonathan says.

They don't stop moving, passing through the warren of small ornate rooms: library, a double parlor where a grand piano is coated with a thick film of dust.

"So, what do you think?" Jonathan asks.

*It's scary,* she wants to say. *It's so far away from anything I understand.* But she doesn't want to hurt him. And honestly she has no idea what she really thinks.

"Let's go upstairs."

She runs her hand along the carved banister—mahogany? a dark-stained cherry?—as she makes her way slowly up the stairs. Patterns of colored shapes dance on the wooden steps like jewels. She looks up—three floors up the winding staircase—at the stained-glass window set into the roof. Ruby red, emerald green, a deep sapphire blue, citrine yellow: a jeweler's house.

"I want you to be happy here," Jonathan says. His arms wrap around her as they reach the second floor. "It may take some time— it isn't what you're used to."

She leans against his chest. She can't tell him what she's thinking— even if she had the words, she doesn't have the heart to tell him that happiness is more than she expects. Contentment, perhaps. A semblance of peace. Fleeting moments of joy such as this one. What she longs for: the absence of pain.

"I will be happy here—I know it."

A white lie, one of thousands of white lies she has already woven so thickly around herself that she sees the world this way: shining, blinding, blanched.

*I don't miss New York.*

*I never think about my mother.*

*All that is behind me now.*

Does she think she's fooling Jonathan? Does she think she's fooling herself? This much she knows is true: She loves her husband. She trusts him as much as she can trust anyone. Look at him! His eyes gazing down at her, *seeing* her. Taking her in. Has anyone ever done that before? Certainly not Ruth. Ruth's attention was predatory, stalking Clara from the other side of a lens. Even now—even as Clara stands at the threshold of her new life—she is being consumed by her mother. *You're mine!* Laying claim to her. *Mine!* Drowning out all that is good.

Jonathan is saying something—he sounds so far away. She struggles mightily to push back into the present.

"What?" She turns to him. Foggy, lost.

"Come. Let me show you our bedroom."

Jonathan holds her hand, leading her down the hall.

THE MOMS ARE SITTING in a wooden booth at Tapley's, killing time, waiting for the five o'clock jujitsu class to let out. Killing time is something the moms have turned into an art form over the years. Crocheting, needlepointing, the lugging around of quality paperbacks—sneaking in a few quick pages here and there—they have learned that a lot can be accomplished in the hours of waiting. Even the dozens of daily miles they clock in their pickup trucks and Jeeps are not wasted. They have discovered motivational tapes and the educational value of radio. And then—on afternoons like this—there's always a quick coffee with the girls.

If only Clara felt like one of the girls. She has never—not from the very first day of Sammy's preschool—felt like she belonged in this group. Before Sammy started school, Clara existed in her own little universe. Taking care of a toddler, helping Jonathan as he started his jewelry shop. But then school opened up a whole world of play dates—and play dates meant hanging out with the moms on carpeted playroom floors while the kids built towers out of blocks or engaged in imaginative dialogue with their Barbies. *Good sharing, honey!* they'd call encouragingly from the sidelines. *Nice work!*

And Clara—Clara always felt she was posing. Did these mothers come from childhoods that had prepared them for this? They were nice enough—Susanna Haber, Tess Martin, Ali Mulvey, the whole gang. But invariably Clara walked away from them feeling that there was a secret club of motherhood, complete with a password no one had ever given her. Why did this all seem so satisfying to them—the cupcake baking, the constant scheduling, the endless games of Candy Land? And what was wrong with Clara, what psychic disease caused her constant yearning for something more? It wasn't that she didn't adore Sammy. She did—with all her heart.

"So what do you gals think," Mary Ann Rowe is saying, "about this new sailing camp opening up? It's supposed to be—"

"Expensive," says Susanna Haber.

"You said it," says Laurel. "Going after the summer people."

"You bet they are."

"Have you heard anything about it?"

It takes a moment for Clara to realize this question is being directed at her. She's distracted, off floating. Usually this is fine. She has existed for so many years among these women, they have stopped expecting her full participation.

"Sorry?"

"The sailing camp. Has Jonathan heard anything about it—maybe from some of his customers?"

"I don't think so."

She's trying to stay focused. Sammy's going to be here any minute, with the rest of the girls from the orange-belt class. Some of them are going out to dinner after—but Clara has declined. She needs to focus. All her energy has been spent on figuring out the next right step in a series of impossibly wrong ones.

"Hey, guys!"

The girls troop in, made smaller by their stiff white uniforms, bright orange belts wound two or three times around their tiny waists.

Clara steels herself. She has been home three days—three days, and Sammy has pulled even farther away from her. Sad, anxious, withdrawn. And so terribly thin. Clara has chosen not to talk to Sammy about the lies, even now that she knows their full extent. A weak heart! Requiring open-heart surgery! Where had Sammy even come up with such a thing? Clara is treading carefully, afraid of anything that will upset Sam more than she already is. Each day, Clara has left messages for the local child psychiatrist—a woman in Bar Harbor—but apparently there's a waiting list.

"Hi." Sam sidles up to her.

Clara's heart leaps. Pathetic—that she is hungry for a simple hello from her daughter. Sam has grown mute these past days. Fading into a mere shadow of herself.

"Hi, sweetie."

"Mom, can I have dinner with—"

Oh, so that's it.

"No, Sammy, we're actually going to—"

"Please?"

"Not tonight."

"Okay." Sam's eyes fill with tears. She crosses her arms and looks away from Clara.

The other moms are pretending not to listen. They have that half glazed-over, sweetly smiling look of *Thank God that's not me.*

Clara hustles her out. She has a plan—and Jonathan has agreed. They can't just do nothing and wait for the child psychiatrist to call them back.

"Where are we going?" Sam is strapped in next to Clara. Her voice barely rises above a whisper. "Why can't I go out with my friends? That's so mean."

Clara grips the steering wheel so hard that her wedding ring digs into her finger. *It's not her fault, it's mine.* She's had to remind herself of that a hundred times a day. Sam hasn't suddenly started acting like this out of thin air. And just in case Clara forgets, Jonathan is always there to remind her. Even if he doesn't say anything, she can see it all over his face.

"We're meeting your father," Clara says. Maybe this will cheer Sam up for now. It's always a special treat, going to Jonathan's shop.

"At home?"

"In town."

This seems to appease Sammy. They drive in silence, the roads narrowed by piles of dirty snow—remnants of what everyone hopes has been the last storm of the season. Clara steals a quick glance at her daughter. Hunched down in the passenger seat, a dark blue fleece unzipped over her jujitsu uniform, her hair stringy and covering part of her face as she stares out the window. The bones of her clavicle jut out, a reminder of just how skinny she's become.

"Did you eat your lunch today, Sam?" Clara tries to keep her voice light.

"Sure."

"Really? Because—"

"I already said I did." Sam gets teary again.

"Okay," Clara says softly. "Sorry."

The drive—usually twenty minutes that zip by—seems to take forever. The easy chatter is gone. She can hear herself breathe. Sammy shifts in her seat, then starts fiddling with the cover of the ashtray.

"Sam, listen. You've got to understand that"—Clara begins the sentence with no idea where its going to end; what exactly does Sam have to understand?—"sometimes there are things that grown-ups have to do."

Sam shifts farther away from Clara in her seat. She's practically pressed up against the passenger door.

"Don't do that, honey. The door could pop open."

Sam acts as if she doesn't hear her. Her small jaw clenched.

Clara rounds the corner onto Main Street. The streetlights are glowing. There isn't a soul in sight. The center of town looks deserted; most of the converted houses and old wooden buildings are closed up until May.

In summertime, there is often no parking to be found on Main Street. But tonight Clara pulls just in front of Jonathan Brodeur Jewelry; only Jonathan's shop and the Pine Tree Market are still open. The sign needs repainting. The B in Brodeur has faded, and the wood is chipped. Instead of appearing elegantly distressed, the sign just looks old and tired, sadly second-rate.

Clara watches as Sam climbs out of the car and over a snowbank.

The bottoms of her white jujitsu pants are dragging on the muddy, salted snow. All these years, Clara has willed herself into believing that Sam has the best childhood possible: pure, simple, all the things that matter. The New York of Clara's own childhood—the fancy schools, the kids sophisticated beyond their years—who needs it? But the last few weeks in New York have seeped into her blood, poisoning her, forcing her to question everything. She thinks about Robin's kids, politely asking for more risotto at the dinner table. Sammy wouldn't even know what the hell risotto is. Tucker is a violin prodigy. Harrison plays chess in the nationals. And Elliot is at Brearley, where she has already tested in the ninety-ninth percentile of those girls who test in the ninety-ninth percentile just to get into the school to begin with.

*What if?* It's the kind of question she rarely allows herself.

Sam runs to the door of the shop and opens it. The wind chimes tinkle their tinny melody. Jonathan's in back, working. How many times has Clara urged him to lock the front door when there's no salesperson in the shop, when he's way back there in his studio? Granted, there's virtually no crime on the island. The newspaper's police blotter always makes for entertaining reading: *Shaye Rice's bicycle was believed stolen from the playground but later was returned to his house by Jimmy from the pizzeria*—that sort of thing.

Laurel was right. Jonathan's windows are particularly beautiful. Lit up and decorated in an early spring display of optimism: plaster made to resemble an underwater reef—Jonathan and Sam must have spent many hours getting it just right—on which a dozen coral pieces, earrings and necklaces, mostly, are scattered, as if lost in a shipwreck.

"Look, Sammy, he hasn't sold it yet!" Clara calls after Sam. A particular pendant—a delicate gold flower with a freshwater pearl at its center—Sam's favorite of Jonathan's current pieces.

"Oh," says Sammy. Like she doesn't really care anymore.

"Hey!" Jonathan crosses from the studio into the main shop in three large steps, his magnifying goggles pushed up on his forehead. He hugs Sammy hello, then kisses Clara, a stiff perfunctory kiss. He smells of metal and soap, a faint hint of cedar from his heavy wool sweater. His crazy gray hair is pulled into a ponytail. He hasn't shaved in days, and his cheeks are covered with long stubble. His skin— ruddy to begin with—is chapped and red from his daily commute in his old lobster boat from their house in Southwest Harbor to the shop in Northeast. Jonathan has always loved it—the ten-minute daily ride from one point of the claw-shaped island to the other—but in wintertime it's brutal. Most people think he's crazy. The windchill out there on the water would be enough to keep any sane person in a heated car, driving the long way around the perimeter.

He checks his watch. His fingernails are dirty, embedded with silver dust.

"Shall we?" He glances at Clara. As if to ask, *Do you mean it, this time?*

She nods.

"Where are we going?" Sam asks.

"Red Sky."

"I *hate* Red Sky."

Clara and Jonathan exchange a look. It had been Clara's idea. Neutral ground. A place where they could sit and talk for as long as was necessary—and Sam couldn't run off, escape to her room, and slam the door.

"It isn't McDonald's, but I'm sure you'll find something to eat," says Jonathan.

Of course they know everyone in the restaurant. Clara hadn't exactly bargained for that tonight. As they settle into a corner booth, Clara spots Sam's piano teacher, Nancy Tipton, on the other side of the restaurant. Then there's Ginny and Dave she-can-never-remember-their-last-name, the couple who run the lobster shack during the summer months. Red Sky is only about half full, so it's hard to ignore people.

"Hi, Mr. and Mrs. Brodeur." Their waitress is Kelly Benson, a high school senior who babysat for Sam last year. "Hey, Samantha, how're you doing?"

"Good." Sam ducks her head.

"Still swimming?"

"Yeah."

Kelly looks confused by Sam's sudden shyness. This isn't the kid she's used to.

"Can I get you guys something to drink?"

"A bottle of the Barolo," Jonathan says. "And for Sam—"

"Diet Coke," Sam says, with a quick glance at her mother.

And Clara doesn't object. Not tonight. A few chemicals are the least of her concerns. Anyway, what about Robin's pantry in New York? Those three kids eat nothing but sugar—all in the form of organic juice boxes, Fruit Roll-Ups, and chocolate-covered raisins. *Christ.* Why can't she stop thinking about her mother and her sister? They've crept into her consciousness and seem to have taken up permanent residence there. She focuses on Jonathan, stretches her leg under the white linen tablecloth, and touches his foot.

He looks at her, surprised.

*Please,* she silently begs him. *Give me a little help here.*

He returns the pressure.

Kelly Benson deposits a steaming basket of French bread on their table. "Are you ready to order?" she asks.

"We need a minute," says Jonathan, opening his menu.

"Sam," Clara begins.

She has to start somewhere. She has to—before she chickens out again. Sam is playing with the paper from her straw, shredding it into confetti-sized pieces.

"Sam? Your mother's speaking to you," says Jonathan. Watching carefully.

"Yeah?" Sam pushes her hair behind her ears.

"I have something to tell you," Clara says. "About why I was in New York."

Now she has Sam's full attention. Now Sam's eyes are trained on her, and there's no going back. Clara remembers—it floats into her head like one of hundreds of fragments that might, if assembled, make a whole picture—the long steep slope behind the house in Hillsdale. As a kid, she and Robin would climb on their sled, holding each other for dear life as they pushed off. Gathering speed—steering to avoid the tree stumps, the stone wall—the world going by in an unstoppable blur.

"I was visiting—" she begins haltingly.

She turns to Jonathan, who is nodding slightly, almost as if he's praying. But he can't do this for her. They've both always known that.

"I went to New York to see—" Clara reaches for her wineglass, but her hands are shaking too badly.

Just say it. *You have a grandmother.*

"A woman named Ruth Dunne," she finishes. She keeps her eyes on Sam. "She's my mother."

Jonathan presses his foot into hers. He reaches across the table and grabs her shaking hand. Sam's eyes, huge to begin with, seem to fill up her whole face.

"What do you mean?" she asks. Her voice, clear as a bell. Nothing stuck in her throat, no words to choke on.

"My mother," Clara says. She fights back tears with her whole being. She isn't allowed to cry, no way; this isn't about her.

"Your grandmother," she manages to get out.

"I thought she was dead," Sam says. A slow, almost transparent veil lowering over those earnest eyes. She's been lied to. How could her mother have lied to her?

"I'm going to try to explain this to you, Sam," Clara begins. "I hadn't seen my mother for many, many years, not since before you were born."

"What do you mean?" Sam practically wails. The piano teacher glances over to their table from across the restaurant, then looks discreetly back at her dinner companion.

"We didn't speak," Clara says. An unfamiliar feeling is washing over her. As if she's speeding down that hill in the sled, Robin's arms around her, but there's suddenly nothing to fear. No tree stumps, no stone walls. Nothing to fight against. No choice in the matter—not anymore.

"Why?" Now Sam is crying. Jonathan has been right all these years. And Clara—Clara has been woefully, terribly wrong. A secret can never justify itself.

"It's a long story."

Jonathan shoots her a warning look. She can't get away with *It's a long story* any more than she can get away with *Not now,* or *Maybe someday.* She has exhausted the limits of evasion.

"She hurt me, Sammy." Her eyes sting.

"Why did you go see her now?" Sammy swipes at her cheeks with a napkin.

"She's very sick," Clara says softly.

"Is she going to die?" Sam asks. What does she know of death? A frozen bird, roadkill, a deer, bloody and stiff, on the side of the highway.

Clara tries to swallow. Her mouth is cracked and dry.

"Yes," she says. "She's going to die."

———◆◆◆◆———

SOMETIMES, during those early years in Southwest Harbor, Clara felt the story of her life gathering inside her, brewing like a storm. First she would feel it somewhere deep in her stomach, a torrent of words all knotted up; then it would slowly make its way up her throat and finally into her mouth. Bitter, explosive. *What's the big deal?* she would argue with herself, during those rare times she was sitting across the table from another mom, a woman who might be divulging some secrets of her own. *It was all so long ago.* Wouldn't it be a relief just to let the words spill out?

The problem was Sammy. At least that's what Clara told herself. Sammy—her spitting image—whom Clara could protect, at least for now. She shuddered to think of Sammy seeing *The Accident.* Or *Clara with the Lizard.* She wondered if she should go talk to someone—Jonathan had often urged her to get professional help— but what could anyone tell her that would change things?

"Who are you protecting?" Jonathan asks her.

They are sitting on the front porch. Sammy is swinging on the brand-new tire swing Jonathan has tied to the low branch of the oak. Sammy: age four. Her dark hair glinting gold in the sunlight. Her tanned legs pumping, arms holding the thick rope. Was this what Ruth had first seen, this simple beauty—this heartbreaking inno- cence? The long line of her neck, the flawlessness of her skin? Clara knows the feeling—now, as a mother, she knows. The desire to devour, the almost physical need to envelop and keep safe. Was this—was this how Ruth had looked at her in the bathtub that day? The mother and the artist so completely inseparable that Ruth was driven to capture the moment, to control it—to *compose* it—and by doing so, freeze it forever in time?

"I'm protecting Sammy," Clara answers.

"Are you sure?" Jonathan is acting as if he knows something Clara doesn't. It's infuriating.

"What are you getting at?"

"I don't know, honey." He rubs her feet. "I just think—maybe— there's going to come a time when—"

"She's four years old!"

"All the more reason to start introducing the whole idea now, so it won't seem like such a big deal, as opposed to someday having to actually sit her down and—"

She jumps up. Needing, suddenly, to get away from Jonathan. He's talking about things he doesn't understand.

"I think you're protecting yourself," Jonathan says quietly.

Her rage feels childish, even to herself. Jonathan's only trying to help. She knows that. But still—

"Let's go," she says. Changing directions, hoping he'll follow suit. It's a quiet Monday afternoon and there's a lot of work to do in the shop. They catch up on paperwork on Mondays, usually, especially in summer when the shop is jammed with tourists during the rest of the week.

"Clara, really, I—"

"Please."

Something in her face must stop him. He adores her—this much she knows—and he feels for her, as much as anyone can. But how long will it be okay with him, the slammed door inside of her? He doesn't entirely realize that she has no intention of opening it ever.

"Okay." He rises from the wicker sofa. "Let's go."

At the shop, Sammy sits cross-legged on the floor, playing with a small pile of gemstones, trying to string them onto thin strands of leather. Jonathan has been letting Sammy play with the loose stones in his inventory since she was old enough to hold them in her hands. Newspaper is spread out beneath her, covering any of the cracks in the wood floor through which a single tiny garnet or freshwater pearl might fall.

"Here are the invoices from Bali." Jonathan hands Clara a pile of fax paper, curled at the ends. "We need to order more of that yellow gold—you know, the kind I've been using for the bracelets—"

"Fine." Clara makes a note.

"Oh, and Marjorie Waller stopped in on Saturday—she was very interested in the black diamond necklace."

"Really!"

Only a few of Jonathan's pieces were priced in the thousands; he just couldn't afford to make them. But once in a while he fell in love with a stone—a black diamond, this time, glistening like wet coal. The necklace had been in the front case, displayed on a white cloth mannequin, for months.

"We'll see what happens."

"Mommy, look!" Sam holds up the leather strand, strung from one end to the other with pearls.

"Pretty, sweetheart."

"Actually, I also forgot to mention that I got a call from a buyer in New York—from a store called Fragments in SoHo."

Jonathan doesn't look up when he says this. He focuses instead on a repair he's working on, a broken clasp.

"What do you mean? How did they—"

"I sent my slides."

"When?"

"A while back."

Marketing and promoting Jonathan's work has been Clara's job. She's the one who sends out his slides to some of the higher-end craft stores around the country. Portland, Boston, Seattle, Minneapolis.

"Why didn't you tell me?"

Finally, he looks up from the broken clasp.

"I don't know," he says. "I just did it on a whim."

*New York. SoHo.* The words don't belong in this room. This cozy little shop with the worn wood floors, the elegant glass cases, the leather chairs propped in the corners in case husbands want to read the paper while their wives browse. *SoHo.* Kubovy's face floats before her, smiling his leonine smile. *Clara, my beauty. Come, let me look at you.*

She feels a sudden hollowness.

"Well, what did the buyer say?"

"She wants me to come down—to show her my stuff in person."

"I wish you had said something." Her voice is sharp, wounded.

"It didn't seem important."

"I don't want you to go to New York."

"You're being ridiculous."

But then he takes her in. Trembling, as if she's in actual physical danger.

"Okay," he says. "I'm sure she can decide from the slides."

---

THE FORSYTHIA outside the kitchen window has started to bloom. Crocuses are pushing their hardy little heads through the still-cold earth in the front yard. And the air has lost some of its harsh late-winter bite. Spring has come earlier than usual to Southwest Harbor. Some years, it doesn't come at all. The endless winter rages on, fading away only when the summer people arrive, claiming the island as their own.

Sam's school is on spring break. Some of the families of Southwest go to Florida this time of year: Disney World, Fort Lauderdale, Key Biscayne. Others try to get in some late-season skiing. Many of the families travel together, rent houses to save money—but no one ever asks the Brodeurs. It isn't that people don't like Jonathan and Clara, quite the contrary. But they do feel—the moms and dads of Sammy's friends—that the Brodeurs are a bit . . . *remote*. Hard to get a handle on. They don't quite fit in.

Clara's on the phone, trying to arrange a play date for Sammy, when the call-waiting beeps. Without thinking—without, for once, checking the caller ID—she asks Jenny Fuhrman's mother to hold and answers the phone.

"Hi, it's me." Robin's voice on the other end.

Clara leans against the counter, her legs suddenly rubbery. She had been shelling peas. These last couple of weeks she has found she has to constantly be doing something with her hands. Chopping

vegetables. Letting down the hems of Sam's jeans. Even crocheting—
something she swore she would never do.

"Hi," she says faintly.

Robin's on her cell phone, somewhere on the street. Clara can
hear the metallic sigh of a bus stopping at the curb, the sound of taxis
honking, the high-pitched beep of a truck backing up. New York
City traffic. Why is Robin calling? In the silence, Clara feels her body
growing ice cold. Is it possible that Ruth—no. It can't be. It's too
soon. Isn't it? But what's this? Her mind is racing, thoughts impossible to decipher as they zoom by, like one of those crawls at the bottom of the television screen gone completely berserk. *Please don't be
dead.* That's all Clara can make out. *Please don't be—*

"Robin?" Her voice thin with tension.

Still, Robin says nothing. Is this some kind of game? Clara hears a
siren through the phone.

"Rob?"

"I—I can't. Clara, it's just too—"

The words are coming out in gulps. Robin is sobbing, Clara
finally realizes. Sobbing. On the street. In broad daylight.

"What happened?" Clara asks. "Is Ruth—"

"No," Robin manages to say. "No. That's not—hello? Clara?
Clara? Oh, fuck. I've lost you."

Clara slowly replaces the receiver on its hook. *Please don't be dead.*
It was the only clear thought she had. What did it mean? Why did
she care? She hadn't planned on ever seeing Ruth again. She was finished with her mother. The slate of her life once more wiped clean.
There was only this mess with Sammy to deal with. Sammy, who had
been asking a few more questions with each passing day.

*How old is my grandmother?*

*Why is she dying?*

*Has she ever asked about me?*

And then, finally: *Why can't I meet her?*

She stands frozen, waiting for the phone to ring again.

"Mom?" Sam has padded into the kitchen in her bare feet. "Was that Jenny's mom calling?"

*Shit.* Jenny Fuhrman's mom. Clara had completely forgotten about her.

"Sorry, sweetheart, let me just try her now."

Clara picks up the phone, manages to dial with her shaky fingers.

"Hi, it's Clara Brodeur—so sorry about that! Anyway, I was hoping maybe the girls could—"

*Beep.* Call waiting again.

"So do you think—okay, perfect. We'll see Jenny here at three."

*Beep.*

Clara lets it ring in her ear until it stops. Sammy peers into the refrigerator, then pulls out some turkey wrapped in wax paper. Blood rushes to Clara's head—a swift sudden vertigo—and she sits down at the kitchen table. Flips through the ever-present pile of catalogs, trying to calm herself down. She has lived her life, all these years, without her mother in it—but with the knowledge, always the knowledge, that Ruth existed elsewhere. Hundreds of miles south, an airplane flight, a long car ride away. Had she somehow counted on that? On Ruth's sheer existence?

"Mom?"

The spinning room slows to a stop.

"I want to see a picture," Sam says in a small voice.

"I'm sorry, sweetie?"

"A picture," Sam says. "Of Grandma."

She walks over to the kitchen table, then sits down, hugging her knees to her chest. Her hair spills over her face, and she brushes it away.

"I don't—" Clara begins, then stops. *Grandma.* Sam has already decided on a name for Ruth. Not *Nana.* Not *Grammy.* Clara doesn't have the heart to tell Sam that Ruth isn't really the grandma type.

She tries again. "Honey, I don't really have—"

*No more lies.* The remnants of her past—the few things she has been unable to part with—are stuffed into a shoe box in the bottom drawer of her dresser, behind the long underwear and dozens of pairs of winter socks.

"Okay," Clara says. Feeling Sam's eyes on her, intent, darting all around her face. Reading her. "Okay." She walks out of the kitchen and up the flight of stairs, past the framed family photos hanging along the landing. How many times has she looked at these photographs of herself, Jonathan, and Sam—on Hunter's Beach, skating on Echo Lake, at picnics and barbecues—and thought *There they are, that's my whole family,* like an artist painting over an unsuccessful canvas, covering the awkward, pained brushstrokes that came before?

Sam is behind her on the stairs, not letting Clara out of her sight. She follows her mother into the bedroom. Clara opens the dresser, feels through the bottom drawer for the shoe box. It's from a store in New York—Harry's Shoes on Broadway—the same box she took with her fourteen years earlier. She pulls it out and opens the lid, sifting through papers and letters, her birth certificate. Baby pictures of her and Robin. A snapshot of Nathan, a rolled-up diploma in his hand, standing on the steps of Low Library at Columbia. And then finally—the one photograph of Ruth that she kept—a photograph that Clara took herself on a sticky summer morning twenty-five years ago.

*Mommy, I want to take your picture!*

*No, darling. Please—no.*

*Why not? You look so pretty. Please let me?*

They were upstate, in Hillsdale, and had just finished shooting *Clara and the Popsicle,* the sugary purple juice dripping down Clara's bare chest. Flies swirled around her in the summer heat. Laughing, Ruth lowered the tripod so that Clara could see into the lens.

*Okay, sweetheart. Just this once. I'll sit right here on these steps.*

Ruth showed her how to turn the lens to bring everything into crisp focus.

*Be careful!*

Clara looked through the lens at her beautiful young mother, sitting in her frayed jeans and tank top on the splintery steps of their country house. Ruth's hair hung in a long braid over one shoulder and she was completely unadorned, not a ring, not a bobby pin. Just plain Ruth. Clara pressed her finger on the button and heard the shutter click, just as Ruth had done thousands of times. *Click. Click. Click.*

*Okay, that's enough.*

Ruth, laughing. An anxious, trilling sound.

*Just a few more, Mommy?*

*No, Clara.*

*Please?*

*No!*

A sharp, almost frightened note entered her mother's voice.

*That's quite enough.*

"Here's your grandmother." Clara hands Sammy the photograph, which is curled around the edges. The only one of its kind. Probably worth a fortune: the camera turned, for once, on Ruth Dunne. Sam holds it gingerly, as if it might disintegrate, and stares for a good long minute at the image of her grandmother. The lean legs in the faded jeans, the skinny arms, the high cheekbones and huge eyes. Clara's waiting. She knows what Sam is going to say.

"She looks exactly like you, Mommy." Sammy puts the photo back in the box and smiles, her first real smile in many days. "She looks exactly like both of us."

Clara reaches for Sammy and wraps her in her arms. Rocks her the way she hasn't since she was a little girl. Back and forth, a silent lullaby. Tears are streaming down Clara's face. Seeing this—her daughter looking at the photograph of her mother, her daughter and mother together at least in this way—has unleashed something she doesn't understand. *Please don't be dead.* There is only one reason. Only one thing left to do.

"Sammy?" She holds Sam's small chin, turns it so her child is looking right at her. "Sammy, do you want to go to New York?"

# Chapter Seven

ON CLARA'S SECOND DAY of fourth grade, she gets off the bus a few steps after Robin, who dashes into school without waiting for her. Robin's been doing this more and more lately—making sure there's distance between herself and Clara, making absolutely certain that everyone knows her mother doesn't take pictures of *her*. The woman who approaches Clara as she gets off the school bus has a round sweet face and short gray hair. Clara's always been told not to talk to strangers, but this woman looks like she might be someone she knows.

"Clara?" The woman smiles. She's holding a book bag from the Metropolitan Museum, and she has a couple of pens tucked into the breast pocket of her shirt. "Can I speak with you for a moment?"

The controlled chaos of drop-off at Brearley. The small yellow school buses from the West Side and downtown, idling curbside. The Upper East Side moms who have walked the few blocks to school with their girls, now standing in clusters. The girls themselves, their long shiny hair pulled neatly back in headbands and ponytails. Clara's friends from the bus scatter. The first bell is in five minutes. She clutches her favorite notebook to her chest—spiral-bound, covered with decals of flowers, her name written in the top right-hand corner: *Clara Dunne, Fourth Grade.*

"I was wondering," the gray-haired woman begins, "if I could just ask you a couple of—"

"I have to go," says Clara. She feels suddenly scared—not scared like the woman is going to hurt her or try to kidnap her or anything. Scared like she just wants to get away before another word escapes the woman's sweetly smiling lips.

"Wow, your mom's pictures are causing lots of excitement, aren't they?" the woman continues, trying a different tack.

"What are you talking about?" Clara asks. She inches her body away from the woman, moving toward the school's entrance. "Who are you?"

"Beth Klinger," she says. She digs into her shirt pocket and hands Clara a business card. NEW YORK POST is printed in big bold type above her name. "We're doing a story on what happened at the gallery yesterday—"

Blood pounds in Clara's ears. What happened at the gallery? Why is this woman at her school? Why does she want to talk to her? She takes a few steps back—she isn't sure what to do—and bangs right into one of the mothers of a girl in the next grade up.

"Clara! Are you all right?"

Clara is afraid if she speaks she'll start to cry. She hands the mother the business card, all crumpled from her fist. The mother scans it, then quickly looks up at the gray-haired woman, who is still standing at the curb.

"You ought to be ashamed of yourself!" The mother says loudly. Clara doesn't understand what's going on. The noise in her head is deafening. She holds her notebook even closer, as if it might shield her.

"She's just a little girl!" The mother moves toward the woman. "Get out of here—before I call the police!"

The police? Clara lets out a small whimper. Everyone is looking at her. And everyone seems to know something she doesn't know. She's about to miss the first bell.

"Come on, honey." The mother leads Clara into school, glancing backward to make sure the reporter isn't following them inside.

That afternoon, the phone calls don't let up. The headmistress calls Ruth. Ruth calls Nate. Nate has one of the partners in his law firm make a threatening call to the *New York Post*. Ruth calls Kubovy. Kubovy calls the *Daily News*—without telling Ruth, of course—and places a blind item about the questionable reporting practices of a certain rival newspaper. The Brearley mother calls a half dozen of her Brearley mother friends. *Bound to happen.* The murmurs swell. *Lovely child. Who knows what's going to become of her?* The eighth-graders talk to the seventh-graders, who tell the sixth-graders, and so on down the line.

"So I heard someone threw a bucket of paint on your mother's pictures of you," one of Clara's friends says at recess, "and wrote some bad words and stuff."

Was that it, what the gray-haired lady had been talking about? Clara looks around the playground for Robin and spots her on the far side, with her back turned. She's talking to some older girls. Is Robin avoiding her?

"That didn't happen," Clara says. She reaches her arms up and grabs the monkey bars. She wants to kick her friend. She feels, all of a sudden, like someone has just thrown paint all over *her*. Black, cold, dripping down her face, suffocating her. The playground hangs over the East River, separated only by a wire mesh fence. Clara wants to climb up and over the fence—to dive into the polluted water and let the current carry her away.

"Oh yes it did," another friend chimes in. "My mother told me. It's in the newspaper."

At the three-o'clock bell, the girls of Brearley depart for their various after-school activities. The West Siders and downtowners board their yellow buses once again; the nannies or mothers—sometimes the nannies *and* mothers—pick up the young ones and take them to piano lessons, golf lessons, aikido, karate, jujitsu. The limos and town cars arrive, and drivers hold doors open for girls who scramble inside, disappearing behind dark tinted windows.

And Clara—she is supposed to be getting on the school bus, as she does every day. She should be climbing the three steep steps and moving to her usual spot in the back, her knapsack bumping against the sides of the seats. But she can't face the bus, not today. She looks up at the windows, the faces of her classmates looking down at her. If she gets on the bus, she'll be trapped with their questions—questions she can't answer. Instead, she waits until she's pretty sure no one is looking and slips away, walking down the street just behind a small group of mothers and some first-grade children she doesn't know. *Do you want to get some ice cream, Molly? Taylor, do you want to come with us?* The mothers have long burnished hair and are carrying identical purses—the size of doctor's bags, fastened with small gold locks.

When they reach Second Avenue, Clara peels off. No one looks twice at a fourth-grade girl in a Brearley uniform walking down the avenue. Some parents let their kids walk home alone, though usually in groups. Clara knows where she's going: the newsstand on the corner of 81st and Second. Inside, past the gum and Life Savers, the Tic Tacs and candy buttons, there is a long wall of every kind of magazine. And under the magazines, piled on the floor, the newspapers.

She picks up the *New York Times* and begins to leaf through, newsprint already smudging her sweaty hands. Which section would it be in? Certainly not the front. Metro? The Arts? She can't find it, and the guy behind the counter—the one with the cigarette dangling from the corner of his mouth—is watching her. She almost loses her nerve, then spots it—in the upper right-hand corner of the front page of the *New York Post:* FOTO FRENZY! And then, in smaller type: FAMOUS FOTOG GETS BLASTED FOR KIDDIE PORN. Porn. Clara doesn't know what the word means, but it sounds ugly to her. Like something spit out—a curse.

"You look, you buy," says the dangling-cigarette man.

Clara digs all the way to the bottom of her knapsack and finds a quarter and a dime. She can't bring herself to look at the man, who seems to be leering at her, like he knows some joke she doesn't. She walks out of the newsstand and heads west. She's never done anything like this before; she's going to be in big trouble. Robin must be wondering what happened to her. She crosses Third Avenue, then Lexington, Park, Madison. The *Post* is folded and tucked into her knapsack, between her notebook and her American history homework. She's waiting for a place where she can sit quietly and read the newspaper; she really needs to focus. Nobody's going to tell her what's going on—she knows that much. She's on her own.

Three-thirty in Central Park. She feels suddenly small. Too small to be here in this vastness alone. She isn't supposed to be in the park by herself, but what's one more broken rule? A Rollerblader balancing a boom box on his shoulder whizzes past her—too close. Packs of moms speed-walk toward Fifth Avenue, pushing the baby joggers that have become all the rage. Somewhere, someone is playing a trumpet.

Clara locates a bench out in the open and sits down next to an elderly couple feeding the pigeons out of a brown paper bag. She pulls the *Post* from her knapsack and opens it to page four. The paper rustles in the warm breeze, part of it almost flying away. She straightens it out. She's afraid to look—but she does. She looks. And there she is, staring back at herself. A gray, grainy newsprint version of *Clara, Hanging,* Ruth's most recent work. Her own arms reaching up, muscles straining. Her legs flopping as she dangles from a thick rope swing—except, wait a minute. A black strip, the size of a piece of tape, blocks out her private parts. And another bisects her flat child-like chest. Her chest! She rubs at the paper. Maybe something is stuck to the page? Slowly—everything is a little blurry, hard to read—she makes out the beginning of the article below the picture:

Is it art? Or child abuse? These are the questions dogging famous lenswoman Ruth Dunne. Last night, at the trendy Kubovy Weiss Gallery, a group of women calling themselves Clara's Angels took matters into their own hands, splattering several quarts of paint over Dunne's latest artwork—if you can call it that, which Clara's anonymous angels sure don't. Clara, Dunne's daughter—

Clara closes her eyes, tries to go inside of herself. She doesn't understand everything, but she knows enough to be frightened. *Angels.* She doesn't want angels. She doesn't want to be someone who needs angels, strangers who think they can help her.

"Young lady?"

She looks around, startled. The old man on the bench is watching her with the unbridled curiosity endemic to either the very young or the very old.

"Yes?" He looks harmless enough, but still she moves a few inches farther away. Nothing feels safe to her. Not the park, not the skateboarders and Rollerbladers zipping by, not this old couple in wool sweaters, warming their wrinkled faces in the afternoon sun.

"Would you like to feed the birds?" He takes the brown paper bag from his wife's lap, offering it to Clara with a shaky hand.

Clara bolts from the bench, pages of the newspaper scattering all around her. The breeze picks them up—she cannot catch them all.

"I'm sorry!" she cries.

"I didn't mean to scare you," says the old man. He looks stricken. "Here, let me help you—"

"No!" She grabs the page with the photo—she doesn't want anyone to see it, ever—and begins to run through the park. She isn't even sure she's heading in the right direction—she's completely without a compass—so she just points herself at the towers looming above the tops of the trees in the distance.

It doesn't take long for Clara to realize she is lost. She's in the mid-

dle of Central Park, in the middle of Manhattan—her city!—but she
has no idea how to get home. *Home.* She doesn't even want be there,
but what are her options? The bridges and ravines all look vaguely
alike. The boat pond is familiar—she has been there dozens of times,
but never by herself. She doesn't know where it is in relation to anything else. And she doesn't want to stop anybody to ask for help.
Who can she trust? Disoriented, she just keeps spinning like a top,
running, then walking this way and that, until finally the park spits
her out at the corner of 72nd and Central Park West.

She knows where she is now. Her breath slows down. The dark
façade of the Dakota rises like a castle before her. A group of Japanese
tourists crowds at the entrance, snapping pictures. It's been two years
since John Lennon was shot, and paper-wrapped bouquets of flowers
still lean against the sides of the iron gates. Someone has spray-
painted LET IT BE in neon orange on the sidewalk. A uniformed
doorman stands over the graffiti with a hose.

It is nearly six o'clock—more than two hours after she would have
been expected—when Clara gets to her own front door. The brass
knob is heavy and cool in her hand. She turns it slowly, as quietly as
possible. She doesn't need her key, and she doesn't have to knock. The
door is—as it always was in those years—unlatched. She lowers her
knapsack to the floor without a sound. Maybe she can manage to get
to her room without anyone noticing. She doesn't want to see anybody. What can be said?

She's going to be in huge trouble, probably. She wishes she could
undo her life—her past, her family, her very existence—like a knot.
Working it, little by little, until the whole thing comes unraveled.
Until there's nothing left but a floppy bit of string. This whole thing
is her fault. If she hadn't been born, then Ruth would never have
wanted to photograph her. And if Ruth had never photographed her,

neither of their names would be in the newspaper. And there would be no group of women calling themselves Clara's Angels.

"I don't care about your stupid rules and regulations!" Ruth's voice, loud and insistent.

Clara stops in her tracks. Who's Ruth talking to? Maybe—is it possible?—Ruth doesn't even realize she hasn't come home until now. She creeps a few steps into the foyer and peeks into the living room. Her mother is pacing back and forth, talking into a cordless phone.

"I know it's only been a few hours, but this is a missing child! What don't you understand about that?"

"I'm here," Clara calls out softly.

"Let me talk to your supervisor." Ruth hasn't heard or seen her. "Nathan? Nathan, will you please get on the goddamned phone and deal with these people?"

It is then that Clara notices her father. He is slumped on the sofa, his head buried in his hands. He's never home from the office this early. She feels suddenly sick to her stomach.

"I'm here!" Clara calls again, hiding half of herself behind the door frame.

A clatter, as Ruth drops the phone on the coffee table.

"Oh, thank God!"

Nathan gets to the foyer a few steps ahead of Ruth. His face is so pale it appears to be almost blue above his starched white shirt. He has sweat stains beneath his armpits. He says nothing, not a word. He simply crouches down and folds Clara into his wide, concave chest. She feels his ribs, the long muscles of his arms, the pounding of his heart. His whole body is freezing cold.

"I'm sorry, Daddy," Clara whispers.

Behind her, she hears Robin coming down the hall from their bedroom, the soft squeak of her sneakers.

"No, I'm sorry," Nathan says. His hands are trembling. He strokes her hair, which has come loose from its ponytail.

"What were you thinking?" Ruth looms over them. Clara looks up at her mother. A vein has popped out in her forehead, and she is panting, out of breath. "How could you—don't you realize—"

"Shut up, Ruth."

Robin and Clara both stare at their father.

"Excuse me, Nathan, but—"

"Just shut up, Ruth."

Nathan's voice is completely calm, as if telling his wife to shut up is part of the regular course of their household business. He has not let go of Clara. He is still stroking her hair, his arms wrapped around her. Rocking her back and forth like she's a baby.

"I went to school, looking for you," Nathan says to Clara. His voice catches. "Honey, you never, ever should have—"

"I know, Daddy."

"I looked everywhere. I thought maybe you had stayed inside, that you were scared by that reporter—"

"I *was* scared, Daddy. That's why"—her words are coming out in big staccato gulps—"that's why I—"

"Sweetheart, you have to promise me—no matter what happens, you must never, ever—"

"I promise."

"Ever again." He has tears in his eyes.

"I promise."

Nathan glances up at Ruth, who is still standing there. Muted. Silenced. For the first time in their family life, it is as if she does not exist.

"And I'm going to make a promise to you, Clara," Nathan says.

"What?"

"The photographs will stop."

"What do you mean, Daddy?"

"Exactly that. There will be no more photographs."

Everything slows down. Inside of her, opposites collide. Joy and terror. Wholeness and emptiness. Hope and impossibility. She can hardly contain it all. She doesn't have any idea what she's feeling, except that she may explode.

"Nathan!" Ruth finds her voice. "We're not going to let a bunch of crazies—or the *New York Post*—dictate how we live our lives! Think about what you're saying. Don't say something you'll—"

Nathan doesn't even glance at his wife. He flicks a hand at her, shooing her away like she's a flea.

"Oh, I won't regret this, Ruth," he says. "There are many things I'm sure I'll regret—but not this."

———◆•••◆———

SAMMY in New York City. Sammy, standing in front of the Apthorp, gazing up at its grand arched entrance like a tourist. It's about as likely a sight as Sammy in a space suit, walking on the moon. An hour-long flight from Bangor—sixty airborne minutes and a bumpy cab ride from LaGuardia—it seems impossible but true. They are here.

"This is where you grew up?"

Clara watches as her daughter stares into the courtyard. The iron gates, the gray stone fountains. The doorman in his navy blue uniform, who nods at Clara in recognition. An older woman with an angular face, her white hair cut into a severe bob, strides through the gates. She sweeps past them without a glance. Sammy watches her as she walks to the corner and hails a cab.

"Yes, right up there." Clara points. "On the top floor."

Sam looks up at the building and squints, as if trying to make out her mother as a little girl. Clara in her Brearley jumper. Clara sleeping in her room. To Sam, it must look like her mother grew up in a castle. Clara can feel it happening: the longing, the desire. Her own childhood, recast in Sam's fantasies as something shiny and sophisticated. Something to envy. Sam turns to Clara, eyes full of wonder. So this—*this*—is where her mother comes from.

Jonathan is holding Clara's hand, Sam's pink plastic Hello Kitty suitcase and their duffel bag by their feet. Waiting—for what? Clara's not quite ready to go inside. There's something still left to say, the one thing that hasn't been said because Sam hasn't known to ask.

"Sam, before we go upstairs," she begins.

"What?" Sammy asks. She looks nervous, like maybe Clara's going to change her mind.

"I want to tell you something."

"Are you going to tell me that Grandma is already dead?"

Sammy looks straight ahead into the courtyard as she says this, her voice breaking. God almighty. Is this what she's been thinking?

"Oh, Sammy—how could you even—of course not! I would never!"

Sam shrugs. A perfect nine-year-old pretense at not caring.

"I just thought maybe—"

"No. Your grandmother is not dead," Clara says. "But I want to prepare you. She looks very thin—very sick—and she pretty much can't get out of bed."

"That's okay," Sam says. "I've seen people like that on TV before."

"Well, it may feel a little different in real life. And another thing. Your grandmother . . ." Clara pauses. Is this really necessary? She's gone back and forth about it. Of course it's necessary. She can no longer choose what to tell or not tell, doling out small nontoxic bits of information like goody bags at a kid's birthday party.

"Remember I told you she's an artist—that she spent her life taking pictures?"

"Yeah."

"Well, I think you need to understand that she's pretty well known."

"What do you mean? Who knows her?"

"She's famous," Jonathan interjects. "She's a famous photographer."

Sam is chewing on her lower lip, a sure sign of stress. When she was a little kid, sometimes she bit her lips until they bled.

"How long has she been famous?"

"Pretty much forever," Clara says.

"When you were a little kid?"

A pause.

"Yes."

Clara pulls her hand away from Jonathan's. She is quickly irrationally furious. She hears the wonder in Sam's voice, the beginning of excitement. Why did Jonathan have to use the word *famous*? Why couldn't he have downplayed it at least a little bit? *Famous.* What does that mean to a nine-year-old girl? Britney Spears is famous. That peroxide-blond rich girl—the one whose tanned sliver of a midriff is always on view—Paris Hilton? *She's* famous, though for what, Clara isn't exactly sure. Sammy's probably imagining hordes of screaming fans surrounding the Apthorp. *Ruth! Ruth! We just want your autograph!*

"Why is she famous?" Sammy asks. She seems to almost taste the word, to savor it in her mouth like a delicious treat.

"Because of some pictures," Clara says.

She begins to walk into the courtyard, ushering Sam inside.

"What kind of pictures?"

*Enough.* Enough questions.

"What kind of pictures, Mom?"

"Honey, one thing at a time. We'll talk about it later, I promise."

They walk across the cobblestones and into the elevator. This time the ride takes almost as long as it used to in the old days: The widow of the celebrated Broadway composer—Clara can't for the life of her remember his name—gets off on 7, the doors open and close for no reason on 10, and then a couple of teenage girls, customized iPod cases attached to their vintage leather belts, get off on 11. Sammy can't stop staring at the teenagers. Heads bobbing, turquoise necklaces swaying back and forth as they listen to their music, oblivious to the three Brodeurs scrunched into a corner to make room for them.

"Do they live here?" Sammy asks, once the girls get off the elevator.

"I have no idea," Clara answers faintly. The doors close, and she feels suddenly, crushingly claustrophobic.

"But it's the middle of the day," Sam says. "Shouldn't they be in school or something?"

"I don't know," Jonathan says. He's tense, Clara realizes. She leans against him, trying to breathe.

When they finally emerge—the long corridor stretching before them—Clara gives Sam the once-over. The shiny dark hair spilling in waves down her back. The pink corduroys, the perfect little white T-shirt, the neckline embroidered with flowers. As much as possible, she tries not to think of Sam's impossible beauty—the knowing eyes, the finely honed cheekbones so startling in a nine-year-old. But that's the first thing Ruth will see, of course. A thought lurches across Clara's mind before she can block it out: Perhaps Ruth will be unconscious. Perhaps in a coma. She feels her spirits lift for a moment, before she realizes what she's wishing for. Evil, terrible.

They walk slowly down the wide dark corridor. Sam's eyes dart everywhere, seeing whatever there is to see: children's galoshes outside of 12B, a note for the dog walker tacked to the door of 12C. Someone has hung a museum poster—a cheaply framed Balthus—on a long stretch of wall. As they approach Ruth's apartment, Clara sees light spilling from the open door. Why is the door already open? They haven't been announced. And there seems to be something—it's hard to tell what it is from here—piled in the hallway. The shape of the pile comes into focus. Suitcases. Two battered suitcases and a knapsack.

"Here we are," Clara says.

She pushes the door farther open.

"Hello?" She pokes her head inside the foyer. No one seems to be nearby. She leads the way in, holding Sammy's hand.

"Why's the door open?" Jonathan asks.

"I don't know."

Sammy stops and stares at the nude hanging in the foyer.

"Did Grandma take that picture?" she asks, pointing.

"No, that photograph was taken by a man named Irving Penn," Clara says. Her head is buzzing, humming, full of infinite noise. The piles and piles of magazines. The dusty beams of eastern light filtering in through the windows. The ink stain—nearly thirty years old—on the edge of the oriental in the foyer. Her childhood and her daughter's, colliding.

She watches Sam's hungry gaze travel around the apartment, or at least the part of the apartment visible from where they stand. What can Sam possibly make of all this? The iconic photographs. The nineteenth-century Turkish rugs. The free-form walnut console, a gift to Ruth from George Nakashima. To Sam, it's all just stuff—her grandmother's stuff—though Clara sees Jonathan taking it in, his eyes widening as he recognizes the Nakashima.

"Where's Grandma?" Sammy whispers.

"I'm sure she's in—"

And then, piercing the deadness of the apartment, the sound of voices screaming behind a closed door. Ruth's voice. Ruth's door. Clara's throat constricts, her fingers tingle. She looks around for a heavy object, or something sharp, to use as a weapon. As she moves closer, she hears the voices more clearly.

"You're fired!" Ruth screams.

"I told you already, I quit!"

Marcy's voice. Marcy, the nurse's aide Clara had hired.

"You're a hideous person!" Ruth screams. "You have no empathy! I don't know how you can look at yourself in the mirror!"

Ruth's door flies open and Marcy comes racing out, looking behind her as if Ruth might follow. She's wearing her usual baggy gray uniform, which she is frantically unbuttoning as if it's choking her. Her eyes are wild and wet, and two red blotches have appeared on her cheeks, making her look a bit like an incensed Raggedy Ann doll.

"In twenty-five years of doing this," she says without missing a beat, as if she had expected Clara to be standing there, "I have never walked out on a job. But she's a nightmare. You have no idea."

"I have some idea." Clara's voice breaks. She feels a wild surge of energy, impossible to contain. Like she might just slam her fist into a wall. She can't do this. Not now. She had run through every possibility in her mind, every way Sam meeting Ruth might go, but she hadn't considered the nurse's aide quitting in the middle of it. *Christ.* Her hands are balled up at her sides.

Sam has sidled up to Clara in the hallway. She stands behind her mother, shielding herself. Jonathan plants himself firmly next to both of them.

"What do you think you're doing?" Ruth shouts weakly from her bed. "There's a word for people like you! Traitor! Deserter!"

Marcy stuffs her uniform into a tote bag. Then she looks once again at Clara.

"She makes me say things I could never—" She cuts herself off, shaking her head, her reddish hair glinting in the thin light spilling into the hall from Ruth's bedroom. "My whole life, I've tried to take good care of people."

"We need to— I can't really talk about this right now," Clara says. Trying to end this. For Sam not to witness another moment of it.

"I've called the agency," Marcy says. "And I called your sister too. She's on her way over. I didn't want to leave Ms. Dunne by herself, even though—"

She shakes her head again.

"Okay," says Clara. Slightly desperate now. Robin's coming? She's not ready for all this at once. She's not ready—and she has no choice.

Marcy registers Samantha, standing behind Clara.

"Oh, my goodness, don't you just look like—"

"What's going on out there?" Ruth's voice. Weakened from all that shouting. "Who's there?"

"We need to go in and see my mother," Clara says.

Marcy just stands there, as if waiting for something.

"So I guess you can go—if you're going to go."

"I'll need my check," says Marcy. "Your sister usually takes care of it."

Jonathan clears his throat.

"I have a checkbook," he says. "In my bag. Out there." He gestures to the front of the apartment.

Marcy follows Jonathan down the hall, leaving Clara and Sam standing alone outside Ruth's bedroom. Sam is pressed up against Clara's leg, cleaving to her mother the way she used to as a very little girl when she needed comfort or protection.

"Are you ready, Sammy?" Clara asks.

A small tentative nod.

"Listen. If you start to feel weird or bad—if you want to leave at any time—all you have to do is say so."

Sammy straightens up. Rising to the occasion.

"*Okay,* Mom. I get it."

Clara takes Sam's hand and walks through Ruth's bedroom door, softly knocking as they enter. Ruth is lying on her back on her hospital bed, covered only by a thin white sheet. Stripes of light from the wooden venetian blinds bisect her body. Her head is turned toward the door—no turban, no baseball cap. Just stark knobby baldness.

At the sight of Sam, Ruth tries to lift herself up. She struggles onto one sticklike forearm, then collapses.

"Raise my bed," she instructs Clara.

Clara strides quickly forward. Her fingers grope for the cord with the controls for the bed. She fumbles, nearly knocking over a lamp. She's shakier than she thought.

"Where the devil—oh, here it is."

The bed creaks upward.

"Okay. Enough."

Ruth's spine can no longer hold her upright. She tries to sit straight, but she lists to the side. She's wearing one of Nathan's old pajama tops, misbuttoned. Her clavicle juts out, a thin ledge of bone. All the while, she stares at Sammy, who is standing motionless between the door and the bed.

"My God," she finally says, her sunken eyes like murky pools of water. "She's you, Clara."

"No, Mom." Clara is swift, a blade slicing this away. They're not going in this direction. Not over her dead body. "She's not."

"You could have let me know." Ruth keeps staring at Sam, drinking her in. "So I could have been a bit more prepared."

She reaches out a hand toward Sammy.

"Come here, darling. Let me take a look at you."

Clara checks for any signs that this is too hard for Sam—her fists might be clenched, she might be picking at her lip or twirling her hair around and around—but no. Sammy actually seems fine. Peaceful, almost. She shyly walks over to the side of Ruth's bed.

"If I had known you were coming, I would have put on my party dress," Ruth says.

Sam looks at Ruth quizzically. Is she joking?

"And heels!" Ruth says. "Now come closer."

Sammy giggles—so easily won over. Of course it's easy. What does she know? She bends forward and allows Ruth to stroke her cheek. She doesn't seem at all afraid of the signs of illness around her. The shape of Ruth's skull, her gray pallor, the bag of bones her body has become—none of this fazes Sammy. All she sees is her grandmother. Finally, her grandmother. It is this—Clara realizes with unbearable clarity—it is this that she has been most afraid of. Not that Sammy might be frightened. Not that Sammy might be traumatized. No. That Sammy might be seduced. Taken in by the all-powerful Ruth Dunne.

"So." Ruth hasn't even glanced at Clara, who has stepped back, as if pushed away by the force field around Ruth's bed. "Tell me something about yourself."

Sam blushes and shrugs. She shifts from side to side, suddenly awkward.

"I don't know."

"I'll bet . . . you're in fourth grade," Ruth says.

"Yeah," Sam says. Chewing on her lower lip. Clara is ready to move toward her. To rescue her. Does she need rescuing?

"And I'll bet . . . you really like school. Do you like school?"

Sam nods.

The sound of heavy footfalls in the hallway. Jonathan's boots. And another voice—Christ, it's Robin. Jonathan and Robin; they have met only a handful of times over the years—and now they fill Ruth's doorway. Jonathan's wild gray hair, his worn jeans and flannel shirt, and Robin, straight from the pages of the Bergdorf Goodman catalog in a trim little shift dress and pointy-toed shoes that must be killing her.

"Looks like there's a party going on," Robin says.

She walks into the room as if it's a boardroom, taking it over. She scans the situation, coolly assessing. Her eyes graze over Clara like she's a piece of furniture, pausing only long enough for Clara to read her expression: *You left me to deal with this, you fucking bitch.*

"Samantha," she says, reaching down to shake Sam's hand. "I'm your aunt Robin."

"Ah, and here's the husband," Ruth says weakly. She extends a hand to Jonathan. Limply. Like a queen.

"Nice to meet you, Ms. Dunne."

"Please." Ruth sits slightly straighter, and some color has returned to her cheeks. "Call me Ruth."

"Mother, what's this about firing Marcy?" Robin asks.

She bustles around to the far side of the bed and begins straightening the dozen or so plastic prescription bottles on the bedside table. She lines them up perfectly so that they appear to be a row of small able soldiers.

"That awful woman," says Ruth. "Goodbye and good riddance."

Robin nods slightly, humoring Ruth. The last couple of weeks have taken a toll on Robin. She looks ragged. Dark circles under her eyes—onto which she has patted too much concealer—make her look like a raccoon.

"Well, that *awful woman,* as you put it, has been changing your bedpan for the past two weeks," Robin says.

Jonathan has moved behind Sam, his hands resting protectively on her shoulders. They look out of place here, in this sickroom high above Broadway, as if they had wandered onto the wrong stage set. *Come on*—Clara fights the urge to grab them and run—*let's get out of here.* She thinks of their house in Southwest Harbor—the empty rooms awaiting their return. The dirty coffee cups they left in the kitchen sink. The unmade beds, rumpled sheets still left with the impressions of their bodies. Home—their home.

"She wasn't doing a very good job of it," Ruth is saying. "She watched soap operas all day long."

"So what?"

"So I don't want to spend my last days on earth watching television for imbeciles. Such stupid people. Who could create such crap?"

Robin crosses her arms, and Clara can suddenly imagine her in court, arguing a case before a judge. She is all angles: elbows and sharp chin; she could hurt you if you don't watch out.

"Who do you think is going to take care of you now?" Robin asks.

"You girls, of course," says Ruth.

"Excuse me, but what the fu—" Robin stops herself, with a quick glance across the bed at Sam. "What are you talking about?"

"In African cultures, there are no nurse's aides," says Ruth. "Families take care of their own."

"Well, we're not in Africa," Robin says, very carefully.

*And we're not a family.* Doesn't it go without saying?

"Could we not fight about this? Marcy's gone, and that's that," Ruth says.

"You bet she's gone. You made sure of it," says Robin. She walks over to the foot of Ruth's bed and grabs hold of the metal footboard. She looks like she'd like to rattle and shake something—anything.

Clara wishes she could see Sammy's face from where she stands. She's standing straight, her posture perfect. Witnessing more ugliness in the last five minutes than she's seen her whole life.

"Samantha." Ruth focuses once more on Sam. "This is quite a way for us to meet, isn't it?"

Sammy lets out a little half giggle. Poor kid. She's self-conscious, not sure how to behave. Nothing in her preteen magazines has prepared her for this. She starts fiddling with her hair, a sign that she's getting overwhelmed.

"And Jonathan—it is Jonathan, isn't it?" Ruth now looks behind Sam—Jonathan hasn't moved an inch—and something hardens slightly in her gaze.

"Yes," he says quietly.

"My daughter tells me you own a shop of some kind. You're— what is it—a jeweler?"

Ruth trots out the word *jeweler* with a flourish, leaving it to hang limply in the air. As if to be a jeweler—in the bedroom of Ruth Dunne, under the watchful eyes of Man Ray and Berenice Abbott— is so absurd that nothing more can possibly be said on the subject.

"That's right," says Jonathan.

Clara moves from the center of the room so that she's standing just behind Sam, next to Jonathan. She puts her arms around them. Her family. A tight little unit. Jonathan blinks, his shoulders tense.

"I work more with semiprecious stones," he says softly. "Topaz, freshwater pearls, tourmalines."

"Interesting," says Ruth. "Do tell us more."

"Please, stop it." The words escape Clara's lips before she realizes that she's spoken out loud. She feels like she's hallucinating.

"What's the matter?" Ruth looks directly at Clara for the first time.

Clara shakes her head. She feels the warmth of Jonathan, next to her. Breathes in her husband and daughter, trying to hold on to what matters.

"Nothing."

"I should think not," says Ruth. She smiles weakly, looking around the room. "Here we are—here we all are."

More footsteps in the hallway now. Did Marcy close the door behind her? Clara almost doesn't care. A burglar would be welcome relief.

Peony pokes her small dark head inside Ruth's bedroom door, and they all turn to look at her. As usual, an array of folders is tucked beneath her arm.

"I just wanted to check to see if you need anything," Peony says, taking in the crowd in Ruth's room without expression.

"Not at all, darling." Ruth waves her away. "My family's here. I have everything I need."

# Chapter Eight

THEY WORKED FOR A WHILE, Nathan Dunne's threats. *No more photographs, Ruth. No more—or else.* He never said exactly what would happen if Ruth went against him, but it was clear from the tone of his voice, the thin, determined line of his mouth, that Nathan meant business.

Clara's father had never so much as raised his voice to his wife, but after what was referred to around the Dunne household as *the incident at Brearley,* or *that thing in the* Post, it was as if something had been unleashed in Nathan. A fatherly fury that was stronger—for the moment—than his fear of Ruth. Or love. Or awe. Or whatever it was.

He came home every night at six. No more four-star dinners out with clients. No more occasional men's poker nights with other attorneys, from which he tiptoed in, cigar smoke clinging to his suit. Weekends, he took Clara and Robin to the park, where they tossed a softball around for so many hours that the girls would beg him to stop. No, Nathan had determined to be around. He had finally figured out that the only way to really understand what was happening in his family was to be there in person. Every day.

And so, for a while, their family life at the Apthorp was similar to the lives of those surrounding them: other Upper West Side families with a couple of kids in private school. They went to Ollie's for Chinese food and stood in line to see *Flashdance* at the Loews on 84th Street. They piled into their Volvo wagon and made the two-hour drive to Hillsdale, where they spent entire days in pajamas and Nathan cooked his one specialty, challah French toast.

Ruth still spent time in her studio, of course. She produced a series of strange still-lifes: a cracked bowl on a kitchen counter, a bed stripped down to its old stained mattress. The photographs were technically magnificent—the silvery precision of Ruth's darkroom technique was unmistakable—but to this day they are seen as a failed experiment and can be had at auction for a fraction of her typical prices.

When she wasn't in the studio, Ruth floated around in a dream world of her own making. She moved more slowly than usual, her lips curved into a half smile. She even did normal things like normal mothers: she went to the gym, picked up clothes at the dry cleaners, arrived home with shopping bags from Fairway filled with fresh vegetables and Italian cheese. It was as if Ruth were acting out a role in a play. *See?* she seemed to be saying. *I can do this. I can be like everyone else.*

How long did life proceed like this? In Clara's memory it is a blink, a flash, nothing more. In reality it may have been eight months, maybe nine. It spanned the entirety of Clara's fourth-grade year. She was the same age as Sam is now. But when she reaches back into her childhood for a foothold, for memories she can feel and touch and taste in her mouth, the year her mother left her alone is blank, like a skipped page in a notebook. A mistake.

It has been picked over by the critics, this gap in Ruth Dunne's Clara Series. Oh, what they have made of it! Whole academic papers have been published on the subject. Clara's personal favorite, "The Interrupted Gaze," written by a professor of psychology at the University of Chicago, is a psychoanalytic meditation on Ruth's work.

The mother—in this case overshadowing the artist—has taken what appears to be a conscious step back, in order to consider the effects of her work on her daughter, a prepubescent girl. Having interrupted her gaze in order to look inward, Dunne then reemerges with an even more powerful assertion of her work, as if her explorations have given her further license, both as an artist and as a mother—or perhaps a renewed acceptance that the two are indistinguishable.

What a load of nonsense. Nathan had to go away on a business trip, is all. Three days in London—and Ruth was suddenly free. Had she always known the day would come when she'd have Clara to herself again—that wild containment in her eye, that aliveness like none other?

"Wake up, sweetheart." The voice, a whisper.

Clara slowly blinks her eyes open. She knows before she knows. This is how it has always been, since that very first day, six years earlier, when she put the lizard in her mouth. She wonders, sometimes, whether somehow she has asked for this, whether she has brought it upon herself—her mother's attention. After all, Ruth has never tried to photograph Robin. Not even once.

"Let's go, Clara."

She stumbles out of bed, rubbing her face. What time is it? The glow of the orange digital clock reads 11:47. It's almost midnight!

"Where are we going?"

"Quiet. . . . We don't want to wake your sister."

Robin. They can't leave Robin alone in the apartment. Surely Ruth knows this. Surely she's thought it through. The inside of Clara's head is a jumble of words, like a game of Scrabble. Nothing is forming, nothing makes sense. As they creep by Robin's door, which is cracked open, Clara catches a glimpse of her sleeping sister. Robin is lying on her stomach, her legs scrunched under her like a turtle tucked into its shell. Through the window, the light of the moon illuminates the long curve of her spine.

Clara wants nothing more than to climb into Robin's bed and curl around her sister's warmth. She can almost feel the slow beating of Robin's heart, her sweet midnight breath.

"Mommy, please, let's not—"

"Ssshhh."

Together, they tiptoe down the rest of the hall to the foyer. Ruth has Clara's denim jacket all ready to slip on over her cotton nightgown. The camera bag and tripod are by the front door.

Finally, Clara finds her voice.

"Mommy, we can't leave Robin alone. What if she wakes up and can't find us?"

The months of not being photographed has given her this bit of strength. She's ten years old now, and she thinks she knows right from wrong.

Ruth stops gathering her equipment for a moment and turns to look at Clara.

"What kind of mother do you think I am?"

"I just—"

"Look in the living room," Ruth says. "Go on, take a look."

Clara peers around the corner into the living room. There, sleeping on the sofa under one of the extra blankets, is Ruth's newest intern, a girl from Pratt.

"Okay?" Ruth whispers harshly. "Are you satisfied?"

Clara is silent. Strangely ashamed. She should have trusted her mother—she should have known better.

The elevator ride takes forever, descending an inch at a time. The wood-paneled interior, the small bench—it reminds Clara of a scene she saw in a recent movie, of a priest in a confessional. And even though she's half-Jewish, even though she's never so much as set foot in a church, she wishes—right now she wishes—that a panel would slide open in the elevator and a priest would be on the other side. *Tell me, my child. Tell me what brings you here.* A warm fatherly voice to whom she could spill everything inside her, washing herself clean.

They're on the fifth floor before Clara speaks again.

"Where are you taking me?" Her voice is small.

"To the park."

*Isn't it dangerous?* The words ricochet, remain unsaid. They pass the fourth floor, then the third. *Just put yourself in your mother's hands.* Whose thought is that? Who is speaking in Clara's head? *Give in to this, give in. You have no choice.*

The doorman doesn't react as they walk past him, onto the desolate street at this hour—as if a mother and her young daughter lugging heavy photographic equipment down Broadway at midnight is in the order of usual business. Clara tries to make eye contact with him as they leave. If anything happens to them, she wants him to remember. So that he can tell the police.

Ruth turns west on 78th Street.

"I thought we were going to the park," Clara says.

"We are going to the park. Riverside Park."

Could she say no? *You have no choice.* That voice again in her head.

"I'm scared," she says.

Ruth stops right there in the middle of 78th Street. She leans her tripod against a building, then crouches down so that she's looking up at Clara.

"Would I ever let anything happen to you?"

Clara remembers her shame from just a few minutes earlier. Ruth is a good mother. Ruth loves her—*so much,* as Ruth would say, *so much,* her thin arms crushing her into a breathless hug.

"No," Clara says quietly. She shakes her head for emphasis. "I know that."

"Okay, then. I'm glad that's settled." Ruth straightens up. "Because now we have work to do."

The park looms before them, black and empty save for the streetlights, their bluish-white halos shining in the misty air like luminous planets. A man in a windbreaker walks a small dog along the edge of the park, his shoulders hunched against the darkness, a small plastic bag in his hand. Clara looks up at the windows of the tall stately buildings along Riverside Drive, searching for signs of life. A white flicker of a television screen. The glow of a bedside lamp, a dining-room chandelier, the end of a very late dinner party. If people peered out their windows, would they see Ruth and Clara, two small figures entering the park? Would they see Ruth move swiftly to the location she has already chosen, just inside the stone walls, where the gnarly roots of an old tree have emerged from the ground?

"Right here, Clara," Ruth says, pointing to the mound of earth between the roots. "This is the spot."

Ruth is breathless from carrying all that equipment—no assistants tonight—and rests for a moment on her tripod as if she's an old woman and it's a cane.

"What do you want me to do?" Clara asks. She can hear the strain in her own voice. Can't her mother hear it too?

"I brought something," Ruth says, pulling a thin white blanket from her tote bag. "Here. Wrap yourself in this."

Clara does as her mother asks. She wraps the blanket around her shoulders.

"No, darling. Take off the jacket and your nightgown—"

That old feeling descends upon her. The numb floating—not altogether unpleasant, really. She can leave the shell of her body behind like those cicadas she's seen littering the ground in Hillsdale. She can shrug out of her skin, the same way she now shrugs out of her denim jacket. She then—quickly, quickly, before she can form a thought about it—pulls her nightgown over her head. The June breeze hits her ribs, the soft flesh of her buttocks.

"Like this." Ruth wraps the blanket around and around her. Mummifying her.

"I can't move!"

"Let me help you."

Ruth cradles Clara in her arms, then lowers her to the ground. The moist spring earth is cool and damp. Clara can feel it, even through the layers of the blanket.

Ruth takes a couple of steps back, frames the image with her hands.

"Beautiful," she says quietly.

She works quickly now, setting up her tripod on a flat patch of grass. She knows exactly what time the moon will be at its fullest, setting in the western sky. There are no pole lights tonight, no generator running power through thick electrical wires. Just this: the enormous, yellow moon, bathing the park in its glow.

Clara tries to breathe. The blanket is tight—too tight. She concentrates on the moon, watching thin clouds drift across its face. When she was a little girl, she always used to be able to find the man in the moon. Now she doesn't see him, no matter how she tries.

"Mommy, I feel bugs in my hair!"

She's not just saying it, she really does feel something creepy and crawly, moving up the back of her neck. Her arms are trapped inside the cocoon of the blanket, so she can't even reach up and swat whatever it is away.

"You're just imagining it." Ruth fiddles with the lens of her camera. "Don't move, Clara. I have to take these pictures very, very slowly, so it's important that you—"

"I'm not imagining it!"

This wasn't Hillsdale either. This was the city—the place where huge rats darted across Broadway at dusk, where cockroaches scattered when she opened the kitchen cabinets late at night. Clara's heart starts to pound against the wall of her chest.

"Mommy!"

"Okay!" Ruth is trying not to look mad. She strides over to where

Clara lies and crouches down, combing her long fingers through Clara's hair. She rubs the back of Clara's neck, her touch more efficient than warm.

"Is that better?" she asks.

Clara nods. It is better. She takes a deep breath, tries to relax. She needs to find that floating, suspended feeling again. To lose herself entirely. Someday—when she is a grown woman with a little girl of her own—she will realize that she has never forgotten a single one of these moments. They are what remains of her childhood, a worn deck of cards that she can shuffle through, again and again. Here— under her mother's lens—is where she is certain she exists. See? In the sharp outline of her pale body in the white blanket, set against the bed of leaves, the rough, knotted roots? This night happened.

"Keep completely still. Close your eyes, Clara."

The shutter clicks. Something is tickling the inside of Clara's nose, and she blows hard, trying to get rid of it.

"You moved!"

Clara opens her eyes.

"But you were finished taking the picture!"

"No, I wasn't. I have to do this at an incredibly slow speed. Each shot takes four or five seconds, because of the light." Ruth shakes her head, as if irritated at having to explain. "Let's try again."

She walks over to Clara, moves her legs a bit to the side. She musses up Clara's long dark hair, then places a few strands across her cheek.

"There, that's better. A bit askew."

"What's askew?"

"Never mind."

Clara closes her eyes again. She tries every trick she knows to stay still. She counts backward from one hundred, slowly, inserting *Mississippi* between each number. She hears the shutter click once, twice. The sound of her mother turning the ring around the camera's wide, fat lens.

"Now turn your head the other way, sweetie," her mother says. "Perfect—now stay just like that."

*Seventy-four, Mississippi.* She's having a hard time floating away— weighed down by the blanket, the way that her arms are pressed to her sides and her legs are stuck together. *Seventy-three, Mississippi.* How long can she do this before she explodes? That's what her body feels like—something ticking. A time bomb. Her blood is raging, her heart thrumming like a small, frightened animal's. *Seventy-two, Mississippi.* She can't do this for another second—she just can't.

Her eyes fly open. Her mother is towering over the tripod, a shadowy figure lit from behind by the moon. *Mommy,* she starts to say. But then the moon starts spinning in the sky—the whole park fragmented, like the inside of a kaleidoscope—and Clara begins writhing, trying to free herself from the blanket.

"Clara!"

"Get this thing off of me!" Clara screams.

"Okay, sweetie, okay—calm down—"

"I can't calm down!"

She's screaming and screaming now. Lights turn on in the apartments just across Riverside Drive, the outlines of people peering out their windows.

Ruth unwraps the blanket, her hands shaking.

"Jesus, Clara, stop. Somebody's going to call the police—"

"I don't care!"

Maybe Clara's Angels will come. She's never met any of them, these strangers who have decided she needs defending. Maybe one of them will swoop down from the night sky, gossamer wings flapping madly, hoping to save her.

"Here, put this on. Quick." Ruth pulls Clara's nightgown over her head.

For the first time in her life, Clara senses her mother's fear. Ruth's whole face is tight, her eyebrows knitted together. She hands Clara her denim jacket, then closes up the camera bag. Her hands are still trembling.

"My God, Clara, you didn't have to—you could have just—"

Clara is beyond hearing her. The screams have died down, but now she can't stop crying. Ruth hoists all her equipment onto one shoulder, then holds Clara's hand, half dragging her away from the park.

In the distance, a siren. The flashing red and blue lights of a police car racing down 78th Street. Ruth grips Clara's hand more tightly. The car stops at the corner, just as they're crossing Riverside, and a young cop rolls down his window.

"Excuse me, ma'am?"

"Yes, officer?"

Never has Clara heard her mother sound quite so obedient.

"There was a report of some screaming—a child screaming?"

The officer looks at Clara, her long hair matted to her wet cheeks.

"Is everything okay, ma'am?"

"Absolutely," Ruth says. "Thank you."

The officer is still staring at Clara. He's not sure whether to stay or go. Is the red-faced girl in front of him the one who was screaming? Is he missing something? Or is there a terrible thing happening—right now—deep inside Riverside Park?

"What's your name?" the officer asks.

It takes a few seconds for Clara to realize.

"Me?" She points to her chest.

"Yes, you."

"Clara." Less than a whisper.

"Clara, are you all right?"

She can feel a pulse beating in her mother's hand. She thinks—in quick succession—of her father in London, her sleeping sister at home, Clara's Angels hovering above her like wispy clouds in the darkness. Does she even think it? *I could ruin everything.*

"Yes," she says more strongly. "I'm fine."

"Okay then," the officer says. His window glides up, cutting him off from them as he engages his siren again—the sound makes Ruth jump—screeches around the corner, and up toward the park's entrance.

<hr />

EACH DAY, as the dawn light filters through the east-facing windows over Broadway, Clara has a moment—a split second—of wondering: *Where am I?* A curiosity that quickly turns into a vague but unmistakable nausea. She hasn't felt sick to her stomach with such regularity since she was pregnant with Sam.

She shifts on the sofa and opens her eyes. Sunlit beams of dust hang in the air, as if from a movie projector. A thin film covers everything. The coffee table, the piles of art books, the ornate black fireplace mantel—all are slightly gray. She looks across the living room at Jonathan and Sam, sprawled on the futons they bought at Laytner's Linens the day they got to New York. *The only way we're sleeping here*, Clara had said at the time, *is if we're sleeping together*. And so together they've slept, for three nights running now. Ever since Rochelle, the hospice nurse, made it perfectly clear that Ruth could not—under any circumstances—be left alone.

"She'll try to get out of bed herself," Rochelle had said. "She won't follow instructions."

"And so?" Robin had asked Rochelle. "What's the worst thing that could happen?" Squinting into her BlackBerry. Multitasking.

"The worst thing that could happen? Okay. Well, she could fall. Break a rib. Break a hip. Be lying on the floor all night, with no way of—"

"All right," Clara quickly interrupted. "We'll call the agency. Ask them to send someone over for the evening shift."

"Mom's not going to go for that," Robin said flatly. "No way."

"Well, what do you think we should do?"

Robin looked up from her BlackBerry.

"I don't know, Clara. Here's a radical idea—why don't *you* decide?"

"Hey," Jonathan said. "Is that really necessary? Everyone's a little tense here. Can't we just—"

"Sorry," Robin said. "But honestly, I've had it."

She pushed back into her chair, then rummaged through her purse.

"Where's my goddamned lipstick?" she asked. Her head was bent forward, her mouth tight. She looked as if she might cry.

*Maybe Peony can*—the words lodged themselves in Clara's throught. *No. That's not right.*

"We'll stay," Clara said quietly.

Jonathan and Sammy both looked at her.

"Really?" Jonathan asked, hesitant. "Honey, are you sure you want to?"

Clara looked at him, the wall behind her eyes crumbling into nothing.

"There's no choice," she said. Finally—it was oddly liberating—no choice.


Sam stirs on her futon. An arm thrown over her eyes, blocking the light. She's been sleeping soundly every one of the three nights they've been here. Sleeping better, eating better. She is—Clara has to admit—a happier child. A weight lifted. A heaviness, an emptiness, gone. Clara hadn't understood this; she still doesn't entirely understand it. How could Sam have felt the absence of something she hadn't even known existed? How could a secret have gathered so much power over the years, rolling into every corner of their lives, gaining strength and velocity with each passing day? And worst of all, how could Clara not have seen it?

"Good morning." Jonathan sits up, rubbing a hand over his face. He's wearing his one pair of striped pajamas; Clara's not used to seeing him like this. At home he sleeps in the nude.

"Hey." She stands and stretches.

Sam's still out cold.

He comes over to her and pulls her close. She can feel his heart beating. He smells different, away from the materials of his work. Guest bath soap, Ruth's old shampoo, the lemony scent of laundry detergent.

"Do you know something?" He speaks softly.

They haven't had five minutes alone since they got here.

"What?"

"I'm proud of you."

She pulls back, looks at him.

"Don't be." The room is suddenly blurry. "I fucked up completely."

"No. You didn't. You're fixing it. Our being here—it's going to be okay."

"You don't know that, Jon." Tears are falling freely now. She swipes at them. It's too early in the day. If she starts crying now, where will she go from here?

"I didn't say it was going to be easy," he says. "But it *will* be okay."

Nothing is as it's supposed to be. And Clara—Clara's just trying to get through it. Her entire focus is on Sammy. This has been the right thing—obviously, painfully, the right thing. But what had she thought? That they'd come down for a day, maybe two, have Sam meet her grandmother, and then—mission accomplished—they'd flee back to their lives and leave Ruth here to die? Is that what she thought? Clara shakes her head hard, angry at herself for her willful naïveté.

She walks into the kitchen and begins sorting Ruth's daily pills into the long plastic pill box labeled for each day of the week. The small powder-white Ativan. The pale blue ovals of Oxycontin. The morphine—a cheery canary yellow. The counter is lined with prescription bottles sent up from the pharmacy downstairs. When Clara was a kid, the Apthorp Pharmacy was an old-fashioned place that sold items like blood pressure cuffs and plastic hair bonnets; it smelled vaguely of alcohol and camphor. Now, its shelves are stocked with fancy French creams, salt scrubs from the Dead Sea. Even the cotton balls are an esoteric brand. But they do still dispense medicine, and it seems Clara is in there at least once a day, handing the pharmacist a triplicate prescription. Ativan, Oxycontin, morphine. *Keep filling these,* the hospice nurse had said. *Even if you haven't run out, keep filling them.* Was she saying what Clara thinks she was saying, a subtle suggestion that they stockpile the medicine? In case there came a time—

The baby monitor on the coffee table crackles.

"Hello?" Ruth's weak, hoarse voice. "Anybody there? Somebody— I need somebody!"

"Coming," Clara calls.

She walks down the hall. Pauses for a moment by Ruth's bedroom door. Over and over again, dozens of times a day, she has to pull herself together, all the fragmented bits. Consciously, with effort. She cannot be unprepared, not for a single second.

She pushes the door open. What does Ruth need? A bedpan? More morphine? The hospice nurse suggested catheterizing her, but Ruth has resisted. The room is dark, the shades drawn. Ruth's eyes have become sensitive, everything about her fragile, disintegrating— she doesn't want to see or be seen. Her life, reduced to shades of gray, soft shadows.

She's sitting on the edge of the bed, a blanket wrapped around her. "What are you—" Clara begins.

"Please, don't say anything," Ruth says. "I can't do this by myself."

"What are you trying to do? Here, let me. Will you just—"

Clara approaches—her unformed plan to take her mother under each arm and swivel her back into bed—but Ruth pushes her away with surprising force.

"Don't tell me what to do!"

"I'm just trying to keep you safe," Clara says.

"I'm not a child, Clara."

Clara stops. Looks down at her mother. The papery skin, the purplish-black shadows under her eyes, the tufted head. Not for the first time since they have been here, she thinks about the book. CLARA. Even her own name, stolen from her by Ruth. Ruth—poring over the images with the ever-helpful Peony, deciding on order, size, commentary—did she think about Clara? The real Clara, not the one on the page? Did she think about what she was doing to her daughter, even for an instant? Clara feels nothing but a sick coldness: icy, dispassionate. *Just die,* she thinks. *Just die, already.* And then hates herself for it.

"Hand me my walker."

There's no way Ruth is strong enough to use her walker, but Clara does as she asks. What's the worst that can happen? A broken pelvis? A shattered femur? It's all going to be in the ground soon enough. It's all just going to disintegrate into powder and dust—isn't it? Ruth has not expressed her wishes. Big funeral or small. Burial or cremation. For all Clara knows, Ruth wants to be preserved cryogenically—frozen so she can come back as herself in her next life.

"Here you go." Clara places the walker in front of Ruth, then stands aside and watches as Ruth struggles to her feet. The cords in Ruth's neck strain from the effort. Her arms quiver. One leg pretty much no longer works at all, and her upper body has wasted away. But she does it. Somehow, she pulls herself up. Wheezing, eyes flashing. She is nothing if not determined.

"Okay," she says, once she has caught her breath. "Okay. Let's go."

"Where are we going?"

"To look at art," says Ruth, her face shining—glowing beneath her papery skin like a child's. She reaches into the pocket of her robe and pulls out a handwritten list: *Sonnabend, Robert Miller, Barbara Gladstone, Feigen Contemporary, Gagosian . . .* The writing is quavery, almost unreadable. Clara can make out the names of eight or nine galleries. "You, me, and Samantha. I want to show her where she comes from."

*Where she comes from?* Clara fights back hard against the venom. *She comes from a small island in Maine. She comes from my belly. She comes from her wonderful father. She comes from—*

"I've hired a car," Ruth is saying.

"This is impossible. You can't be serious."

"We're doing this, Clara." Ruth is panting just from the attempt to stand still. "It's not up for discussion. Now help me get dressed."

Up until now, Clara has successfully avoided anything tactile, anything . . . *intimate* . . . as it relates to her mother. Ruth is looking at her expectantly, like a toilet-trained toddler waiting for a wipe. This is another test, Clara thinks. Another way for Ruth to push and push until finally Clara snaps. That's what Ruth wants, isn't it? She wants to see what will happen if the façade Clara works so hard to maintain is blown—truly blown to bits. What does Ruth think she'll discover in the rubble? Rage? She knows all about Clara's rage. Disappointment? Loneliness? Sorrow? Is it possible she thinks—or hopes against all hope—that perhaps all that will be left is love?

"I think I'll wear a caftan," Ruth says. She starts to try to move to the bedroom closet, then stops. "We can just pull it over my head. That would be easiest."

*I can't do this.*

"Could you pick one out for me, sweetheart?"

As if sleepwalking down a flight of stairs—insensibly descending—Clara enters Ruth's walk-in closet. The scent hits her in a single breath: camphor, mothballs, sweet old sachets layered between shawls and scarves. She inhales all the longing of her childhood. Those hundreds of hours spent hiding inside Ruth's closet—sifting through her blue jeans, the piles of indistinguishable black tops, the few elegant dresses wrapped in plastic garment bags—as if on a secret mission to find her mother's true spirit.

Now there are dozens of caftans. A rainbow of unreasonably bright hues. When did Ruth ever start wearing color? Bright pink, beaded coral, lime green, iridescent turquoise. Crinkled silk, soft cotton—it seems important, somehow, to choose the right one. What possible difference can it make? Still, Clara can't decide. She stands there, transfixed.

"The pink one," Ruth says, after a minute or two.

"Which pink one? There are a few different—"

"Oh, for God's sake, hurry up!"

Clara looks at Ruth, bent over her walker. Maybe she'll exhaust herself, standing there. Maybe she'll realize this whole outing is an insane idea. Clara is stalling, she now realizes, as she pulls a pale silk caftan, the color of a ballet slipper, from its hanger. Where did Ruth find such a thing? It looks as though it might have come from a Turkish souk, an open-air bazaar. More likely, it was purchased at one of those stores Clara has passed on Madison—windows displaying artfully ripped jeans and embroidered tops inspired by Woodstock.

She doesn't want to undress her mother.

Ruth unties her bathrobe with one hand.

"Help me, Clara."

Clara summons a memory: dressing Sammy for all those years before Sam started to dress herself. The soft downy body. The unblemished skin, the pure ripple of her ribs. The sweet smell—how Clara used to sniff Sam whenever she hugged her close! She tries to keep those images and that smell in mind as she tugs Ruth's robe off, laying it in a crumpled heap on the bed. Then the nightshirt—an ancient man's dress shirt, actually, torn at the elbows. Is it possible that it's one of Nathan's? Blue-and-white stripes, an attorney's uniform, faded now, all the starch gone out of it after so many washings.

She closes her eyes, but she can't keep them closed. Like a child who knows she's not supposed to look at the sun, she blinks open—and, like the sun, what she sees imprints itself upon her. Damaging her. Her mother's body: the crescent-shaped scar running up the side of her chest, where one lung was removed. The flaky yellow pallor of skin that has been buried under sheets and blankets for months. The bump—a tumor?—rising knoblike from the right hip bone. And superimposed on all that: Ruth Dunne, young and beautiful and easy in her nakedness. Stepping out of the shower, dashing to answer the phone—so flawless, so lovely. Is this what we come to—all of us? Even the ones who seem untouchable?

"My bra and panties," Ruth says. "Top drawer, on the right."

Clara does as asked, now. Her movements quicker, robotic. *Let's get this over with.* At the other end of the apartment, she hears Sammy's high-pitched giggle. Awake, now. *Don't come in here, don't come in.* Clara slides the panties up, one stick-thin leg at a time. Puts on the bra—one strap, then the other, reaching around Ruth's back to hook it in a gesture that could almost look like a hug. Then the caftan, which floats easily over her head.

"Now what shall I wear, a hat or a scarf?" Ruth muses. "Or perhaps baldness is in order?"

This is important to her—how she presents herself to the world on this of all days.

"With the caftan, a scarf, I think," says Clara. Suddenly a fashion stylist.

"Very well—that white one." Ruth points to a simple white silk scarf hanging from the closet doorknob.


The Apthorp was not designed to be handicap-accessible. Not for the first time, Clara maneuvers Ruth's wheelchair out of the elevator, down the two steep stone steps to the courtyard. The three generations of Dunne women—Ruth, Clara, Sam trailing behind them—make their way over the cobblestones and out onto Broadway.

"Good to see you, Ms. Dunne!" The doorman tries to contain his reaction; Ruth's deterioration is obvious. "Out and about, are you?"

"Is that our car, Joseph?" Ruth asks.

A dark blue town car is waiting at the curb.

"Yes, ma'am."

"Sammy, help me get Grandma inside," Clara says.

"Allow me, ma'am."

Clara steps back and allows Joseph to help her mother into the back of the town car. Sammy scrambles in next to Ruth. Clara concentrates on the apparatus itself, releasing the levers from the back of the wheelchair, folding it flat. The thing must weigh forty pounds, and the size of it is awkward; she staggers, trying to hoist it into the car's trunk.

Joseph comes around the back of the car. "Let me give you a hand." He lifts the wheelchair easily. There are dozens of elderly people living in the Apthorp; he's gotten this down to a science.

He slams the trunk closed, then turns to Clara.

"Poor Ms. Dunne," he says. "How much time does she have?"

Clara stares at him, amazed—though she shouldn't be. When it comes to birth and death, people seem to feel they can ask anything. The normal rules of civil discourse do not apply. When she was pregnant with Sam, perfect strangers used to reach out and pat her belly. *When's the baby due? Is it a boy or a girl? Are you having natural childbirth or using an epidural?* Now—with death—it is much the same. *What's wrong with her? It's cancer, right? The big C. What do the doctors say?*

"Not much," Clara says faintly. "She doesn't have much time."

Joseph shakes his head. "Such a shame," he says. "My own mother went fast—it was in her liver."

"Sorry to hear it." Clara tries to look through the tinted back window of the town car. She can see only shadows, the vaguest outline of two heads.

"Ms. Dunne's a great lady," he says.

He goes around to the other side of the car and holds the door open for Clara; she slides in so that Ruth is in the middle. How many hundreds of trips have they taken together, in the backs of taxis and cars like this one? In the close confines of the backseat, she feels panicky. But she's not allowed to panic—not, at least, in any way that Sammy can pick up on. Clara should have brought Jonathan. Somehow it had seemed simpler to do this without him. Easier, not to subject him to Ruth's complete and utter condescension. *It doesn't surprise me that Clara married an artist,* she had said to Jonathan just last night. *Or rather—should I say artisan?*

"Here, let me help you buckle up," Clara says. She leans over Ruth, who is slumped down and tilted slightly to the right, as if she might just topple over.

"I don't need a seat belt," says Ruth. She lets out a small wheezing laugh. "Really, if there were ever anyone who didn't need to worry about a seat belt—"

"It's the law, Grandma," says Sammy. Clara tries to fasten her own seat belt, then abandons the effort. The twisted shoulder strap, the buckle wedged deep in the crease of the seat—everything, even this, feels impossible.

Ruth has a point, she really does. A yellow light, a speeding car, a high-impact collision—that would be the best way for her to die, wouldn't it? Given the current alternative? Ruth would never know what hit her. Except—here is where the thought goes astray—Clara and Sam would be with her. Clara finds her hand on the door latch. Ready to bolt at the next red light and pull Sammy out with her.

"Go down Ninth!" Ruth calls to the driver. They're already passing Lincoln Center, just before the road splits. "Ninth Avenue!"

Clara can barely stand it. Something about being out in the open with Ruth, speeding down the wide open expanse of the avenue—the Afghan restaurants, the low seedy buildings, the concrete barricades in front of the Port Authority—she feels brittle. Breakable. She sneaks a glance at Sammy. How is she doing? She's staring out the window, taking in every single thing. No conflicted emotions there. Nothing but excitement. And Ruth: her elegant profile, emaciated, the white scarf appearing like a turban. The dangling earrings—

Moroccan gold—that Ruth requested just as they were leaving the apartment. As the car crosses 34th Street and heads down into Chelsea, Clara pulls out her cell phone and punches Robin on the speed dial.

"Robin Dunne." The crisp, efficient voice, answering her own phone for a change.

"Hey there," Clara says. Ruth is watching her. Who does Ruth think she's calling?

"Where are you? I called the house, and there was no answer—"

"We're on our way to Chelsea." Clara pauses. "Mom wants to go gallery-hopping."

"You're kidding." A long beat on the other end. "Clara, please tell me you're kidding."

"Um—no."

"Let me talk to her." Ruth holds out a hand for the phone.

Clara leans back into the soft, comfortable leather seat. At least there's this. At least there's plushness and privilege, tinted windows and climate control. She can hear the tinny sound of Robin lecturing Ruth over the cell phone.

"Stop it." Ruth holds the phone away from her ear. "Robin, I don't have to listen to this." She looks at the key pad, squinting. "How do I hang up this thing?"

"Give me that!" Clara grabs the phone away. "Hello? Robin?"

"This is insanity," Robin says. "She's going to kill herself."

Suicide by gallery-hopping. Clara hears beeping in the background, phones ringing. An entire switchboard lit up, waiting for her sister.

"Robin, could you please—"

"Oh, I've got to take that," Robin says hurriedly. "Sorry."

The line goes dead. *Breathe,* Clara tells herself. *Just keep breathing.*

"There's a show at Robert Miller I want to see," Ruth says. "Twenty-four artists—'The Subjective Figure'—and the fuckers didn't ask me."

"Mom! Watch your language!"

"Oh, really, darling. When you were a child, you heard far worse."

"Are you sure you want to see the show, then?" Clara asks. The last thing she needs is an angry Ruth.

"Diane, Jean-Michel, Lucien, Alex Katz, Mapplethorpe." Ruth continues as if Clara hadn't spoken. "It's absurd." Her hand is wrapped around the door handle, knuckles white.

Sammy is watching them, eyes darting back and forth. How much is she understanding? What can she possibly make of any of this? In Southwest Harbor, grandparents are old people who live in Florida. Tennis-playing, golf-cart-driving leathery creatures smiling from ceramic picture frames.

The car turns right onto 24th Street, a block completely unfamiliar to Clara. What is this neighborhood? She has no recollection of ever being here before. The Chelsea of her childhood was a place to drive through on the way downtown, a blur of crumbling brownstones and gay bars. Now, all the galleries she remembers from SoHo—fifteen, twenty years earlier—are here: the polished glass expanses of Mary Boone, Matthew Marks, Metro Pictures, one right after the other. As if the whole art world just simply up and moved.

"What happened to SoHo?" Clara asks Ruth. "Are there still galleries—"

"God, no." Ruth is fiddling with her head scarf. "SoHo's full of bankers. The artists drove up real estate values. The place is a mall now."

"What do you mean?"

"Chanel, Louis Vuitton . . . you name it." She pauses. "Pottery Barn. Oh, and J. Crew. Banana Republic."

"So the galleries—"

"One by one, they moved here. Matthew was one of the first. Now, everybody's on these couple of blocks." Ruth pulls a compact from her purse, flips it open, and studies her face. Since when does she use a compact? Clara can't even recall her ever carrying a purse. Nathan was in charge of the money. Ruth was like a queen, gliding through life without such pedestrian necessities as cash or identification or house keys.

"You can pull over here," Ruth says to the driver. "Just in front of that hydrant."

Clara climbs out of the back of the car and Sammy hops out after her. A few kids in their early twenties are smoking cigarettes in front of Metro Pictures. They give Clara and Sam a quick once-over, then go back to their conversation. Just another uptown mother and daughter doing a bit of gallery-hopping. Clara goes around back and pops open the trunk. The wheelchair is easier to lift from this angle—still, she struggles under its weight. It bangs against the curb as she tries to open it. Nobody thinks to help her. Why would they? They're kids. Kids with black portfolios under their pale, emaciated arms: art students, most likely. They're focused on each other, on this glorious sunny day—on this fantastically unassuming block where the keys to their careers are in the hands of just a few gallery owners who can turn a starving graduate student into a star overnight.

Clara sets the wheelchair on the sidewalk. *Thanks for nothing.* The driver has opened the door for Ruth and is standing at attention, as if expecting Ruth to get out under her own steam.

"Excuse me." Clara bends over her mother, half dragging her to the wheelchair.

"Let me help." Sammy grabs an elbow.

"I can do it myself," Ruth says, her legs flopping like a rag doll's.

"Please, just cooperate," Clara says.

The art students stop talking and turn to watch, as if this whole exercise is some sort of strange new installation, a performance put on especially for them.

"Are you all right?" Clara lowers Ruth into the wheelchair.

"I'm fine." Ruth shifts until she's sitting up straight. She squares her shoulders and raises her chin, staring at the front door of Metro Pictures. Clara watches as her mother's whole demeanor—no, more than her demeanor, her very *aura*—transforms.

"Let's go inside. I must say hello," Ruth says.

Ah, Clara realizes. Of course. Her mother is summoning every bit of her strength—one last time—to become Ruth Dunne.

The frigid air inside the gallery hits Clara like an icy wave. A shiver goes through her whole body. Goose bumps rise on her forearms. Why keep things so cold? It must be sixty-five degrees. Sammy's going to freeze in her capris and cotton T-shirt. Ruth isn't going to be able to tolerate this for very long, in her thin silk caftan, with no layer of body fat to protect her. Well, at least her head is covered.

"What is this show?" Ruth asks, as Clara begins to wheel her around. "I don't understand it—do you?"

Clara studies the walls. The entire show is comprised of six gigantic photographs, clearly destined to be hung in enormous lofts. The photographs are oddly bright, a kind of heightened acid-trip Technicolor. The background of each picture appears to be a jungle. Superimposed on the dense green thicket are normal, corporate-looking people—men wearing suits, women carrying briefcases—and they are falling, weightless.

"I have no idea," says Clara.

"An ironic comment on the post-nine-eleven universe," says Ruth. "It's a jungle out there. Blah, blah, blah."

"I think it's cool," says Sammy.

Ruth reaches up and grasps Sammy's hand.

"Samantha, let me explain," she begins. "Art—real art, *good* art— does not strain the way this work does. Its metaphors are intrinsic, organic to the work itself. Not this overly stylized stuff that thunks you over the head—makes you think it's *about* something, when really it's just—"

Sammy's brow is furrowed. She's nodding, trying to follow Ruth. And Clara—Clara doesn't know whether to laugh or cry. *Metaphor? Intrinsic? Organic?* Does Ruth really think these words are in Sammy's vocabulary?

A gallery assistant appears at their side.

"The photographer is twenty-two," the assistant says. "This is her first solo show."

"I see," murmurs Ruth. "Clara? Can we move on?"

"But I thought—"

"Next!" Ruth says a bit too loudly.

Out on the street, Ruth looks so pale that her skin seems to be molting.

"Ridiculous," she says to no one in particular. "To think my work has hung on those very same walls."

Clara wheels her down the street. Sammy sticks close to her mother—nervous, perhaps. And with good reason. Ruth talks the whole time. Where is her energy coming from? Snatches of what she's saying drift up to Clara like bits of debris from the sidewalk. *Derivative* and *silly* and *conceptual overintellectualized crap.* Ruth looks tiny from Clara's vantage point behind the wheelchair. Her legs are a phosphorescent white, poking out from the hem of her caftan, useless against their metal rests.

"Over here. Let's see what Andrea's up to." Ruth points to the glass doors of the Andrea Rosen Gallery. "She usually has good taste. Ah, a group show. I always like a good group show."

Clara pushes Ruth slowly around the perimeter of the gallery. Ruth's gaze is careful, assessing. She nods slightly at a moody black-and-white portrait of an old woman, a tight close-up by a southern photographer.

"Now that"—she grasps Sammy's hand again and points at the wall—"that is genuinely evocative. Unforgiving." She gazes up at Sammy. "Do you know what I mean by that?"

"I think so," Sammy says. "You mean we can see everything?"

"Exactly!" Ruth beams at her young pupil. They keep moving.

Next, a delicate, extremely intricate pencil drawing—truthfully, it looks like an elaborate doodle, something the artist might have drawn while on a very long phone conversation. Then, a large piece—the largest of all—a photograph of a furry extraterrestrial creature in the midst of a fancy cocktail party.

"Lord. Will you look at that," Ruth says.

Clara peers at the plaque next to the photograph.

"He's a Los Angeles artist."

"Would you get me the catalog and price list, Clara?"

No one seems to be in the gallery—literally no one, not even an assistant. Clara picks the price list off a clear Lucite table and brings it over to Ruth.

"Incredible," Ruth murmurs, looking through it. "All these kids, two years out of art school—"

"What?"

"The prices! Sixty thousand dollars," she says. "For E.T. drinking a martini."

Ruth looks around the whole room. "Over there. Samantha, do you see that Chuck Close? Do you know who Chuck Close is?"

"No."

"A genius," Ruth says. "One of the greats. And do you know why he's in this show?"

"Why?" Sammy is nearly breathless. Overwhelmed, Clara can see. Pulled into the force field of Ruth's vision.

"To lend credibility to the rest of this mediocre stuff, that's why." Ruth slaps the catalog on her lap. "I'm disappointed in Andrea."

"Please, Mom," Clara finally snaps. "Keep your voice down."

The familiar embarrassment. The desire to distance herself—to pretend that she has nothing to do with Ruth Dunne.

"Why? No one can hear me. And anyway, if you display your work, you invite criticism. The problem with the world is that everyone is too polite. This is terrible work—terrible!"

Ruth's voice cracks.

Clara feels a cruel streak rise inside of her. *What's wrong?* she almost asks. *Are you afraid that when you die you're going to disappear, just like the rest of us? That your work is going to end up stored in the back rooms of galleries? That—in the end—what you did just didn't matter that much?*

"Let's go," commands Ruth. "I can't bear it."


Outside, the street is filling up with the lunchtime art crowd. A couple of gray-haired men in jeans and tailored jackets. A tall woman in a black suit, talking into her cell phone. A skateboarder weaves by, carrying a portfolio under his arm.

Ruth really does look like she's about to keel over. Clara looks up the block for the dark blue town car. Now there are several town cars just like it, idling outside of gallery doors.

"Do you remember that trip, Clara?" Ruth asks dreamily. "When we visited Barbara Gladstone in Todi?"

"Not really," Clara says.

"Samantha."

Sam looks up.

"When your mother was a little girl," Ruth begins, "no more than five or six, the owner of this gallery rented an old rectory in Italy. It was the most marvelous place—"

Wait. An image hovers just around the edges of Clara's consciousness. An old village square. A vineyard. A small café table beneath an arbor, and herself—on the other side of Ruth's lens. Clara had fallen and wound up with a black eye, and Ruth had shot a close-up of her that way: eye swollen shut, looking like a prizefighter. Clara had forgotten where all of that had taken place: upstate New York, the Italian countryside—what difference does it make? *Clara and the Black Eye* is all that remains.

"We must stop in to see Barbara," Ruth says, pointing to the floor-to-ceiling windows of the Barbara Gladstone Gallery.

"I really think we shouldn't," Clara says.

"Really, Clara, we must." Ruth sits up straighter. "I want to introduce her to my granddaughter."

Clara wheels Ruth inside, across the cracked cement floor. Dread spreads its cold black waters inside of her. *This—she can't—what will Barbara—the comparisons—not not not—Sammy—*

A young woman, dressed in—could it be?—two layers of black cashmere, is seated behind a small desk displaying the usual catalogs and price list.

"Excuse me," Ruth says.

The young woman, her dark hair slicked back into a chignon, slowly raises her swanlike neck and blinks at Clara and Ruth through angular black-framed glasses.

"Can I help you?"

"Is Barbara in?" Ruth is erect in her wheelchair but, even so, her head doesn't come quite to the top of the high desk. The young woman looks down at her. In the bright whiteness of the gallery, her black silhouette is as sharp as a pencil drawing.

"No, she isn't."

She says this as if the question itself is absurd, somehow brazen.

The price list on the polished desk has tiny blue dots next to each piece. It's a Richard Prince show, and it appears to be entirely sold out.

"When do you expect her?" Ruth asks. A slight edge—undetectable to anyone but Clara—has crept into her voice.

"Mom, would you like to look at the work?" Clara asks quickly. She wants to wheel Ruth away.

"I have no idea," the girl says.

Clara begins to pull the wheelchair back. In the center of the loft-like main room, a sculpture of what appears to be a car's hood rests on a wooden block, paint dripping down the sides.

*Don't say it, don't say it, don't say it.* Clara silently begs the back of her mother's head. She knows what's coming, what has to be coming.

"You don't know who I am, do you?" Ruth asks. Petulant and incredulous as a child.

A pair of perfectly arched eyebrows rise above the tops of the black-framed glasses. The girl is perhaps twenty-one. The year she was born, Ruth was nearing the end of the Clara Series.

"I'm sorry. Should I?"

"Ruth Dunne." Each word bitten off. "When Barbara gets back from Umbria, or from having her pedicure, or wherever the hell she is, please tell her that Ruth Dunne stopped by."

Ruth's shoulders are shaking. She sits there, waiting for the slow dawning of recognition on the girl's face. A sign that she's screwed up. That she's in the presence of unexpected greatness. Something. Anything.

"Ruth Dunne." The girl slowly writes the name on a message pad. "Is that spelled D-O-N?"

"D-U-N-N-E," Clara chimes in. Please, not this. Not now. Not in front of Sammy. "The photographer."

The girl looks up, pencil poised, her face as smooth and placid as a lake at dawn.

"Fine. And what may I say this is regarding?"

Ruth reaches up for Clara's hand and squeezes it. Sam is standing close to her grandmother, close enough to see her trembling. Ruth's palm is clammy and cold. Does she whisper the words or merely think them?

*Please, Clara. Take me home.*

# Chapter Nine

"WHERE ARE WE GOING NOW?" Sammy is exhausted, no doubt from the morning of gallery-hopping. Showing herself—finally!—to be a nine-year-old child. She's been acting altogether too mature since they got to New York. She probably needs to put her feet up and watch reruns of *Full House* for a couple of hours. Or go on Ruth's computer and e-mail her friends back home.

Instead, they are standing in the vast lobby of the Museum of Modern Art—the size of a European train station—the sounds of foreign languages echoing all around them as they trudge up a long flight of stairs.

"Do we have to do this?" Sam goes on. "I'm so tired."

It may not be the best timing, but timing is not on Clara's mind. Something is propelling her, something cold and hard against her back. From the moment they left the galleries, Clara knew what she had to do. First, she took Ruth home and straight into bed, no arguments there. Gave her an afternoon cocktail of Ativan and morphine, pulled the bedsheets up around her. Ruth fell asleep almost instantly, still in her caftan and white scarf. Then Clara found Jonathan, just back from a run in Central Park and still slightly out of breath in his sweatpants and T-shirt. She wanted the two of them to take Sam to

MoMA, she told him. Right then—not later. He began to question her, but in an instant he understood. Sam at MoMA. Of course.

The museum of Clara's childhood, while not exactly a cozy place, has been replaced by this staggering open space that makes her dizzy. The art itself is immense. Rodin's Balzac rising like a mountain in front of the sculpture garden. And here—on the second floor—four enormous Twomblys, magnificent in their chaos of color and scribbles. Clara can hardly bear to look at them. They feel like the inside of her head: random words, hard to make out. Everything just slightly out of reach.

"I know you're tired, Sam," Clara says, "but you'll see." *Trust me,* she wants to say. But she isn't sure she's earned the right to say it. And she doesn't want to see that look crossing Sammy's face, the look that says, *I can't.*

Arrows point in every direction: ELEVATOR. ESCALATOR. STAIRS. She isn't sure which way to go, but Jonathan leads the way. Jonathan, who has always been able to make himself comfortable in any environment, from the docks of Southwest Harbor to the concrete caverns of high art. As they slowly rise on the escalator to the third floor, Clara sees a sign for the Edward Steichen Photography Galleries.

"Mom?"

Clara quickly looks at Sam. Does she get it yet? Does she suspect?

"I'm hungry. Can we go to the café downstairs?"

It's all so elemental: exhaustion, boredom, hunger. Why would Sammy have any idea, especially after this morning? Nothing exists in Sammy's world, up until now, that would make her even consider the possibility that her grandmother's pictures might be hanging on the walls of this museum.

"Maybe in a little bit, Sam. There's something I need to show you first."

The Steichen galleries are in a space more intimate than the lower floors, a warren of rooms that begin with what Ruth would refer to as *the granddaddies.* Steichen, of course. The streets and churches of Walker Evans. A small group of tourists are standing in front of a whole wall devoted to Weston nudes.

Sammy's eyes widen as she sees the nudes.

"Isn't that one in Grandma's apartment?" she asks, pointing to one in a series called *Nude on Sand.* An elegant nude—one Clara has always loved—facedown, her long legs open, feet slightly pigeon-toed. Her head resting on crossed arms, a tangle of dark hair.

"Yes, it is," says Clara. She's distracted. Looking around. MoMA has such a huge permanent collection—they rotate it constantly—she isn't exactly sure where Ruth's work is hanging. Clara scans what she can see of the next room, but most of it is out of view. Jonathan has walked ahead of them, already there.

"Let's keep going, Sammy."

Clara leads the way, taking in one image at a time. The room seems to be arranged in some sort of chronology. Here, Diane Arbus's twins. There, Warhol's *Chelsea Girls.* The photographers who came of age in the sixties and seventies, one generation before Ruth. Clara's gaze revolves slowly around the room: she is like a bodyguard, a sharpshooter, looking everywhere for danger. She sees unfamiliar images: a crisp wartime photograph of a boy lying on his side. A single tree rising up from an otherwise desolate field, like a hyperkinetic Ansel Adams. And then—Jonathan is standing in front of them—three photographs, grouped together. Ruth Dunne, accorded nearly the same amount of wall space as the Weston nudes.

She clenches and unclenches her fists. Repeats the motion several times as if trying to get her blood moving, remind herself that she is made of flesh. The images are a blur so far; she has not determined which of the Clara Series is hanging, only that they are there. The unmistakable silvery prints. A hint of wild grass, open sky. A sliver of skin. A mass of wavy hair.

A lone young woman with a bandanna tied around her head—an

art student, most likely—is standing beside Jonathan. Her head is cocked to the side, appraising. From the back, she looks like every intern who has ever worked for Ruth. There is awe in her very posture. It's all Clara can do not to rush at her, knock her away. *Stop staring!* And Jonathan? She knows Jonathan has seen all these and more. From the very beginning, he made it his business to see the photos— to understand her. But she has never *seen him seeing.* This is the man who has made love to her a thousand times. Who has held her head when she's vomited. Who has stood and watched as she pushed a newborn into the world. Why does she feel so exposed?

Two guards stand in the wide arch between the two rooms, guarding against—what? Bombs? Art thieves? What about Clara's Angels? Do they still exist, or have they grown old and retired? Maybe they've moved to the suburbs. As far as Clara knows, it's been a long time since anyone has thrown a bucket of paint at a photograph of Ruth's.

"Mom? Hello?"

Sam is looking at her strangely.

"What, darling?"

"You're talking to yourself."

*Snap out of it, Clara.* She has forgotten—for a long dreamlike moment, the glimpse of the photographs has made her forget—her purpose in being here. How long has she been standing frozen in the middle of the room?

"Come with me."

She pulls Sammy over to the photographs. Quickly, quickly. Moving next to Jonathan. Their tight little family huddled together in front of the huge prints.

"Excuse me," she says to the art student, who is standing too close.

She moves slightly to the side, and Sammy looks up at the first photograph, then the second, and then the third, moving across them as if they are movie stills. As if they might tell a single story.

"What are these?" Sam asks, the words becoming rhetorical even as they form and hang in the air. Clara watches her carefully. She watches as the images sink in.

"Who am I looking at?" Sam asks again.

*Evocative.* Clara looks at the first photograph. *Unforgiving.* Her mother's highest praise. And then, that terribly shaky voice: *Don't you know who I am?*

"Who is that?" Sam's voice rises above a whisper in the quiet of the gallery. Too loud. The art student moves away from them, focusing now on the Warhol.

Clara bites her lip to keep from speaking. She wants Sammy to come to it on her own. And besides, Clara doesn't trust the way her own voice might come out: strangled, the tendons in her neck tight with tension.

Jonathan puts his arm around her, creating a shelter. *Clara with the Lizard* is the first of the three photographs, which are hung close together, almost like a triptych. In the middle is *Clara in the Fountain.* And finally—as if some curator's idea of creating a narrative— *Naked at Fourteen.*

Sam stares for a long moment at the middle photograph, the one Clara would say, if asked, is the most bearable. She is naked, yes—she can still feel the cold water of the fountain, the pennies beneath her bare feet—but *Clara in the Fountain* is one of Ruth's few photographs that doesn't make her feel ill.

Sammy takes a few tentative steps over to where the plaque is affixed to the wall. Clara moves over to Sammy—she can't stand to have her more than arm's distance away—and reads along with her.

RUTH DUNNE (1947–   )

The blank space after the date of her mother's birth begins to break apart, become pixilated until a date of death begins to form.

"So in the pictures, that's—that's—"

"Your mother," says Jonathan, his voice choked up.

"What do you want to know, Sam?" Clara asks. "You can ask me—you can ask me anything." She gives herself over to an unfamiliar feeling. What is it, resignation? Relief? The muscles in her body—the tightness in her neck, her legs tensed as if ready to jump—all of it just melts away. Suddenly, she's exhausted. She could curl up right here, on the stone floor of the museum, and go to sleep.

The art student is now looking at them with intense interest, focusing first on Sammy, then on the photographs, then back at Sammy. A glimmer of confused recognition.

Sammy looks closely at *Clara in the Fountain*. She seems almost to be ignoring the others. Of course, Clara realizes: In that photograph she's almost exactly Sam's age.

"What are you doing? Where are you?"

"In the fountain at the Apthorp," Clara says. "In the middle of the night."

"Why are you naked?"

"I was always naked."

"In all the pictures?"

"Pretty much."

Sam nods slightly—almost as if Clara has confirmed something she had already begun to suspect. Then she turns her attention to *Clara with the Lizard*.

"How about that one?"

"That was the first picture," Clara says. "The first ever."

The chemical taste of rubber fills her mouth. Her skin feels damp.

"How old were you?"

"Three."

"And that one?"

Sam points to *Naked at Fourteen*.

"That—well, that was the last."

"Why? Why was it the last?"

The questions are rapid-fire. For a moment, Clara can't find her voice. There are so many answers to choose from. *Because it never should have happened. Because I wanted to die. Because I should have found a way to stop it the year before, or the year before that, or the year before that.*

"Because it had to be," Clara finally says.

Sam nods again. That knowing look in her eye. Was all this somehow inside of her already, this knowledge? She looks once again at the photographs, as if committing them to memory.

Then she turns to Clara and Jonathan.

"That's cool, Mom—you're in a museum. So now can we go to the café?"

⸻ ◆•◆•◆ ⸻

RUTH and Nathan Dunne did most of their fighting outside of the house. From the time the girls were born, Ruth and Nathan agreed that their children shouldn't be exposed to their arguments, which, though rare, could spiral into a place full of scalding rage. And so, with a few notable exceptions, they went out. To restaurants, to bars, to park benches where they sat, warming their hands around Styrofoam coffee cups while they tried—two fragile creatures trembling with anger—to make themselves understood to each other.

But not on this particular night. On this particular night—Clara is on the cusp of her eleventh birthday—the shouting starts only moments after Nathan returns from the office. Something, it seems, has happened. Clara doesn't know what, and she sees on her mother's face that Ruth doesn't know either. But Nathan's thin face is pale with fury, his lips dark red against the whiteness, as he sets his briefcase down by the front door.

He grabs Ruth by the arm and pulls her into the kitchen.

"We need to talk."

"Not now, Nate. The girls—"

"The girls! Don't you dare use the girls as an excuse!"

"What are you—"

Clara tries to follow them into the kitchen, but they've already moved on. Nathan has dragged Ruth through the kitchen, out the other side, and into her studio, closing the door firmly behind them.

"What's going on?"

Robin has emerged from her bedroom. A Walkman dangles around her neck like a piece of tribal jewelry, and an algebra book is tucked under her arm.

"I don't know."

Robin scratches her head. Her expression is blank. She has just become a teenager and has instantly developed a teenager's feigned boredom in all situations.

"I'll bet I know," she says.

"What?"

Clara can hear her father's shouts, even through the layers and layers of soundproofing. He must be yelling really loud.

"Dad came home during the day today. I had just gotten back from school."

"Yeah? So what?"

"So he went into the studio."

Clara starts to feel a little nauseated. Like suddenly she might throw up.

"Was Mom there?" she asks. "Was Mom in the studio?"

"No. She had a doctor's appointment."

Now, the sound of a crash—something actually being knocked over and broken. Even at his angriest, Clara has never seen her father be physically destructive. It just isn't like him. Maybe it's Ruth. Ruth is more capable of breaking things.

Robin stretches her arms overhead and moves them from side to side as if she's in a calisthenics class. Her T-shirt pulls out of her jeans, exposing a wide swath of belly. She lets out a yawn and then turns and starts heading back to her room.

"Where are you going?" Clara asks.

"I have to study." Robin waves her algebra book in the air.

"But—"

"Oh, come on, Clara. What am I supposed to do, stand here like an idiot and listen to this?"

Robin shakes her head in disgust. Suddenly, she looks a lot older than thirteen. For a strange brief second, the veil separating the present and the future rises, and Clara can see her sister as the grown-up she will someday be. The tight little face, bunched up with worry. The business suit and briefcase, just like Nathan's. The padlocked eyes that let no one in.

"I mean," Robin tosses over her shoulder as she walks away, "it's not like it has anything to do with *me.*"

Clara starts to speak, but no words come out. She has nothing to say, and she knows better than to say something stupid. Deep down, she is certain that there can be only one reason for her parents fighting in the studio. It's her, of course. The shattering crash on the other side of the wall, the awful sound of her father's shouts—it's all about Clara. Only Clara.

Alone now, she sinks to the floor and leans her head against the wall. She can hear the pitch and tone of her parents shouting but can't make out a word. She looks around the living room, gray shadows falling over the furniture in the early evening light. The huge old sofa, strewn with pillows. The threadbare wing chairs. The massive fireplace mantel, darkened with soot. And on the walls—hanging, leaning everywhere—the photographs. What was so special about them? She didn't get it. When she had asked her mother, Ruth responded with the small smile she reserved for things she was certain Clara couldn't yet understand: *It's how a picture makes you feel, deep inside.*

Clara looks slowly at all the pictures: the nude, the picture taken from high up in the sky, the crystalline image of a suburban family on their lawn. What do any of them make her feel? She focuses hard—anything to block out the sounds coming through the wall. Nothing, she decides after a few minutes. There must be something wrong with her. She feels nothing—no, less than nothing. A maw inside of her, a cavernous emptiness.

The door to the studio opens and Ruth flies out, her face swollen, cheeks wet with tears. She takes a couple of long steps across the room, looking wildly around. She doesn't even see Clara at first, sitting there on the floor.

"Get back in here, Ruth. We're going to finish this."

Nathan's voice, strung tight.

"I wasn't *doing* anything with them," Ruth shouts. "Why can't you just accept that?"

"Because it's not the point."

Nathan emerges from the studio. From Clara's vantage point she can see his shirttail hanging out from the back of his suit jacket. Ruth wheels around and glares at him. Her mouth is trembling with rage.

"What *is* the point, Nate? What made you think you had the right to go through my work?"

"Because I knew you were lying to me!" Nathan shouts.

"I had to lie to you! You gave me no choice!"

"Bullshit, Ruth. You could have stopped. You promised you would stop. We both agreed that—"

"Please." The word bubbles up from inside Clara—no more than a whisper.

"I wasn't planning to show the work," Ruth goes on. "Kubovy hasn't even seen it."

"Oh, *Kubovy* hasn't seen it," Nate says. "Well, I guess everything's fine, then."

It is as if Clara is in a terrible magical bubble. She can see and hear her parents, but she is invisible to them. She holds a hand in front of her face, flexing her fingers. Why can't they see her?

"Did you ever stop and think, Ruth? Or are you just too fucking selfish to—"

*"Please."* Clara says it a little louder this time.

They both wheel around and look down at her.

"Oh, baby," Ruth says, stricken.

The two of them—Ruth and Nathan, who in this, at least, are completely, utterly together—crouch down so they're face-to-face with Clara.

"We're sorry, honey, you shouldn't have—"

"Please," Clara repeats. It seems to be the only word she knows.

"Please what, sweetheart? Talk to us. Tell us—anything."

"Please." She pushes past the lump in her throat. "Don't fight."

⬥•◆•⬥

IT HAS BEEN so many years since Ruth's dining room has been used for dining that it has become an extension of her office. The table itself—a Nakashima covered by thick protective pads—is piled with the overflow of magazines and newspapers from the foyer. A stack of recent invitations to gallery openings hasn't even made it into the studio. It seems that Peony's responsibilities now revolve solely around Ruth's book; she has gone from intern to nursemaid to secretary to, now, a kind of glorified personal assistant whom Ruth can't live—or die—without.

Clara removes the piles, one by one, and hands them to Jonathan, who stacks them neatly in a corner next to the sideboard.

"Sammy, can you give me a hand with these?"

Old coffee-stained issues of *Harper's, The Atlantic Monthly,* and *The New York Review of Books,* some of them dating back to 1998. Ruth could never bear to part with anything, not even a bunch of magazines. Maybe she really believed that one rainy day she'd sit down and read all these back issues, cover to cover.

"Why don't we just throw them out?" Sammy asks.

Clara stops thumbing through a *Harper's* essay about the first Gulf

War, suddenly struck by the thought that, yes, she could indeed take these piles and walk them down the hall to the incinerator. She could do this—and Ruth would never know.

Her stomach lurches, a queasy excitement.

"You're absolutely right, Sammy," she says.

Jonathan is standing there, a big stack of old pale-pink *New York Observers* in his arms.

"Let's start with those." Clara eyes them.

"Are you sure?" Jonathan asks. "We can just—"

"Oh, I'm sure," says Clara. Suddenly she feels a high degree of certainty. No, more than that: a near-euphoric clarity. This, at least, she can do. She can purge her mother's apartment of all that is unnecessary. She can remove every single unessential thing.

They march out of the dining room—the three Brodeurs—past Peony, who has just come in from some no-doubt urgent errand, carrying her ever-present black portfolio.

"What are you guys doing?" she asks.

Clara searches Peony's tone for an edge, a hint of judgment.

"Throwing out some of these old papers and stuff," Clara says. "They were really piling up."

"Don't you think we should . . ." Peony trails off.

"What?" Clara asks sharply. There it is—she knew it—that reflexive loyalty to Ruth. Peony, who doesn't have the slightest idea. Peony, the champion of All Things Ruth. *She wasn't your mother!*

"I mean," Peony falters, "don't you think we should use the recycling bags?"

"Oh," says Clara. "Right."

She shifts the pile of magazines she's carrying to one hip, then uses her free hand to open the door. The garbage room is only a dozen steps or so down the corridor. Five trips—each of them carrying as many teetering piles as they can handle—and the dining room actually begins to resemble a place where a family might eat dinner.

Robin, Ed, and the kids show up a little after seven o'clock, carrying two bulging plastic bags full of Chinese food. Harrison and Tucker are still in their tennis whites, fresh from their weekly lesson, and Elliot is wearing her Brearley jumper.

"Sorry we're late," Robin says.

"You're not—"

"General Tsao's chicken," says Ed, walking with the bags into the kitchen. "Sesame noodles, crispy orange beef, and that stuff with the pancakes, what do you call it?"

"Ed." Jonathan shakes Ed's hand. "Good to see you."

Sammy stands next to Jonathan, her eyes darting from one cousin to the next to the next. Who are these children and how can they be—how can they possibly be—related to her? Something around the eyes, the shapes of their faces; they look familiar. They have the same grandmother. And they had the same grandfather, though none of them ever knew him. This, at least, they share.

"Harrison, Tucker, Elliot," Robin says, "this is your cousin Samantha."

One by one, Robin's kids shake Sammy's hand as if she's a bride on a receiving line. Clara's stomach churns at the formality of their gesture. In another life, these children might have played together every weekend: Frisbee in Central Park, movies on Sunday afternoons. And holidays—all the holidays: Christmas, Thanksgiving, Halloween. As it is, it's taken days to arrange this visit. She's practically had to beg Robin. *She wants to meet her cousins. Please, Rob. Whatever's between us, let's not infect our children with it.* Clara shuts her eyes for a second. She should have reached out before. All these years—there must have been a way, but which she had never found, to give her daughter some piece of her family. And now, here is Sammy, already her own little person, trying to make sense of the fact that there are three of them and one of her. Never has she looked so small and alone.

Clara is about to swoop in, try to make it better, when the oldest, Tucker, says, "Hey, do you guys want to play Monopoly? I think Grandma has a game in the other room."

"Okay."

They all troop out, Sammy swept up in the group. She has a look on her face that Clara recognizes. The thinnest veneer of pride. She has cousins now.

Robin is rummaging through the refrigerator. From behind, in her low-slung jeans and cashmere sweater, she looks like she could be sixteen.

"So what's going on with Ruth?" she asks.

"She woke up once," Clara says. "She was in a lot of pain. I gave her more morphine."

"Did you talk to her about the help situation?"

"She wasn't in any shape to discuss it."

Robin turns to the Chinese food. She places the white paper cartons on the kitchen counter, lining them up according to size. Clara can see a small vein in her temple throbbing.

"We should have ordered from Shun Lee," Robin says.

"It doesn't matter," Clara says.

"Of course, it doesn't matter. I'm just saying."

The kids voices rise and fall; Clara strains to hear Sammy. They're in the living room. It seems that Clara and Robin's old Monopoly board, amazingly still intact, is the great equalizer. The language of Boardwalk and Park Place, Short Line Railroad and Jail—*No, I want to be the banker!*—sliding them easily past any awkwardness.

"Can I get you a drink?" Clara hears Ed ask Jonathan, as if Ruth's apartment is his own. They're with the kids in the living room, next to the liquor cabinet, which probably hasn't been opened in years.

"Excellent idea." Jonathan's voice, sounding forcefully cheerful.

The bonhomie of men with nothing in common—just like the children—looking for a way to connect. Snatches of conversation drift into the kitchen, where Clara and Robin are setting out the plates and silverware, buffet-style. *Are you a bourbon man? She has some Knob Creek in here.* Clara expects they'll be talking about sports next.

"Robin." Clara takes advantage of a moment alone with her sister. "We need to make some sort of schedule."

"Aren't we using chopsticks?"

"There aren't enough."

"Be sure to put out a plate for Peony," Robin says.

"Of course," says Clara. Peony's entrenchment has gone a step further, from glorified assistant to member of the family.

Did Robin not hear her?

"A schedule," Clara says again.

"What do you mean?"

"I don't know, maybe switching off nights staying with Mom—"

"Not possible."

"What do you mean?"

Robin crosses her arms, as if prepared to make a closing statement. "I have three children. And an incredibly demanding job."

"I didn't realize this was a contest," Clara says. She tries to keep her voice mild, her face expressionless.

"Believe me, I'm not competing with you, Clara. I'm just stating the facts."

Despite the best efforts of cosmetic dermatology, small areas of Robin's face show signs of stress: the ever-present throbbing in her temple, a small, almost imperceptible twitch below her left eye.

"So you expect me to stay here every night with Sam and Jonathan?"

"I don't expect anything. I'm just telling you what my limits are."

"Then we need to find somebody," Clara says. "I'm not going to be able to—" Her voice cracks. "I mean, there's no way I can handle it."

There, she's said it.

"No way," she repeats, for emphasis.

"I can help." Peony appears—as she always seems to—out of nowhere. She has floated into the kitchen on her little cat feet.

"No!" Clara blurts out. "I mean, it's not your job."

"I don't mind."

"That's very kind of you, Peony," says Robin. "But it's not appropriate. Clara's right. We need to get the agency to send someone."

"Mom's not going to stand for it," says Clara.

"She's not going to have a choice," says Robin. She rolls her neck from side to side, trying to release tension. "Anyway, pretty soon it won't matter. She won't know the difference."

"That's true." Clara pauses. "How long before that happens, do you think?"

"How can you talk about her like that?" Peony's cheeks have turned bright red, the first time Clara has seen her betray any emotion whatsoever.

"Excuse me?" Robin turns to her.

"How can you talk about Ruth like she's just some . . . I don't know . . . some piece of garbage?"

Robin and Clara stand shoulder to shoulder. Clara can feel a force field of heat around her sister's body.

"I'm going to pretend you didn't just say that," Robin says.

"No, hold on a minute," says Peony. "Do you both realize what an amazing—I mean, she's a role model for a whole generation of—"

"A role model," Clara repeats.

"Yes." Peony seems to have grown two inches taller. She squares her shoulders, buoyed by the full force of her self-righteous indignation.

"She was—she is—our mother," says Robin. She's speaking very softly now, as if to a young child.

"That's what I'm saying!" Peony cries out. "How can you not understand how lucky you are?"

———◆◆◆◆———

THE KUBOVY WEISS GALLERY—in the dead center of the
1980s—was on the Rolodex of every Wall Street investment banker
and bond salesman looking for a creative way to spend whatever was
left over of his year-end bonus after buying the Porsche and the house
in the Hamptons. Clara sometimes wondered what would have happened to Ruth's career if she had been working in a different place
and time: Nebraska, say, in the 1950s, or Paris at the turn of the cen-
tury. Would the strange, explosive confluence of subject matter, art
form, and marketplace have come together some other way to turn
Ruth into a star?

No, of course not, and a silly game to play, though still she plays
it: *What if?*

What if there hadn't been so much money floating around New
York just as Ruth was immersed in the Clara Series?

What if Kubovy hadn't known exactly how to stoke the egos of
young bankers: accompanying them to auctions, commending them
on their good taste, inviting them to candlelit dinners at his SoHo
loft that were then written up in *Vanity Fair*?

And what if—speaking of *Vanity Fair*—Ruth hadn't been quite so
beautiful, quite so alluringly photogenic herself?

If it is possible to pick a moment, a single moment when the balance tipped forever in the life and career of Ruth Dunne—another
useless exercise—it might very well be the long-anticipated opening
of Ruth's new work at Kubovy Weiss.

It's a sultry night in early summer. Town cars and limos are lined
up outside of Kubovy's new space—he has moved a few blocks north
to a huge loftlike gallery on West Broadway between Prince and
Spring—and there are photographers, paparazzi types, lurking outside the glass doors, waiting to see who'll show up. Rumor has it that
Ruth Dunne has become a bit of a Hollywood darling, collected

by studio heads and actors. Dennis Hopper owns at least three Dunnes, and Angelica Huston recently bought *Clara with the Lizard* at auction.

Kubovy, of course, has milked Ruth's year of vanishing for all it's worth. Ruth's newest photographs in the Clara Series have come, according to the press materials,

> out of a deepening sense of the fragility of motherhood. Witness the centerpiece of this series, *Clara in the Shroud.* The photograph—technically masterful—has an ominous, other-worldly glow, and the child is presumed to be dead. Is this a parental nightmare? A terrible fantasy? We are left to ponder multiple layers of meaning which have grown exponentially during Dunne's time of pulling back and reflection.

"Well, will you look at that."

Nathan whistles under his breath as they round the corner from Prince onto West Broadway and see the crowd already spilling from the doors of Kubovy Weiss. They are fashionably late for Ruth's opening: A quick drink at Da Silvano spiraled into two drinks for Ruth and three for Nate. Ruth stumbles as her high heel catches in a grate, then rights herself. Clara and Robin exchange a look. At eleven and thirteen they are old enough to understand that their parents— who rarely drink—are already tipsy before they even get to the opening.

"Kubovy said there might be a crowd," says Ruth. Her tone is weary, but Clara knows she's just pretending. "Maybe even some Hollywood people."

All day, Ruth has been humming under her breath, something she only does when she's in a state of excited anticipation. Ruth spent most of the afternoon figuring out what to wear. She pulled dresses, pants, silk blouses, and camisoles from her bedroom closet, trying on outfit after outfit. The faded blue jeans and black silk blouse she's wearing now, the seemingly careless way her hair is gathered into a loose ponytail, the slash of berry-colored lipstick on her otherwise bare face—there is nothing accidental about the way Ruth looks tonight as they walk through the strobe of paparazzi flashbulbs.

"Ruth, darling!"

"Over here, my love!"

"Clara! Clara, look over here!"

One photographer—a guy in a T-shirt and tan vest—steps in front of Ruth and Clara, angling his body to be sure that Nathan and Robin are out of the picture.

"Excuse me." Nathan pushes him to the side.

"Hey!"

"Get away from my family," Nathan says.

The photographer keeps pressing.

"Just one more," he says. "Come on, Clara, let me see your face."

A curtain of hair has fallen over Clara's eyes, and she likes it that way. She won't push it to the side. She's just going to stay like this all night, hiding inside a cave of her own making. She can feel Robin next to her: rigid, angry, a little bit frightened. Clara can always tell what's going on with Robin. *I'm sorry,* she wants to say. But she can't apologize, she knows she can't. *It's not my fault.* But she can't say that either. She's not even sure if it's true. So instead, she turns and whispers in her sister's ear.

"It's okay. Don't be scared."

But then Nathan shoves the photographer harder this time, and the guy staggers back a couple of steps, banging himself on the steel gallery door.

"I could sue you for that, you motherfucker," the photographer shouts.

Nate smiles his best attorney smile.

"Go ahead," he says.

"Stop it, Nate," Ruth says through clenched teeth. "I know this is hard, but please—"

"There you are!" Kubovy comes outside, a plastic cup of white wine in one hand and a price list for the show in the other. He pays no attention to the photographer, as if scuffles with the paparazzi are a regularly occurring event outside his gallery.

"Kubovy, what's going on?" Ruth asks, as Kubovy ushers them through the crush of the people by the front door.

"Isn't it obvious? You're *huge*," Kubovy says to her.

He hands the price list to Nate.

"Here, take a look at this," Kubovy says. "Your wife—I'm not even sure I can explain it. People are going insane for this work."

Nathan holds the list at arm's length, squinting. Lately his eyesight has been getting worse. His face registers nothing: not surprise, not excitement.

"What?" Ruth asks impatiently. "What does it say, Nate?"

All around them, Clara notices, people are watching them in that way very particular to New Yorkers who find themselves around celebrity. *I'm not really noticing you.* Their eyes slide past with only a flicker of recognition. *I'm not impressed.*

"Kubovy has raised your prices." Nate gives the list to Ruth.

Ruth inhales sharply as she stares at the laminated paper. Clara can see all the red dots indicating another sold-out show.

"What did you do, Kubovy?"

"It's simply what the market will bear, my dear." Kubovy pauses. He pulls off his glasses and wipes them with a handkerchief. "You now have a wait list more than fifty people long."

Nathan moves away from them all, walking over to the wide expanse of wall where *Clara in the Shroud* hangs by itself. He's seen it, of course. He saw it in Ruth's studio that day, months earlier. But that was a small image on a contact sheet. Nothing like this—blown up, almost life-sized.

His back is curved like an old man's as he looks at the photograph, lit and displayed to perfection. In just three years, he will slump over his desk with little more than a sigh. He will die instantly—*never knew what hit him.* But for now he examines the photograph, which has sold out its printing at $60,000: the darkness of the park, the articulation of the dead leaves even within that darkness—and the ghostly paleness of the girl in the cocoon. Is she a corpse? Is she a moth in a chrysalis, waiting to turn into a butterfly?

Nathan runs a hand through his thinning hair. Then he looks back at Clara, who has been watching him. She knows—even at the age of eleven, she knows—what he wants from her, what he can never dare ask. He wants her to know that he stayed for her. That had he left, he would have been embroiled in a custody battle so public and so ugly that it might have destroyed both of them. He has made a choice: these scars, not those.

*I understand.* She tries to tell him with everything she has. *I forgive you.* It radiates from her every pore, from her skin, the backs of her eyes.

# Chapter Ten

*NOT A PROBLEM. I'll take her to the park.* That's what Peony had said. *You guys go ahead.* Still, Clara wasn't sure. *Sammy? Do you want to come with us?* But Sam was thrilled—beyond thrilled—to stay with Peony. The object of her little girl's crush.

Certainly, it wasn't unprecedented. Ruth's interns had often doubled as babysitters for Clara and Robin throughout their childhood, an endless parade of them. Every fall, as the academic schedules of Parsons, Pratt, the School of Visual Arts, the New School, and Columbia got under way, an eighteen-year-old intern would be deposited on the doorstep of Ruth Dunne's studio like an infant swaddled in a blanket.

Nina, Aimee, Lois, Mathilde, April, Beth. They spent hours playing endless games of Sorry! and Candy Land with Clara and Robin. They took them to the very same playground in Central Park where Peony is now—right now, as Clara and Jonathan walk the streets of SoHo—hanging out with Sam.

A poetic symmetry or a gross abuse of young talent, depending on how you look at it.

"I don't know," Jonathan says. They're standing in front of Fragments, the jewelry boutique in SoHo that had been so interested in his work five years earlier. "It's been a long time."

"It can't hurt to go in and ask," Clara says.

"You're supposed to make an appointment for this sort of thing."

"I know. But you brought your stuff."

"Who knows if the same buyer is even there?"

She looks at him. Trying to let him know—it's too hard for her to say it—how aware she is that she's held him back. She's kept herself invisible, yes. And along with herself, she has slowly erased Jonathan from the landscape. He shouldn't be selling his work only out of a small seasonal shop in Maine. His jewelry should be here, in the heart of the active world.

"Let's go," she says. Opening the door.

Inside the boutique, there are two horseshoe-shaped glass cases filled with every well-known jewelry designer: Mallory Marks, Cathy Waterman, Renee Lewis, Malcolm Betts. Delicate platinum-and-diamond bracelets of woven leaves and vines. Tougher hammered-gold rings with unusual stones—pink sapphires, yellow diamonds. Beautiful mesh necklaces, light as gossamer.

Jonathan's work belongs here—she's always known it. His pieces have an angularity and elegance, and at the same time somehow feel rough and alive. Of the earth that made them. JONATHAN BRODEUR. Next to these established names. Out there. Visible. Two blocks from the gallery that turned Ruth Dunne into a star.

"Can I help you?" A skinny guy with sculpted jet-black hair that stands straight up from his head.

"I was wondering if Julie Becker is in," Jonathan asks.

"She's here. Do you have an appointment?"

"No, but we spoke a while back and—"

"She's very busy."

The guy stares at Jonathan for a moment. Assessing. What does he see? The wild gray hair. The shirt—one of Jonathan's nicest ones—from the Eddie Bauer catalog. His bright blue eyes—confident, easygoing. Clara knows he must be nervous inside, but he doesn't show it.

"Let me see what I can do," the guy says. "What's your name?"

"Jonathan Brodeur."

He disappears behind a closed door in the back of the boutique. Jonathan lets out a sigh. Is he angry at Clara? He must feel something about all the lost years—well, not really lost, but still he put his ambitions on hold. He lowered his sights. Portland, Maine. A small crafts place in the Back Bay. Shops in university towns: Madison, Ann Arbor. But he stayed away from the big leagues for Clara. He decided—it must have been a conscious decision—that the risk to her wasn't worth it.

She rests her head on his shoulder as he looks at some necklaces hanging in a case against the wall. Feathers on leather strands. The less expensive stuff.

"Jonathan?"

An attractive woman in a floaty black ensemble—do all New York women wear black?—walks over, hand outstretched.

"You finally made it!"

"Hi there, Julie." Jonathan shakes her hand. "This is my wife, Clara."

"Did you bring samples?" Julie gets right to business.

"I did," Jonathan says. Opening his knapsack. Pulling out one silk pouch after another. "I did indeed."

Julie takes the pouches to a table in back and opens them onto a black velvet board. The freshwater pearl earrings with dangling teardrops of angel skin coral. The hammered-gold bracelet, slices of watermelon tourmalines imbedded into each link. The brown diamond necklace, tiny stones strung together on an oxidized chain.

She puts on a pair of tortoiseshell glasses that had been hanging around her neck. She lifts up the brown diamond necklace, cupping it in her hand, weighing it. Examining it.

Jonathan is watching, trying to read her. His face is pinker than usual.

She holds the pearl earrings up to the light. Nods. What does nodding mean? Jonathan gives Clara a quick, nervous look.

Julie studies each piece slowly and doesn't speak until she's finished.

"Great stuff," she finally says. "Really great."

"Thanks." Jonathan inhales sharply. Trying not to show his relief.

"I've always known I was going to love your work."

She pushes back from the table and folds her arms.

"So how many pieces can I have for summer?"


It's the middle of the afternoon by the time they get back uptown. Clara has been so immersed in Jonathan's news that she actually hasn't thought about her daughter for a couple of hours. Twelve pieces to start. Great placement in the front counter. Jonathan's name included in group ads. Clara and Jonathan stopped for a beer. Sat in an outdoor café on West Broadway, just across the street from the old Kubovy Weiss Gallery, which was now a new gallery full of Leroy Neiman prints and old movie posters. *See? I can be here. I can do this,* she thought to herself. *It's all different.*

Now they are back at Ruth's apartment. A sparkly pair of sneakers—the only pair of shoes Sammy brought on this trip—by the front door. So they're not in the park. Maybe Sam got tired and Peony brought her home.

"Hello?" Clara calls. Feeling suddenly cold. "Hello?"

"In here!" A voice calls from the living room. Peony's voice.

Sam and Peony are sitting side by side on the sofa facing the fireplace, a large book open between them.

"What are you guys—"

The very sight of Peony sitting so close to her daughter—Peony's dark hair pulled messily into a clip, her small pretty face, skinny jeans, and thick-soled boots—makes Clara uneasy. It's as if the girl has slowly morphed into a modern-day Ruth. She blinks sleepily up at Clara.

"Mom, look at this!" Sam tilts the book so that it catches the light.

It hadn't occurred to Clara. It really hadn't—and the shock of it causes her to take a step back, nearly tripping. She can see the spread of two photographs, even from this vantage point—*Clara with the Pumpkins; Clara, Hanging*—how is it possible? The book isn't supposed to be published for months.

"The bound page proofs," Peony says proudly, as if she had bound them herself. "They just arrived from Steiffel this morning."

"Is that so."

"Yeah—and they look so amazing. Do you want to see?"

"Um—no."

Does Peony somehow not hear the edge in Clara's voice, or is she merely ignoring it? It's impossible to tell.

"Ruth hasn't looked at them yet; she's been sleeping. I'm just so happy that Steiffel got these to us while she's still—"

Peony stops, finally seeming to take in the fact that Clara hasn't moved a muscle.

"I mean—" She falters. "I called them last week to see if they could rush—"

"How thoughtful of you." Blood is pounding between Clara's ears. "I'm sure my mother will appreciate the gesture."

"What's wrong, Mom?" Sammy asks.

The contrast between the two girls—the false guile of the older one and the genuine guile of the younger—is so stark that Clara has to restrain herself from striding across the room and grabbing Peony by her black Rolling Stones T-shirt. *Who the fuck do you think you are?*

"This should have been my choice," Clara says. Staring at Peony. Her voice cold. "Whether or not I wanted to show my daughter—and when. You had absolutely no right to—"

She feels Jonathan's hand on her back, warm through her shirt. Steadying her. *Not in front of Sammy. What's done is done.*

Clara stops. She flashes one more withering glance at Peony—she wants the girl to melt down into her thick rubber-soled boots and disappear. Is she actually malicious? Or just young and stupid?

"I'd better check on Ruth," Clara says. But she's not going to leave Sam sitting on the sofa next to Peony, not for another second. She forces her voice to soften. "Sammy, why don't you come with me?"

Peony closes the book. Clara can see the front cover of the page proofs. The wavy hair, the braided rug, the close-up of her face. The black paper sash running across the image, obscuring her nakedness. The black paper sash—CLARA—like a mourner's armband.


Ruth's head is turned away from the door. Her chest rises and falls beneath the covers, accompanied by the high-pitched wheezing that has become part of her every breath. It's impossible to tell, from the doorway, whether she's awake or asleep.

Sammy precedes Clara around the hospital bed—she's unafraid, matter-of-fact in the face of this wasting away—and softly whispers, "Grandma?"

A thin stream of drool runs from the side of Ruth's mouth down to the pillow, where it has created a damp spot.

"Grandma?"

Something is happening behind Ruth's eyes. A consciousness. A flutter.

"Sweetie, maybe we should just let Grandma rest," Clara says.

This is the best it can be, for now: Ruth, seemingly not in pain, unconscious.

"No." A very small voice, muffled by the pillow.

The eyes struggle to open and make it halfway. Clara swears Ruth's dark brown eyes have become lighter these past few weeks— they appear to be a yellowish green—as if she is being scrubbed away, bit by bit.

Ruth's gaze rests on Sammy. She blinks a few times, as if trying to clear her vision—as if perhaps she's imagining the girl leaning over the iron rail of her bed.

"Is that you, sweetheart?"

"Yes, it's me," Sammy says in a whisper.

"I'm so happy to see you, darling."

"Me too."

"How long has it been?"

Ruth reaches a shaky hand up to stroke Sammy's bare arm. They're in their own little zone. Protected, impenetrable.

"I've missed you so."

Sammy looks across the bedroom at Clara, her face clouded by confusion. She just saw her grandmother this morning. What does Ruth mean?

"I saw your book, Grandma," Sammy says. "It's really beautiful."

Clara swallows hard, past the lump in her throat. Sammy thinks the photographs are beautiful.

"What book?" Ruth asks. Her voice weak.

"Your—"

"Come closer, my darling girl."

Sammy moves her face even closer to Ruth's. The afternoon light catches the peach fuzz on her smooth cheeks. Her eyes are a clear amber brown.

"I want to tell you something," Ruth says.

"What?" Sammy's hands are wrapped around the rail. She's all ears, hanging on to Ruth's every word.

"I want to say—" Ruth stares at Sam intensely. Too intensely. She struggles to lift her head from the pillow.

*Give them room,* Clara thinks to herself as she watches her mother and her daughter. Fighting the urge to pull Sammy from Ruth's bed, to drag her out of this room and away from whatever comes next.

"I know that I hurt you," Ruth goes on.

"What do you—what do you mean?" Sam stammers.

"I mean, I'm an artist. You understand me, Clara."

*Jesus Christ. She thinks—*

Clara takes a step toward Sam. But then she stops. She can't help it. She wants to hear more.

"Sometimes—" Ruth is starting to lose her voice. "Sometimes I think—" Every word is costing her something. A tear leaks out of the corner of her rheumy eye and trickles down the side of her face.

"It's me, Grandma," Sam bursts out. "It's me. Sam."

Sammy is a little scared now. Ruth doesn't seem to hear her.

"Forgive me," Ruth says.

Sammy doesn't know what to do. She searches Clara's face for an answer, but Clara—Clara is crying too hard.

"Grandma, I— It's not—"

Ruth reaches a hand out once more and holds Sammy's forearm.

"Please. Just say you will."

Sam is silent. Her face is bathed in the golden light streaming in from the west-facing windows. Who is she—to Ruth? Is she *Clara in the Shroud*? *Clara in the Fountain*? *Clara, Hanging*? Does she look like the artist's model? Or the artist's daughter?

Clara looks at her mother. Ruth's eyes are glued to Sammy's face. Waiting—waiting for something that doesn't come. After a few moments, Ruth's lids drift slowly down. Her breath deepens. Her chest rattles as she falls back into the netherworld between sleep and death.

◄•••►

THE SEVENTH GRADE at Brearley. The seventh grade anywhere, really—but more so at certain New York City private schools: Brearley, Spence, Chapin, Fieldston, Riverdale, Dalton. These schools have always had their own special version of early adolescence. Girls whose mothers take them to Eres on Madison for their first bras. Girls who pay a visit to their mother's dermatologist at the sight of their first pimple—as if that teenage rite of passage, acne, can be fixed like everything else if only you know where to go. Girls who seem to sparkle through their most awkward of ages, with clear skin and straight teeth, shiny hair, and lovely little bras beneath their school uniforms—whatever turmoil, if any, well hidden beneath their preternaturally polished exteriors.

Not so Clara. She is beautiful, yes—no one can deny that—but she has a face that shows her feelings. A face that registers every embarrassment, every slight. Every single moment she wishes the floor would open up beneath her and allow her to just . . . disappear. There are daughters of movie stars at Brearley, daughters of politicians, even daughters of white-collar criminals whose names have been splashed across tabloid front pages—but none of these girls incites quite the swell of whispers and murmurs that surround Clara like a rustling breeze wherever she goes.

It's the piece in *Vogue* that tips the balance. *Vogue,* the one magazine that every Brearley mother reads without fail. Had the photographic essay on the work of Ruth Dunne appeared in *Bazaar* or *The Atlantic Monthly* or even *Newsweek,* at least some people would have missed it. Or had the essay been done years before, when Clara was still a little girl, perhaps her friends would not have noticed. But twelve-year-olds are not known for their kindness toward each other. They are not about to look the other way.

So when the first dog-eared copy of the September *Vogue*—featuring a blond model in faded jeans and a Christian Lacroix jacket on its cover—makes its way into the halls of Brearley, it doesn't take long for the chain of whispers to extend all the way back to Clara. She hasn't heard about the essay—Ruth neglected to mention it—but Clara does know that, whatever the gossip, it somehow has to do with her.

Elizabeth Ridgeway is the first to say it straight to her. Elizabeth, whose nickname is Buffy and whose father owns a football team—Clara has never paid attention to which one. Buffy's lank brown hair falls halfway across her face. She peers at Clara curiously with one unobscured eye.

"So how does it feel?" she asks.

Clara hugs her books to her chest.

"How does what feel?"

"You know," Buffy says, braces glinting.

"No, I don't." Clara feels herself beginning to flush. She tries to think cool thoughts. Ice cubes. Air-conditioning. A freezing lake. Even though she doesn't yet know what she's supposed to feel—or what it's about—she doesn't want Buffy to see her squirm.

Buffy bends down, rummages through her knapsack, and pulls the copy of the magazine out from between her French and algebra textbooks. She thumbs through it, frowning. Clara sees a blur of color—perfume ads, fashion spreads, glistening lips, kohl-rimmed eyes—until Buffy stops on a page that is black-and-white. She thrusts it at Clara.

"Here," she says. "This."

The double-page spread that opens the essay has three photos and very little text. The first image is a recent one: after *Clara in the Shroud,* Ruth became interested in covering parts of Clara but leaving other parts exposed. In this one—Clara has never seen it before, though of course she remembers posing for it—she is lying in bed, a rumpled sheet pulled in what appears to be a haphazard way across her body, her chest—the very beginning of her prepubescent breasts— exposed. Her eyes closed, grimacing. Her arms trapped beneath the sheet.

"It looks like you're . . ." Buffy trails off.

"What?" Clara asks. Honestly, she has no idea.

"You know."

"Will you stop saying that?"

The heat is rising up Clara's neck to her cheeks. She feels herself blushing. Now there's nothing she can do about it.

Buffy leans forward. Her breath tickles Clara's ear.

"Masturbating," she says.

Clara's hand flies to her mouth. She's heard about that—she's never done it, not yet anyway—but now, when she looks at the enormous photograph of herself on page 246 of the September *Vogue*, that's all she can see. Her hands beneath the sheets. That look on her face. What was it Ruth had said that day? *Try to look like something is hurting you, Clara. That's right. Close your eyes. Beautiful. Just like that.*

Buffy shakes her head, as if she is truly sorry.

"I thought you knew," she said.

She tries to pry the magazine from Clara's hands.

"No," Clara says. She grips it tighter.

"Come on. It's mine—give it back to me."

"No!"

"I stole it from my mother. You have to give it back!"

Other girls are starting to look at them. Clara stands her ground. Sweat is pouring down her back, but she doesn't let go.

Finally, Buffy releases the magazine. She lifts her chin slightly. Even though she's shorter than Clara, she appears to be looking down at her.

"Fine," she says, with a small, closed smile. "That's fine. There are millions and millions of others."

---

CLARA SINKS to the living-room floor, her back against the soft velvet of the sofa. Her favorite spot. How could she have forgotten? The threadbare oriental, worn in the same patches. The bit of missing fringe. She was three years old here. She was four, seven, twelve, sixteen. The space between the sofa and coffee table. Near the fireplace. A haven. A warren. A place to burrow and be safe.

She closes her eyes against the swirling images. *God almighty, Ruth!* Clara hears her father's voice. *Look outside of yourself for once!*

The ghosts of Nate and Ruth of decades past, standing just on the other side of the coffee table. Ruth, her hair sprung from its braid, eyes wild. Her bathrobe hanging halfway open, a breast exposed. Nathan in his navy blue suit—getting ready to leave for the office—afraid to go. Afraid of what might happen. *Promise me.* His voice cracking. *Promise me you'll leave her alone.*

"Here, Mom." Sam sits down next to her. "Here. You should—"

Clara sees what Sammy is carrying. The fucking book again.

"No, Sam. I don't want to."

Jonathan sits down on her other side. She is sandwiched between her husband and her daughter.

"Take a look," Jonathan says. "There's something you should see."

She starts thumbing through the page proofs from the end back toward the beginning. Angry, resentful. Why should she be looking at this? There are no surprises. What could possibly be a surprise? She was there for all the photographs. She had posed for them under bright metered lights. From *Naked at Fourteen* all the way to *Clara with the Lizard.* The narrative of her entire childhood as created by Ruth Dunne. She closes the book. So what? She'll do the best she can to pretend it just doesn't exist.

"You missed something," Sam says.

Her small fingers pry open a page toward the very beginning. The dedication. *To Clara and Robin,* in the center of the page, and then simply the words, *Without whom.*

Without whom? Without whom what? Clara's heart is pounding, skipping beats.

"Excuse me?" Peony appears, as she always seems to do, at the worst possible moment. How does she walk so quietly in those heavy boots?

Clara looks up at her, startled.

"What?"

"I'm worried about Ruth's breathing," Peony says. "I think we should call Rochelle."

Clara checks her watch. "She's due any minute."

Jonathan gets up without a word and quickly walks down the hall toward Ruth's bedroom.

"She's gasping. She's having trouble taking in air." Peony looks stricken. Clara almost feels sorry for her. Almost. Someday, when Peony is a famous photographer herself, she will be interviewed about her time in the household of Ruth Dunne. She will speak with authority, mincing no words. *Her daughters just couldn't see Ruth for who she really was. Her genius was lost on them.*

Clara pulls Sammy close to her. The child is shaking. She shouldn't be here for this, she shouldn't be—

"She's having trouble." Jonathan comes back into the living room. "It's true."

Clara begins to shake herself.

Jonathan sits down next to her, pushing the page proofs aside. He puts his arms around her. She looks up at him—his eyes clear as they have always been.

"Come into the bedroom," Jonathan says.

---

SHE IS FOURTEEN when she figures out a way to break free of her mother. It begins on a rainy afternoon, after school. A group of girls is walking down Lexington Avenue—their destination a soft-serve ice-cream shop—when one of them suggests that they hop on the subway downtown instead. They aren't allowed to do this, of course, which only makes the idea that much more appealing.

"Where are we going?" one of them asks. They are so cosseted uptown. Their neighborhood haunts consist of a soda fountain, a deli, and the park benches along the edges of Central Park, where the more rebellious among them smoke cigarettes and sometimes pot.

"I know," Clara says casually, as they wait for the train under the fluorescent lights of the subway station. Where did the idea come from? It seemed to spring to her mind, fully formed. "I heard about a place where we can get tattoos."

It was true that she had seen a small tattoo on one of Ruth's interns—a tiny bird flying above her ankle—and it was also true that Clara had asked the girl who had done it. A guy on Eighth Street, the girl had told her, and then described the building: a brownstone tucked between some taller buildings, a buzzer with no name, a five-story walk-up. Clara took in these facts and tucked them away for months and months in the back of her mind.

"Oh my God, isn't that illegal? There's no way can I do that," one of her Brearley friends says.

"That's okay," says Clara. "I will."

In the tattoo parlor's waiting area—separated from the room in back by a bright orange curtain—Clara looks over a wall-sized display of designs: birds, flowers, flames, Sanskrit mandalas. It's more expensive than she thought—two hundred dollars cash—but her friends all help her out, pooling their money. The girls are all hyped up, hysterically giggling, but Clara—Clara is calm as can be, just as she was a few months ago, when she walked into her bathroom at home and hacked her hair into an uneven chin-length bob. *What have you done to yourself?* Ruth shrieked when she saw her.

Soon she will dye her hair jet-black. She will pierce her nose. She will try to gain weight, adding heft to her skinny frame.

"This one." She points to a delicate winding vine. "We'll do this around my arm."

"Maybe you should do something smaller," one of her friends says.

"No, this is good."

Her arm. There's pretty much no way to photograph her without her arm being in the picture. This is what she's thinking about as she lies down on the cold hard table covered by white tissue paper. *You sure you're old enough to be doing this?* the guy asks. He knows she's not—but after all, they're talking about degrees of breaking the law. As the thin needle pokes her skin a thousand times, like being stung by a swarm of bees, she concentrates on what Ruth will say.

*You aren't my daughter.*

*I don't recognize you anymore.*

*How could you do this to your beautiful body?*

Clara focuses on the ceiling of the tattoo parlor. The spot where the incongruously floral wallpaper is peeling away from its seams. The framed safety instructions about washing the area with anti-bacterial soap.

By the time she is finished, her whole arm is aching and her friends have left, bored and anxious to get home before dark. She walks slowly down Eighth Street toward the subway. Dusk settles around her. The rush-hour crowd streams past. She pictures the vine, its dark green leaves snaking around her bicep. A thing of permanence. A thing that no one—not even Ruth—can take away.

------•••••------

WHERE IS EVERYBODY? Clara kneels at the side of the hospital bed, her face inches away from Ruth's. She finds herself praying, a murmured jumble of words and phrases. *Our father who art in heaven . . .* then the Hebrew words of the Shema. She's praying for her mother and she's praying for herself, her very posture one of supplication.

"I tried Rochelle on her mobile," says Jonathan. "She must be underground."

Ruth's breath rattles. She's choking—she can't get enough air—but her face is peaceful, as if her brain has disconnected from her physical self. Or so Clara hopes. The sound is awful, terrifying. Please, somebody get Sammy out of here.

"Jonathan?" Clara jerks her head in Sam's direction. "Could you—"

"Don't make me leave," Sammy says. "Please don't make me."

"Robin's on the way," Jonathan says. He's pacing by the foot of Ruth's bed. His face looks soft, open—vulnerable. He's frightened, Clara realizes. They've been preparing and preparing, as if preparation is possible—as if this is a final exam, a tough test they have to pass. They've known Ruth was going to die, but is this it, actually? Is this what dying looks like? Clara has no idea. She reaches for her mother's hand. Tries to remember everything she's read: Sontag, Kübler-Ross, Stephen Mitchell.

"It's okay," she whispers into Ruth's ear. "Just let go."

*Just let go.* What a fucking hypocrite she is. Her head feels like it's going to split open, even as everything around her slows down. Only what is essential remains: breath. A heartbeat. The weak, erratic pulse fluttering beneath Clara's fingertips. *I have hated you for so many years,* she thinks. And then—like an overlay, a transparency on top of the thought—*and I have loved you.*

She lowers the bed's railing and moves even closer to Ruth. Stroking her papery forehead, etched with fine lines—the skin still warm, the blood still flowing—she runs her fingers along the sides of Ruth's face. Her touch is maternal; this is how she touched Sammy as a newborn. With wonder, with an elemental disbelief.

"We have to do something!" Peony's voice, loud, slightly hysterical. She's lurking just outside the bedroom door.

"There's nothing to do," Jonathan says.

But is there? Clara looks wildly around the room. The collection of prescription bottles on the bedside table, the walker, the wheelchair, the commode. *I'm killing her*—she seems to have no control over her thoughts—*it's my fault she's dying.*

In the far distance, the sound of a door opening and closing. An efficient bustle down the hall.

"What's going on?" Rochelle asks, moving quickly to take Ruth's blood pressure, which seems—given the circumstances—beside the point.

"Her breathing," says Jonathan. "It changed about half an hour ago."

Rochelle listens, watching Ruth carefully.

"Can't you help her?"

The hysterical Peony.

"She's not in pain," Rochelle says. She assesses the situation in Ruth's bedroom, then says to Peony, "Come. Come with me."

"But—"

"We need to leave these good folks alone," says Rochelle.

"Sam, go with Rochelle," Clara says.

"Mom? Dad?"

"Come, Sam."

Rochelle quickly takes Sammy by the hand and leads both her and Peony out of the room. Clara can hear them as they move down the hall. *Where are we going?*

"Am I doing the right thing?" Clara turns to Jonathan. "Should Sammy be with—"

"There is no right thing," Jonathan says quietly.

"I don't think Sam should—"

"Then that's your answer."

The choking sound worsens. There's no break in it now, no pause between gulps of breath. Just that endless rattle, like nothing Clara has ever heard.

"I'm here." Robin bursts into the room: breathless, sweaty, her blouse hanging from the waistband of her skirt. "The traffic—I ran all the way from the Sixty-fifth Street transverse."

She walks to the foot of Ruth's bed and looks down at her.

"Oh," she says.

"Come here." Clara turns to her.

Without another word, Robin kneels next to Clara on the floor. They hold hands the way they haven't since they used to cross the street together as little girls. *Quickly! The light is turning red!* They feel the warmth of each other's bodies as they watch their mother fight for air. Jonathan stands behind them, just outside this small closed circle of Dunne women.

"I don't know what to say, Clara," Robin whispers.

"Say goodbye," Clara says softly.

She wonders if her mother can hear her. There is no movement behind her eyes, no crease between her brows. The choking stops.

"Goodbye," Clara says, again and again.

# Chapter Eleven

"It's been taken care of," says Kubovy.

He paces the living room near the windows overlooking Broadway. He has not stopped moving since he walked through the door an hour ago: raking his fingers through his hair, folding and unfolding his arms, shrugging his shoulders. If he were to be still for a moment, he might fall apart. He pulls a pack of clove cigarettes out of his jacket pocket.

"Do you mind?" he asks.

"Yes," Robin snaps. "Our mother just died of lung cancer, for God's sake."

"These don't cause cancer," he says.

"What do you mean, it's been taken care of?" Clara asks. Can they just stay on one subject?

"My dear," says Kubovy, "I called the *Times* months ago."

"How—"

"We want a proper obituary. They like to have a heads-up whenever possible. And the best news, really, is that Roberta Smith wrote it—"

"You called the paper in advance?" Clara asks. Everything is coming slowly to her, as if through a scrim. An obituary has been sitting in some drawer at *The New York Times,* just waiting for Ruth to die?

"What's an obituary?" asks Sammy. She's curled up next to Clara on the sofa. She's said very little since Robin, Clara, and Jonathan emerged from Ruth's bedroom. Since the emergency medical technicians came and carried Ruth out in a zippered plastic body bag. *Where are they taking her, Mom?* Clara wanted to cover Sammy's eyes with her hands. A nine-year-old shouldn't be this close to death. A nine-year-old shouldn't hear the squawk of emergency radios or see the impassive faces of the men who do this for a living. *To the funeral home, darling.*

"It's sort of a short biography," Clara says.

"Only very important people get written about in the *Times* when they die," adds Jonathan.

There it is, the fame thing again. Why does he do this? Frustration and incomprehension rise like a wave inside her, but just then Jonathan's earlier words come floating back. Clara feels them with the force of a revelation: *The worst thing you can do is keep her from knowing you—really knowing you.* And Clara is—no matter how hard she has tried not to be—the famously photographed daughter of a famous mother. Of a famous dead mother. Her mother is dead.

"That's true," she says softly. "Kubovy, do you know if they're running a picture?"

"I would imagine," says Kubovy.

"Which one?"

"We have no control over that."

"She would want a good picture."

"We'll see tomorrow," he says. "It may even make that little box at the bottom of the front page—depending on who else died today."

"Frank Campbell's?" Robin asks, holding her cell phone. "Have we agreed on Frank Campbell's?"

"It's the only place that makes sense," says Clara.

"But Dad's funeral was at Riverside. Don't you think their funerals should be at the same place?"

"Dad was Jewish."

"It just seems weird, that's all."

Clara feels as if she's floating. None of this seems real. It's as if they're all actors in a stage play, reciting the lines they've rehearsed. She gets up off the sofa, goes over to the windows, and cranks them open. The smells in the apartment are suddenly unbearable. The dizzying mixture of disinfectant, peroxide, plastic, metal, and the vaguest hint—perhaps she is imagining it—of decaying flesh.

Below, an ambulance screams by, siren wailing.

Kubovy stands by an open window now, lighting up.

"I thought I asked you not to—" Robin starts, then stops. She closes her eyes for a moment, then shakes her head. A small smile crosses her lips. Clara knows what's going through her sister's mind: Who the fuck cares, really, at a time like this?

"So what else needs to be done right now?" asks Jonathan. He moves behind Clara and hugs her. She very nearly collapses into him.

They all want to *do something*. Anything but stand around here and stare at one another. If they just keep busy with their checklists and phone calls—Robin has already contacted the rental agency to pick up the hospital bed and wheelchair—then they won't have to think. Much less feel.

"I hope she wasn't in pain at the end. I hope she didn't know what was happening."

Peony—who can always be counted on to go straight into the black heart of the matter—has walked out of the kitchen, where she made herself a cup of tea. She blows into it, steam rising around her face.

"I can't believe I wasn't there," says Sammy from the sofa. She says it with a childish naïveté, as if talking about missing the good part of a movie.

Kubovy clears his throat. "There is much to discuss," he says. "The eulogies—we must call Matthew, and James Danziger, and the galleries in Europe—"

"We're not going to have that kind of funeral, Kubovy." Robin's voice is firm.

"What do you mean?" Kubovy blows a thin stream of smoke out the window. "But we must—"

"We'll have a memorial service later on," says Clara. She and Robin have discussed this and are in complete agreement. There will be no line of black town cars blocking traffic on Madison Avenue. No chic art-world crowd who barely knew Ruth using the funeral as a see-and-be-seen occasion. No air-kissing in the aisles.

"Your mother would have wanted—"

"Our mother isn't here," Robin says.

"Didn't you discuss—"

"She never wanted to talk about it," Clara says.

"She didn't think she was going to die," says Robin.

"Ah," says Kubovy. He leans out the window and stubs out his cigarette on the newly pointed brick. "That's where you're wrong."

"What do you mean?"

"Ruth discussed matters with me at great length," says Kubovy.

"Listen," Robin snaps, "we're not having a circus of a funeral, and that's that!"

Kubovy blinks at her slowly, like a sleepy reptile.

"I wasn't talking about the funeral, my dear." He crosses the room and sinks into the wing chair by the fireplace, finally exhausted. "I was talking about the way your mother left things."

"Her will? She's been dead for two hours, Kubovy," Clara says. "Could we please just—"

"What?" Robin interrupts. All attorney. "What were you going to say?"

Kubovy colors slightly as he looks around the room at all of them—Peony, Jonathan, Robin, Clara, Sam—as if it has just occurred to him that perhaps this isn't the moment to start talking business.

"Never mind," he says. "We have plenty of time."

"No, Kubovy. You can't just come out with something like that and then drop it."

"Robin," Clara says. "Robin, let's not—"

"I want to know," Robin says. She stares at Kubovy, her chin quivering. "How badly did she screw us?"

"Robin! Not in front of—"

Kubovy shakes his head sadly, as if he's observing this from a great distance and feels sorry for the whole lot of them.

"With all due respect, you have no idea what you're talking about," he says.

"Then tell us."

Clara feels a queasy embarrassment on Robin's behalf. Why is she fixating on this? Why now, when their mother's body isn't even in the ground?

"We will make an appointment to talk about it," Kubovy says. "After the funeral."

———◆◆◆◆▶———

THERE WAS A *BEFORE,* though she hardly remembers it: before *Clara with the Lizard,* before every breeze sounded like a whisper, before a strange harsh light descended upon the Dunne family, capturing them forever in its glare.

An autumn weekend in Hillsdale. Clara is not quite three. Weekends are distinguished from the other days of the week, in her preschooler's mind, by the fact that both parents are home from work. Nathan is not at the office until midnight, trying to make partner. Ruth is not racing out the door, her canvas tote bag heavy with equipment and books, late to catch the train to her teaching job at Bard. For these two short days, Clara and Robin have their parents all to themselves.

But not today. Today, Clara is playing with her Legos—was she building a birdhouse?—when she hears her father say something about company coming over.

"Oh, no, Nate!" her mother says. "Please, not another one of these goddamn business lunches."

A quick shared glance at Clara, playing there. *Whoops.* They're not that kind of parents, the kind who curse in front of their children. Except Clara is so young. Clara doesn't say much, and certainly any small household tensions are bound to go over her head. Ruth and Nathan are both in their twenties, practically still kids themselves. They can be forgiven for not understanding that Clara absorbs every word.

"It's not like that, Ruth."

Ruth's hands are busy. She has taken to baking on the weekends— pastries, breads, cookies, pies—and right now her palms are covered with flour as she kneads a piece of dough. She lets out a huge sigh. Clara doesn't know how her mother can have that much air inside of her.

"You don't get it. You just don't get it. I have nothing in common with these people."

"First of all, just because they're lawyers doesn't mean that you should dismiss them out of hand," Nathan says. "And anyway, that's not what—"

Ruth stops kneading the dough. She slaps her hands against her apron, releasing a small cloud of flour.

"How do you think it feels," she says slowly, "to be asked if I'm still doing that photography thing. Like what I do is some sort of hobby that I might have moved on from. Like—I don't know—needlepoint."

"That's not what they mean, Ruth. They just don't know what to say to you. They're not used to talking to artists."

"Well, it makes me feel bad. All they care about is money—and since my work isn't in some big gallery and they've never heard of me, they just dismiss me. You should see their eyes glaze over."

Ruth's barrette has come undone. Her hair falls across her face, and she swipes it away.

"Listen, this is silly," says Nate. He walks over to Ruth and rubs her shoulders from behind. "I invited a new client for lunch. I know it's last-minute, but this is someone I think you'll really like."

"No lawyers?" Ruth asks hopefully.

"No lawyers."

Robin comes into the kitchen now, dragging a Raggedy Ann doll behind her on the floor.

"Hello, darling," Ruth exclaims. "You were playing so quietly by yourself, I almost forgot you!"

She's kidding, of course. Of course she's kidding, but Clara sees a little cloud drift across her five-year-old sister's face, then disappear.

"Come, girls. You can be my helpers," Ruth says. She hoists them both up on the kitchen counter and gives each child a small piece of dough to work with. She begins chopping apples, her movements quick, careless.

"Do you want me to do that for you?" Nathan asks. He's afraid she'll slice her finger open.

"No, I'm fine," Ruth says. "So tell me, who is this fabulous client? I hope he likes strudel."

Nathan's client arrives an hour late for lunch. He is flustered, pacing back and forth on the front porch, his long hair—jet-black, not yet gray—windblown from the ride upstate in his convertible. He's wearing jeans and a navy blue blazer. A bright-red cashmere muffler is wrapped around his neck, obscuring the bottom part of his face.

"These country roads," he says by way of introducing himself, when Ruth opens the door. He hands her a bottle of wine. "My apologies."

"Not at all," Ruth says. She's slightly mystified by this man on her porch. Nathan hasn't told her much about him. "Please, come in."

Robin and Clara are watching television in the family room when Ruth brings the stranger through.

"Girls, please say hello to Mr. . . . ." She trails off. "I'm sorry, I don't know your name."

"Weiss," he says. "Kubovy Weiss." He crouches down so he's at eye level with the girls. "But you can call me Kubovy."

"You made it!" Nathan comes bounding in from out back. He has bits of dried leaves and twigs on his fisherman's sweater; he must have been hauling in firewood.

"Nathan." Kubovy straightens up, offering his hand. "Thanks for having me."

Clara keeps looking at the man with the long hair and the funny name. He's different from the people her father usually brings home, and it isn't just the hair either. He looks like a drawing in one of her picture books. A Maurice Sendak animal, all curls and angles and watchful eyes.

"So you are the photographer," Kubovy says to Ruth.

"Yes," Ruth answers faintly. Her forehead knots with anticipation as she waits for the usual questions. *Where have I seen your pictures? Can you make a living at that?*

"I'd love to see your work," Kubovy says.

"Oh." Ruth's hands fly up, a reflex. "I don't really—"

"Kubovy is an art dealer," Nathan says.

Something comes over Ruth. Her pupils widen, her nerves bristle with attention. She is suddenly more alive than before.

"Really," she says. Her voice gives nothing away. She is cool, oh so cool. "Do you have a gallery?"

"Yes, in SoHo," says Kubovy. "On Prince Street, though we're about to move into a larger space on West Broadway."

Nathan hums a little tune under his breath as he uncorks a bottle of wine. He walks into the kitchen and emerges with a platter of cheese and a small bowl of olives.

"Please." He gestures to the sofa. "Make yourself comfortable."

Kubovy sinks into the deep food-stained pillows. He struggles to sit upright as Nathan hands him a glass of wine.

"My husband tells me you're his client?" Ruth asks. She's still trying to make sense of all this. The thoughts practically gallop across her face.

"Our firm is handling a dispute between Kubovy and one of his former partners," Nathan says.

"Mommy?" Clara looks up from *Sesame Street.*

"Yes, sweetie?"

"I'm hungry."

"We'll have lunch soon, Clara."

"Clara. What a beautiful name," says Kubovy. Then he turns to Ruth. "So. I am serious, you know. I hope you will show me your work."

"Maybe after lunch," Ruth begins. "I don't know what I have here. Most of my work is in the city."

"Whatever you like." Kubovy shrugs.

"Contemporary photography is Kubovy's specialty," says Nate.

Ruth nods, as if unsurprised. It must be a lot of work, acting as if none of this matters to her.

"Please, my dear," Kubovy says. He sounds much older than he is—he is perhaps in his mid-thirties. "Don't be nervous. I don't bite."

"I'm not nervous!" Ruth says.

Kubovy does a slow-motion blink. "Of course not," he says. "My mistake."


After lunch—after the charcuterie, the crumbling Asiago, the thick slices of saucisson and hunks of fresh baguettes, after the wine—

Ruth slips upstairs and comes down a few minutes later carrying a large black portfolio.

"These aren't my most recent—" she says. The color in her cheeks is high: two bright pink spots. "I mean—"

"That's fine," Kubovy murmurs. "Let's have a look."

He brushes away the bits of cheese and bread crumbs, then spreads the portfolio open on the dining-room table.

From the kitchen, the sound of running water, clanking dishes. The hum of domestic life. Nate has absented himself from this process, taking the girls with him. *Here, Robin. Stack these dishes. Clara, honey, could you hand me that towel, the one over there, hanging by the stove?*

Ruth stands behind Kubovy, looking over his shoulder as he slowly flips through the pages of her portolio. There are fifteen photographs in all, sheathed in plastic. His manner—relaxed until now—is focused, fastidious.

"Those are landscapes," she says, and shakes her head. "Obviously."

Kubovy doesn't respond. He's not making this easy for her. No comments as he takes in each photograph. No sign of what he's thinking. He pauses over one image, a photograph of the local garbage dump: the rusted gates, the pickup trucks, the huge vat of empty bottles glistening in the silvery light.

He closes the portfolio, placing his thick square hands on top of it. Ruth sits down next to him at the table. She isn't going to give him the satisfaction of asking, *Well? What do you think?* She stares at him, waiting for a verdict.

"Interesting." He purses his lips, blowing out air. "Not quite there yet—but interesting. Quite beautiful. "

She waits for more, but no more is coming.

"What's not there?" Ruth asks.

"My dear, that's what you need to figure out." Kubovy pauses, fishing for a cigarette. He lights up, then flicks his ash onto a salad plate. "I'll tell you what: Figure that out and come see me in a year."

"Hi, Hilary." Robin greets the saleswoman on the fifth floor of Barneys by name. "My sister here is looking for something simple and black."

"Any designer in particular?" the saleswoman asks, turning to Clara. Sizing her up. She's certainly happy to see Robin, who must be one of her better customers.

"I don't know," Clara says. She looks around the floor at the spare well-placed racks on which dozens of shapeless garments—mostly black—hang. She's never heard of half these designers. Costume National. Rick Owen. Junya Watanabe. She feels she's been living under a rock—or at least in the pages of the L. L. Bean catalog.

Sammy has already found a bag she likes in the Prada department. She carries it over to Clara.

"Look, Mom. Isn't this cute?"

Clara takes it from Sammy and looks at the price tag. Thirteen hundred dollars for a few stitched-together pieces of leather.

"Robin, this is insane," Clara says.

"Well, it's Prada."

"No, I mean being here. It's too weird."

"You need something to wear. You can't go in blue jeans—which, as best as I can tell, is all you own."

"I'll just borrow—"

"I'm a size two," interrupts Robin.

"No, I was going to say—" Clara starts, then stops. What *was* she going to say, that she'd wear something of Ruth's?

"Is it for a special occasion?" The saleswoman—Hilary—returns with an armload of black. Skirts and sweaters, blouses, dresses.

"Our mother's funeral," Robin says.

"Oh!" Hilary looks from one to the other, as if wondering for a moment if Robin is joking. Then realizing.

"I'm so sorry," she says, ushering Clara into a large windowed dressing room.

Couldn't Robin have lied? Did Hilary with the crimson lips and powdered face really need to know their family's business? Clara strips down to her bra and panties. She averts her gaze from the three-way mirror. The last thing she wants to do is look at herself from any angle—much less every angle—well lit and naked.

She pulls a black sweater over her head, but she can tell before she even gets it all the way on that it doesn't fit. Then she climbs into a pencil skirt, tugging it up over her hips, which have become curvier since giving birth to Sam. She gives herself a quick glance in the mirror: awful, like a sausage stuffed into its casing. She keeps going. Layers of black chiffon (inappropriate), a black wool thing that wraps around and around her body (bizarre), until finally she slips into a black short-sleeved dress and zips it up the back.

On the other side of the dressing room curtain, she can hear Robin and Sam discussing the finer points of shopping. *My favorite color is pink,* Sammy says. *What's yours?* Clara strains to listen. Pathetic, that she doesn't know her sister's favorite color. *Gray,* Robin says.

Clara forces herself to meet her own eyes in the mirror, and when she does, her knees almost give way beneath her. How long has it been since she's seen herself in anything other than jeans and a sweatshirt? The dress fits her perfectly. She looks—she has tried so hard not to, but she looks—elegant and beautiful. Her skin is pale, stark against the darkness of the dress, and for a moment she has the eerie sensation that her mother is in the mirror, gazing calmly back at her.

Suddenly dizzy, she sits down on the plush little ottoman and crosses her legs. *Focus.* Whose voice is she hearing? Ruth's—or her own?

"Clara?" Robin's voice sounds far away.

The dressing room might as well be a space capsule. She has been catapulted into orbit, snipped loose from earth's gravitational pull.

"Clara?"

*She's dead.* Clara's mouth forms around the words. She reaches back, pulls her hair out of its usual ponytail, and shakes it loose. She keeps staring into the mirror. *Dead. My mother is dead and gone.* She imagines Ruth's body, lying in its casket at Frank Campbell's.

"Mom?"

There's Sammy—real as can be—parting the curtains of the dressing room. Eyes like saucers.

"Oh my God, Mom—you look so pretty."

And then Robin, just behind her.

"Well, well. Look who cleans up nicely."

"I can't do this." Clara struggles not to cry.

Robin looks at Clara with a notable lack of sympathy. *Suck it up,* she seems to be saying.

"Of course you can."

The three of them take in Clara's reflection in the mirror. Everything will be different from now on. And nothing will ever, ever change. Clara's relationship with Ruth—now frozen in amber. Tears roll down her cheeks, and she wipes them quickly away.

---

SHE KNOWS this will be the last time. When her robe falls from her shoulders and she stands in the hot white glare of the pole lights, when she shivers at the suddenness of it, she knows she will never, after this, have to pose for her mother again.

It is late at night when Ruth pulls her from a deep sleep.

"Come," she says, her voice gentle. "Come with me."

The studio is brightly lit. Ruth has hung a heavy cream-colored tarp along the length of the far wall. The tarp spills halfway onto the floor, pooling there like the train of a wedding dress. Ruth recently started to take commissioned portraits for *Vanity Fair* and uses the studio for the shoots: Sting has come through, and Meryl Streep, and even Madonna, who just starred in *Who's That Girl?* Near the door a leather-bound guest book, a gift from Kubovy. Someday it will be full of famous signatures, from rappers to presidents.

"Stand over there, Clara." That quiet voice. Does Ruth use the same tone when she shoots her celebrities? Clara steps onto the tarp, the canvas rough beneath her bare feet. Her mother has never taken her picture in the studio before. All the other pictures have been staged: the lizard, the wet bed, the Popsicle.

She waits, her senses alert, the thick terry-cloth robe still wrapped around her. She doesn't allow herself to be detached—not like she has always been before. No. This time she needs to be fully present for what happens next. What happens when her robe drops to the floor.

Ruth fiddles with the lights, then moves a reflector so that it's aiming up at Clara like a silvery moon. Ruth is muttering to herself as she works, concentrating on getting the exposure exactly right.

In the arched windows of the studio, Clara can see her own reflection against the darkness of the night. She imagines people down on Broadway—walking their dogs before bed or coming home late from a party—looking up at the bright glow coming from the top floor of the Apthorp and wondering what's going on up there at this hour.

"Okay," Ruth says. "Let's get to work."

Clara pauses for a moment. Nothing will be the same after this. Lately, she has managed to hide herself. She has worn black bulky leggings and sweaters beneath her school uniform. She has locked the bathroom door when she's taken showers. She has changed quickly into her pajamas. The only noticeable change has been her hair, that short black choppy cut she gave herself a few months ago.

"Come on, Clara."

Ruth is impatient. Everything is set up and ready to go. Clara sheds her robe the way a high diver might before walking out onto the board. Preparing to somersault, to flip backward, to slice clean through the water like a blade.

"Oh, my God."

The first words Ruth utters. She doesn't see Clara head-on, but, rather, through the lens of her camera. She lifts her head up and stares at her, her mouth ajar. "What the hell is that?"

At fourteen, Clara's thighs have become fleshy, thanks to a steady diet of ice cream and doughnuts after school. The weight she's gained hasn't made her fat, exactly. She's what could be described as solid. For the first time not a waif, not a frail thing. But it's the tattoo Ruth can't handle, the dark green garland of leaves and vines snaking around Clara's upper arm like a misplaced Christmas wreath.

"What have you done to yourself?" Ruth's voice has lost its gentle, coaxing tone. Her voice is stretched so thin it sounds like it could snap. And Clara—Clara just gazes at her mother calmly. As if watching a movie unfold from a comfortable seat in a darkened theater. Ruth has no way of knowing how hard Clara's heart is pounding. How she feels her entire spine is made of ice.

Ruth puts aside her equipment, then approaches Clara slowly, almost nervously. She lifts Clara's arm and examines the tattoo for a moment, then rubs her thumb over it to see if perhaps it's just painted on.

She stands inches away from Clara, her chest heaving.

"Who did this to you?"

Clara can't seem to talk.

"Do you realize it's illegal to—my God, Clara. You could have gotten an infection. You could have died."

Ruth is still staring at the tattoo, willing it to go away. And Clara is wondering. Is that what's really bothering her mother?

"Say something!"

Clara is silent. Her body speaks for itself.

"Goddammit!" Ruth cries. Then she turns around and stalks back to her camera.

Clara bends down to collect her robe.

"What do you think you're doing?" Ruth asks.

"Getting dressed," Clara says.

"Oh, no. We're still going to work."

The ice in Clara's spine turns to water. She feels herself melting—all that hardness, all that bravado falling away.

"What?" she asks.

"You did this to yourself, to your beautiful—" Ruth's voice cracks. "Why?" The word comes out in a wail.

"So you'd stop," whispers Clara.

Ruth doesn't move a muscle. She stands behind her camera and looks at her daughter for what seems a very long time. Lost—somewhere way, way deep inside herself—in thought. Outside, on Broadway, a car alarm goes off, a long series of high-pitched beeps. The radiator hisses and rattles. A mouse scratches its tiny claws inside one of the thick walls.

"We'll document this," Ruth finally says.

"I don't want to," Clara says.

"It will be the last time, Clara." Ruth closes her eyes. "I promise."

*Click.* Clara is standing naked in all her tattooed, black-haired solidness, holding her bathrobe like it's a teddy bear. Her breasts are hints of the woman she is becoming. A shadow between her legs. *Click.* Her left arm red from where Ruth had grabbed her so tightly. *Click.* Tears—is she angry or sad, relieved or mournful?—standing still in her eyes.

———◆•••◆———

AFTER THE FUNERAL—town cars lining Madison Avenue despite the attempt to keep it private—after the eulogies and flowers, the casket lined in a purple velvet Ruth would have hated, after the guest book scrawled with signatures, the sea of famous faces, Kubovy ushers Clara and Robin into a café two blocks from the funeral home.

"Why now, Kubovy?" Robin fumes. "There will be people waiting at the apartment. People who want to pay their respects."

"I'm leaving for Europe tonight." Kubovy looks first at one sister, then the other. "I know this is difficult, but—"

"We should be doing this in her attorney's office, not here"— Robin gestures at the marble and chrome, the gleaming espresso machine—"sitting in this fucking fishbowl."

And it is a fishbowl. They're seated by the floor-to-ceiling windows of E.A.T., where all of Madison Avenue can see them. The tables are crammed close to one another. An older woman in a tweed jacket is right next to them, eating her scrambled eggs and lox. Clara realizes, with a start, that this is precisely why Kubovy has chosen this place. Total visibility. He's trying to avoid any possibility of a scene. But why would there be a scene? She doesn't care how Ruth left things, and she can't imagine that Robin does either. Robin certainly doesn't need any more money. And Clara—Clara doesn't want it or expect it. She hopes her mother left her entire estate to a museum— or to Kubovy, for that matter. She just wants to go back to her life in Maine. She wants all of this to close up around her like skin healing over a wound.

"Your mother"—Kubovy speaks carefully—"wanted me to be the one to explain to you the terms of her will."

"Fine." Robin takes a sip of her espresso. "Let's get down to business. The kids are waiting."

Clara watches Robin—her sister's body is rigid and tense. Robin is nervous. But why?

"All right." Kubovy pulls a legal-sized envelope from his briefcase. It's hard to see his eyes behind his green-tinted glasses.

"Robin, your mother appointed you executor of her estate," Kubovy says.

Robin's shoulders slump with relief. She wanted this, Clara realizes. She wanted Ruth to pay attention to her—in death, if not in life.

"Well, that makes sense," Clara says. Hoping to smooth things over.

"What, you mean because I'm an attorney?" Robin asks.

"No. Because you're the older daughter."

Kubovy clears his throat. The woman eating her scrambled eggs is hanging on to their every word, all the while pretending to be immersed in the current issue of *The New Yorker.*

"And Clara—" Kubovy says, drawing out the words. "Clara, your mother has given you the—" He stops, shaking his head, as if he can't bear what he's about to say.

"Come on, Kubovy," says Robin.

"A little respect, my dear." Kubovy's lids are heavy, his pallor gray beneath his tan. Clara almost feels sorry for him. Almost.

"You have control over the work," he finally says in a rush. "Ruth left all decisions regarding the disposition of her work up to you."

The din of the café falls off. What did Kubovy just tell her? It makes no sense. Her thoughts are just out of reach.

"That's—but that's everything," says Robin. Looking suddenly a bit shaken.

"Hardly," says Kubovy. "You're going to be dealing with the investments, the apartment, the country house—which of course you two will split down the middle—"

"What does that mean, the disposition of her work?" Clara asks. She thought she didn't care. She thought there wasn't anything about this conversation that could possibly matter to her. So why is she gripping the sides of her chair so tightly that her knuckles have turned white?

Robin turns to her.

"It means that you'll decide," Robin says. "Galleries, museums, retrospectives, future sales of Ruth's photographs—"

"And the book," Kubovy says quietly.

"What about the book?"

"Oh, Clara, don't be so naive," Robin says.

"Don't say that. I haven't done anything to—"

"I'm sorry," Robin says. "I just—"

She stops, swallowing hard. Then she scrapes her chair back and walks quickly in the direction of the ladies' room.

Clara and Kubovy sit in silence, across the small table from each other. He is watching her carefully, searching her face for signs of how she's taking this news. And Clara—Clara is looking out the window. The nannies pushing strollers up the avenue, the bike messenger locking his front wheel to a meter, a handsome older couple carrying shopping bags from the Sharper Image.

"Why did she do this, Kubovy?" she asks. "After a whole life of—" She breaks off. "I mean, she never— I don't get it."

Kubovy reaches across the table and grabs Clara's hand, as if he needs to touch her in order to make himself understood. For the first time in all the years she's known him, Clara sees—is it possible?—the thin sheen of tears in Kubovy's eyes.

"She wanted to do right by you, my dear," he says.


The plane back to Bangor rumbles down the runway. Clara—sitting in the middle seat—holds Sammy's hand, counting the seconds until takeoff: *five, four, three, two* . . . They rise quickly above the runway's wavery heat. Home. They're going home. Clara leans her head against Jonathan's shoulder, finding the spot just above his collarbone where she can rest and think about normal things: How they'll pick up Zorba from the kennel. How the roses will be in bloom—that is, if they've survived the weeks of neglect. How their house, in all its creaky paint-chipped comfort, will be waiting for them just the way they left it. Jonathan's pajama bottoms still on the bedroom floor. Dirty coffee cups on the kitchen counter.

Sammy extricates her hand from Clara's.

"You doing okay, sweetie?"

Sammy nods.

"Anything you want to talk about?"

She shakes her head.

Clara pushes through the silence.

"Do you miss Grandma?"

Sammy's quiet for a minute.

"I don't exactly miss her," she says. "Mostly I feel—lucky."

"Lucky?" It's the last word Clara was expecting.

"Yeah. That I got to know her."

Jonathan's listening to this exchange. Clara wishes she could turn to him and say *Don't be thinking what you're thinking. I get it. I know that it isn't over. The waves will come—one crashing after the next and next.* But instead, she says, "Me too."

"Me too, you miss her?" Sammy asks.

A pause. "Me too, I'm glad you got to know her."

Clara orders a glass of airplane wine, trying to switch gears. City to country. Past to present. It feels like they've been gone for a long, long time. Everything is different now. Ruth—no longer in the world. Secrets—no longer necessary. Money—for the first time in their marriage, she and Jonathan will be without the constant weight of financial worry. *How are we going to pay the bills this month? Much less save for Sammy's college fund?* All that—gone. Gone forever.

"Things are so . . ." She trails off.

"What?" Jonathan prompts her.

"I don't know," she says. "Strange."

"Which part do you mean?"

"Ruth being gone," she says, surprising herself. Hasn't her mother been gone—as far as Clara has been concerned—for all these years? But no, she can sense it now. Some important piece of her, a vital organ, has always been shut down. She had never experienced its absence, but now, the rush of feeling, the absolute *presence* of . . . what? She hardly knows how to describe it: aliveness? Fullness?

"What about how Ruth left things?" Jonathan asks.

"What about it?"

"How does that make you feel?"

"I don't know, Dr. Freud. How does it make *you* feel?"

She tries to make light of it—her old way of dealing with things—but the new Clara doesn't seem capable of just brushing difficult thoughts away. *She wanted to do right by you.* Kubovy's words float through her mind. What did Kubovy mean by that?

Clara takes a sip of sour wine. She looks over at Sammy, who has curled up in her seat, sound asleep, her mouth open.

"I don't know if I'm wishing this or if it's actually true," Clara begins slowly, piecing an idea together. "But I think—finally—Ruth *knew.* She knew what all of it—"

She breaks off. Suddenly choked up.

"What it did to you," Jonathan finishes her sentence. "How it hurt you."

"Then why didn't she stop?" Her own voice sounds, to her ears, like a child's.

"She couldn't stop," Jonathan says.

"That's bullshit!"

Jonathan smiles softly, almost sorrowfully.

"Maybe," he says. "It's hard to say."

"But why did she leave me with all of it?" Clara goes on. "The photographs, the incredible responsibility—" She stops.

Ruth's face, that afternoon—in the dim light—watching as Clara flipped through the dozens of photographs. *It's not about you. It was never about you.*

"What?"

"She wanted me to have control," Clara says, "over the work. The pictures of myself. The book."

Jonathan looks at her, unfazed. He's already figured this out—he's just been waiting for Clara to arrive at it herself.

"It's up to me," she says, as if she can't quite believe it. "She left it all in my hands."

She imagines Ruth, propped up in bed. Nearly too weak to sign her own name. *Are you sure you know what you're doing?* Kubovy must have asked. And Ruth—ignoring him—moving her pen slowly, deliberately, across the page. Focusing hard.

The plane banks to the left, beginning its initial descent. The jagged coastline of Maine is spread out beneath them, the islands dotting the sea.

*She loved me.* The thought—until now, for all these years, unbearable. She feels her veins expanding, making room to receive it. *She loved me.* Because it never mattered—because it wasn't enough. Because it was too much. *She loved me.* Clara stares out the window, feeling herself drift slowly down to earth.

# Epilogue

The glass doors of Jonathan Brodeur Jewelry are open to the sidewalk, people spilling onto the street despite the snow flurries in the bitter December air. Inside, the place is so hot and crowded it's hard to move. The bar is in back, bottles set up on a long jewelry case. Jimmy Scanlon, who runs the school cafeteria, is the bartender tonight, doling out plastic cups of white wine. Some of the high school girls are passing around trays of cheese cubes stuck with toothpicks.

Everyone is here. The parents from Sammy's school, a healthy mix of artists, construction workers, acupuncturists, social workers, and attorneys. Laurel Connolly, who has brought her daughter Emily; Emily and Sam are in the back office, stringing beads that Jonathan has set aside for them. Oh, and there's George Odlum from the hardware store. And Nancy Tipton, Sammy's piano teacher. And Ginny and Dave from the lobster shack. It seems like the whole island has shown up.

"How's my beautiful wife?" Jonathan's hand on the small of Clara's back, steadying her. A habit, really, since she doesn't need steadying tonight.

"Great," Clara says.

"That guy is here," Jonathan says. "From the *Times*."

"Okay." Clara looks around the room for someone who looks like he might be a *New York Times* reporter. She spots him. The shirttails hanging from beneath his jacket are a dead giveaway. The men in Southwest Harbor tuck their shirts in.

"Do I need to go talk to him?" Clara asks.

"Not right now." Jonathan surveys the scene. "Hey, check out Kubovy. He looks like he's wandered onto the wrong stage set."

Clara spies Kubovy in the far corner, standing next to a case displaying Jonathan's new collection. She laughs. Of all the people, he's caught in the net of old Mrs. Reynolds, the retired school crossing guard, who is shaking her finger at him. He may have a nervous breakdown any minute.

"I'd better go rescue him," says Clara.

"Oh, but why? It's so much fun to watch him squirm."

Just as Clara starts to make her way through the crowd toward Kubovy, Robin, Ed, and the kids come through the gallery doors.

"You made it!" Clara hugs her sister close. "I wasn't sure, with all the snow—"

"Oh, please," Robin says. "But I'll tell you, these streets aren't made for walking." She lifts up one foot, examining a scuffed three-inch heel.

"Where's Sam?" Harrison asks.

"In back, making a necklace. Do you want to join her?"

He makes a face.

"So where is it?" Robin shrugs off her shearling coat.

"Hot off the presses. We have tons of them," Clara says. "They sent like six cartons."

Robin pulls off her kids' down jackets, stuffing their mittens into the pockets.

"I want to see," she says.

The crowd seems to part for Robin—something about her New York energy. She walks over to a jewelry case on which a pile of books is stacked in a pyramid. She picks up the one from the top. Gazes at the cover for a good long minute. The blurred close-up. The black paper band around it. The letters cut out: CLARA.

She opens the book, fingering the thick glossy pages.

*"To Clara and Robin,"* she reads on the dedication page. *"Without whom."* Robin pauses, squinting at it. "Without whom what?"

"Fill in the blank," says Kubovy. He has managed to ditch Mrs. Reynolds and find his way over to the only people in the whole room he knows.

"What do you mean?" Robin's voice gets edgy. It takes almost nothing for Kubovy to annoy her.

"Without whom none of it would have been possible," Kubovy says. "That's what she meant."

"How do you know?"

"Could we stop?" Clara asks. "Please?"

Robin does. She stops and takes in Clara. Beautiful in the black dress from Barneys. Her lips outlined in red.

"You're getting some use out of that thing," she says.

"Well, you know. Funerals. Book parties."

"Speaking of which," Kubovy says. "I would like to have an event celebrating this publication in New York." He pauses. "And L.A."

He looks at Clara, as if waiting to be challenged.

"That's fine," she says faintly. "Whatever's best. This party here—this is the only one I care about."

She looks once again around the room. Sammy's cousins have found her and brought her back into the crowd. Sammy's drinking a cup of soda and wearing a necklace of bright blue beads strung onto a piece of leather. She looks—Clara's throat thickens with something like joy—she looks proud. Her face is lit with pleasure at this moment. Her grandmother's book. Her mother in the center of the room. Her family surrounding her.

Robin slowly turns the pages of the book. The silvery unmistakable images caught in the tiny spotlights dangling over their heads like stars.

"Steiffel did a great job," she says.

"Yes, they did."

"Did you think about stopping them?" Robin asks. "You could have, you know."

Kubovy leans slightly forward to better hear the answer.

"Of course I thought about it," Clara says.

She catches a glimpse of herself, reflected in a tall mirror behind one of the display cases. Her hair pulled back. Her mouth red. The black dress. Her own young daughter out there in the crowd. The past, rushing up to meet her. And Clara does the only thing—she understands this now—the only thing possible. She turns to face it, head-on.

## ACKNOWLEDGMENTS

For support and sustenance, I would like to thank the good people of the Mayflower Inn in Washington, Connecticut, who kept me caffeinated and made me feel at home while I scribbled away in their midst. Lisa Hedley, Jack Rosenthal, and Jeanette Montgomery Barron were early, invaluable readers. Jane Tawney provided me with an insider's view of Mount Desert Island. Marion Ettlinger has always inspired me from both sides of her lens. Jordan Pavlin, Sonny Mehta, Leslie Levine at Knopf, and Jennifer Jackson at Anchor—thank you for being everything I could hope for in a publisher. Thanks also to Sylvie Rabineau and Andy McNichol. Jennifer Rudolph Walsh—you're spectacular and I adore you. And finally—to my husband, Michael Maren, whose influence and love are reflected on every single page of this book.

## A NOTE ABOUT THE AUTHOR

Dani Shapiro's most recent books include the novel *Family History* and the best-selling memoir *Slow Motion.* She teaches at Wesleyan University, and her work has appeared in *The New Yorker, Granta, Elle,* and many other publications. She lives with her husband and son in Litchfield County, Connecticut.

A NOTE ON THE TYPE

This book was set in Adobe Garamond. Designed for the Adobe Corpora-
tion by Robert Slimbach, the fonts are based on types first cut by Claude
Garamond (c. 1480–1561). Garamond was a pupil of Geoffrey Tory and is
believed to have followed the Venetian models, although he introduced a
number of important differences, and it is to him that we owe the letter we
now know as "old style."

*Composed by Creative Graphics, Allentown, Pennsylvania*

*Printed and bound by Berryville Graphics, Berryville, Virginia*

*Designed by Robert C. Olsson*